ROPE BURN

THOSE JENSEN BOYS!
ROPE BURN

WILLIAM W. JOHNSTONE
and J. A. JOHNSTONE

PINNACLE BOOKS
Kensington Publishing Corp.
www.kensingtonbooks.com

PINNACLE BOOKS are published by

Kensington Publishing Corp.
119 West 40th Street
New York, NY 10018

PUBLISHER'S NOTE
Following the death of William W. Johnstone, the Johnstone family is working with a carefully selected writer to organize and complete Mr. Johnstone's outlines and many unfinished manuscripts to create additional novels in all of his series like The Last Gunfighter, Mountain Man, and Eagles, among others. This novel was inspired by Mr. Johnstone's superb storytelling.

All Kensington titles, imprints, and distributed lines are available at special quantity discounts for bulk purchases for sales promotions, premiums, fundraising, educational, or institutional use. Special book excerpts or customized printings can also be created to fit specific needs. For details, write or phone the office of the Kensington sales manager: Kensington Publishing Corp., 119 West 40th Street, New York, NY 10018, attn: Sales Department; phone 1-800-221-2647.

PINNACLE BOOKS, the Pinnacle logo, and the WWJ steer head logo are Reg. U.S. Pat. & TM Off.

ISBN-13: 978-0-7860-4430-6
ISBN-10: 0-7860-4430-6

First printing: March 2020

10 9 8 7 6 5 4 3 2 1

Printed in the United States of America

Electronic edition:

ISBN-13: 978-0-7860-4431-3 (e-book)
ISBN-10: 0-7860-4431-4 (e-book)

THE JENSEN FAMILY
FIRST FAMILY OF THE AMERICAN FRONTIER

Smoke Jensen—*The Mountain Man*

The youngest of three children and orphaned as a young boy, Smoke Jensen is considered one of the fastest draws in the West. His quest to tame the lawless West has become the stuff of legend. Smoke owns the Sugarloaf Ranch in Colorado. Married to Sally Jensen, father to Denise ("Denny") and Louis.

Preacher—*The First Mountain Man*

Though not a blood relative, grizzled frontiersman Preacher became a father figure to the young Smoke Jensen, teaching him how to survive in the brutal, often deadly Rocky Mountains. Fought the battles that forged his destiny. Armed with a long gun, Preacher is as fierce as the land itself.

Matt Jensen—*The Last Mountain Man*

Orphaned but taken in by Smoke Jensen, Matt Jensen has become like a younger brother to Smoke and even took the Jensen name. And like Smoke, Matt has carved out his destiny on the American frontier. He lives by the gun and surrenders to no man.

Luke Jensen—*Bounty Hunter*
Mountain Man Smoke Jensen's long-lost brother
Luke Jensen is scarred by war and a dead shot—
the right qualities to be a bounty hunter. And he's
cunning, and fierce enough, to bring down the deadliest outlaws of his day.

Ace Jensen and Chance Jensen—*Those Jensen Boys!*
Smoke Jensen's long-lost nephews, Ace and Chance,
are a pair of young-gun twins as reckless and wild as
the frontier itself . . . Their father is Luke Jensen,
thought killed in the Civil War. Their uncle Smoke
Jensen is one of the fiercest gunfighters the West has
ever known. It's no surprise that the inseparable Ace
and Chance Jensen have a knack for taking risks—
even if they have to blast their way out of them.

CHAPTER ONE

The soldier with the ugly scar on his cheek cursed and shouted, "I'm gonna whale the tar outta you, you stinkin' little whelp!"

Ace Jensen held his hands up, palms out, and said, "Take it easy, mister. He didn't mean anything by it."

"Like fire I didn't mean anything!" Chance Jensen, Ace's brother, said. "If that lout doesn't get his hands off her, he's going to get the thrashing he deserves!"

Through gritted teeth and from the corner of his mouth, Ace said, "Blast it, Chance. We're outnumbered four to one, here."

"I don't care. I'm not going to stand by and allow him to manhandle that poor girl like that."

The man with the scar grinned at his fellow cavalry troopers. "This is gonna be fun, boys."

"You want us to help you, Vince?" one of them asked.

"Naw. I won't need any help with this little pipsqueak. Just sit back and enjoy the show."

The soldier clenched his fists and stalked toward Ace and Chance. He had the three yellow stripes of a sergeant sewed on the sleeve of his blue uniform shirt. His brawny shoulders stretched the fabric of that shirt. His forage cap was pushed back on his bullet-shaped head.

"Fun, he calls it," Ace muttered. "I'd like to know how come we keep winding up in so much *fun*."

"Just lucky, I guess," Chance told him.

Behind the bar, the apron-wearing drink juggler said nervously, "Sergeant MacDonald, why don't you and these fellas take your problem outside?"

"Too late for that," the three-striper replied. "I want Honey to see what I'm gonna do to this little varmint."

He rushed at Chance, swinging a roundhouse punch at the young man's head.

Chance ducked under the sweeping blow and hammered a right hook into the sergeant's mid-section. It was like punching a wall and didn't do a thing to slow him down. The sergeant's momentum carried him into Chance, and his weight drove the young man against the bar. Chance cried out in pain as his back struck the hardwood's edge.

As a general rule, Ace let his brother fight his own battles, but hearing Chance yell like that triggered anger inside Ace. He stepped in and slammed the side of his right fist against the sergeant's skull, just above the left ear. That was enough to distract the man from his attempt to get his hands around Chance's throat while he had him pinned to the bar.

It set off the sergeant's companions, too. One of them yelled, "They're gangin' up on the sarge, boys! Let's get 'em!"

The seven men surged out of their chairs and rushed from the table where they had been sitting and passing around a couple of bottles of forty rod. They came at Ace and Chance like a buffalo stampede. The saloon's other customers, already edging away from the battle between Chance and the sergeant, stampeded, too—toward the batwing doors to get out of there. Behind the bar, the apron howled in dismay at the beating his establishment was about to take.

The scarred noncom still crowded Chance against the bar. Chance cupped his hands and clapped them over the man's ears as hard as he could. The pain from that, combined with the blow to the head that Ace had given him, made the sergeant stagger back a couple of steps.

That gave Chance enough room to go after him. Knowing it wouldn't do any good to punch the man in his rock-hard belly, Chance went after his face instead. He landed a swift left-right combination, the straight right landing solidly on the scar that ran from the left corner of the sergeant's mouth up past his left eye. Somebody had laid his face open with a knife in some previous fracas.

Meanwhile, one of the other troopers had reached Ace. The man tried to grab him, but Ace got hold of the man's arm instead, pivoted, threw a hip into him, bent, and hauled the man off his feet. The trooper let out a surprised yell as he flew through the air and crashed down on his back.

Over by the table where the men had been sitting, the heavily painted saloon girl who had set off this explosion of fisticuffs by yelping when the sergeant got too rough in his pawing of her clapped her hands to her cheeks and screamed. The cry had sort of a perfunctory sound to it, as if she had witnessed dozens of brawls like this and knew the part she was supposed to play in it.

Ace tried to avoid the other men who came after him, but there were too many of them. Two of them seized his arms and forced him back against the bar. Another man loomed in front of Ace, fists poised to move in and pound him while the other two held him.

Instead, Ace drew his legs up and lashed out with them. His boot heels caught the attacker in the chest and flung him backward, completely out of control. He came down atop a table, the legs of which cracked under the impact and dumped him on the floor amidst the debris.

That only worked once, though, because as Ace's legs dropped after that kick, a second man took the first one's place and pummeled him, throwing hard fists into the young man's face and rocking his head back and forth. Ace tasted blood in his mouth and his vision began to blur.

A few feet away, Chance still battled with the sergeant. Chance was stronger than he looked, so he was able to stand toe to toe with the burly noncom and slug it out for a few moments. The real advantage Chance had was his quickness. He avoided some of the punches, drew the sergeant in, and then reached behind him to pluck a bottle of whiskey off the bar. He had spotted it a second earlier from the corner of his eye. Holding the bottle by the neck, he slammed it over the sergeant's head.

Chance expected the bottle to break, but it landed with a dull thud and remained intact. The sergeant grunted and his eyes rolled up in their sockets. He managed to keep his feet, but he was only half conscious. Chance dropped the bottle, lowered his right shoulder, and rammed it into the sergeant's chest as he drove hard with his feet. That knocked the sergeant backward into the men holding Ace.

Legs tangled, and everybody went down, including Ace and Chance. The wild melee continued on the floor now, where sawdust damp from spilled beer and spit soon coated the clothing of all the men. A fight like this had only one rule: survive. Ace and Chance punched, kicked, gouged, and even bit.

Ace scrapped his way to his feet. One of the troopers made it upright, as well, and clambered onto the bar. Ace wasn't sure what the man had in mind, but then it became clear as the trooper started trying to kick him in the head.

Ace jerked aside and avoided the first kick. Before the soldier could try again, his other foot slipped on a puddle of beer on the bar and that leg shot out from under him. He windmilled his arms in a frantic attempt to keep his balance but toppled off the bar, bouncing on the backbar and taking down several shelves of whiskey bottles. These broke with a great shattering sound, and the liquor's raw reek filled the air.

Chance grabbed hold of the bar and pulled himself to his feet next to Ace. The brothers, battered, filthy, in torn clothes, stood back to back and cocked their fists, ready to continue the battle if need be.

Only three of the troopers were still in any shape to fight. The others, including the scarred sergeant who seemed to be their ringleader, sprawled around in various stages of stupor, groaning and shaking their heads. The three who had suffered less stumbled upright and looked at each other, obviously unwilling to carry on but not wanting to be the ones to surrender, either, especially when they still outnumbered the two young strangers.

The boom of a shotgun blast took the decision out of their hands. Everyone in the saloon still coherent enough to do so turned to look at the entrance, where a man had just slapped the batwings aside and come into the place. He leveled the Greener in his hands, with its still unfired barrel, at the men standing in front of the bar and yelled, "The next man who moves is gettin' a load of buckshot in his guts, and I don't care who else gets ventilated, neither!"

CHAPTER TWO

The stocky, middle-aged newcomer had a graying mustache, a beefy face, and perhaps most important—other than the shotgun—a badge pinned to his vest. His eyes flashed with anger, and he looked perfectly capable of pulling the trigger and scything down several of the combatants with hot lead.

"Hold your fire, Marshal," Ace said, being careful to keep his hands in plain sight, in a nonthreatening manner. Beside him, Chance did likewise. The three soldiers who were on their feet didn't try anything, either. Nobody wanted the lawman getting trigger-happy.

The badge-toter stomped forward a couple of steps and gestured with the shotgun. "You soldier boys get over there by the bar," he ordered. "I'd ask what's goin' on here, but that's pretty obvious, ain't it?" He raised his voice. "Hey, Putnam! Where are you?"

Ace recalled the sign painted on the saloon's false front. He and Chance had seen it when they rode into the small settlement of Packsaddle, Arizona Territory, about an hour earlier. PUTNAM'S SALOON, the sign read, so it was reasonably safe to assume that the bartender was also the proprietor, since he'd been the only one working in the place other than the blond girl.

She spoke up now as she pointed a trembling finger toward the bar. "He's back there, Marshal. One of those soldiers fell on him when all those bottles got knocked down and busted."

"Putnam!" the lawman called again. When he got no response, he told Ace and Chance, "Move on down there with those troopers. Don't try anything."

"We won't, Marshal," Ace said. "We're not looking for trouble."

"That's a blamed lie," one of the soldiers said. "They came in here and picked a fight with Sergeant MacDonald for no good reason!"

Chance started to respond hotly to that, but Ace said, "Keep your shirt on. We'll get a chance to tell our side of the story."

He hoped that was true.

The lawman herded Ace, Chance, and the three soldiers down to the far end of the bar, then said to the girl, "Honey, you take a look back there and see if Putnam is all right."

She looked like she didn't want to do that but was too scared not to obey the order. She approached the bar, rested her hands on it, and leaned forward, sticking her head out and craning her neck to see.

Then she took a fast step backward and cried out again.

"What in blazes is wrong?" the marshal demanded.

"It . . . it's Mr. P-Putnam," Honey said. "I think he's dead!"

"Dead! What in blazes?"

The marshal kept the shotgun trained on his prisoners as he moved around the far end of the bar and looked along the floor behind it. He started to curse and sounded as surprised as he did angry.

Ace risked leaning over the bar to have a look for himself. He saw the sprawled body of the trooper who had fallen off the bar while trying to kick him in the head. He appeared to be out cold, but his chest rose and fell.

Underneath the trooper lay the bartender. Broken glass from the bottles and a big pool of spilled whiskey surrounded both men. At first glance, Ace couldn't tell what Honey and the marshal were talking about, but then he looked closer, saw the unnatural angle of the bartender's neck, and realized that the man's eyes were open and staring sightlessly at the ceiling.

"Is he . . . ?" Chance asked in a half-whisper.

"Yeah," Ace said. "Looks like he broke his neck when he got knocked down."

"It was that trooper who did it—"

"That's a lie!" a soldier yelled. "It wasn't Haygood's fault! That varmint right there done it!"

He leveled an accusing finger at Ace.

"Me?" Ace said, his eyes widening. "I didn't do anything—"

The marshal said, "All of you, shut up. I'll get to the bottom of this." Without taking his eyes off Ace, Chance, and the other men, he said to the girl, "Honey, what happened here?"

"It . . . it wasn't my fault, Marshal—"

"I didn't say it was. Just tell me what happened."

Honey took a deep breath, which lifted the creamy half-moons of her breasts that showed above the low neckline of her short, spangled dress. "It was just a normal evening," she began. "Sergeant MacDonald and those other troopers from the fort came in, and those two fellas I don't know"—nodding toward Ace and Chance—"and some other men from here in town. Vince—Sergeant MacDonald—and the others seemed to be in kind of a hurry at first, but then they started drinking and they weren't in as much of a rush after that. Vince wanted me to sit with them . . . he's kind of sweet on me, I think . . . and I didn't mind, but then he pulled me onto his lap and he was getting kind of rough, and . . . and I kind of let out a yelp—"

"He was mauling her," Chance interrupted before Ace could stop him. "And I can't stand to see a woman being mistreated like that."

"It was none of your business," a trooper snapped at him.

"I *made* it my business," Chance responded defiantly.

"Anyway," Honey went on, "that stranger told Vince to leave me alone, and Vince didn't take it kindly . . . Vince never took many things kindly, you know . . . and that was how the trouble started. Pretty soon they were all fighting, all the soldiers against those two young strangers. I . . . I really don't know what happened after that. It was all a blur."

"You didn't see Putnam get killed?"

Honey shook her head emphatically as she bit at her bottom lip. "I saw that soldier fall on him, but that's all. I didn't have any idea he . . . he . . ."

She covered her face with her hands again. Ace wasn't sure she was really quite as grief-stricken as she was acting, but she did seem to be genuinely shaken up.

The soldier who had blamed Ace for the saloon-keeper's death spoke up again. "I can tell you what happened, Marshal. It's this man's fault, right here." Again he pointed an accusing finger at Ace.

"How's that possible, when it's Private Haygood layin' on top of Putnam?" the marshal wanted to know. "He's got to be the one who knocked him down and broke his neck."

"Yeah, but it was this young peckerwood who *pushed* Haygood and made him fall on Putnam. Poor ol' Haygood just climbed up on the bar to try to get away from these two loco coyotes."

"What!" Chance couldn't hold in the startled exclamation. "That's the craziest thing I've ever heard!"

"He wasn't trying to get away," Ace said. "He climbed up there so he could try to kick me in the head. And I didn't push him. He slipped in a puddle of beer. What happened to Mr. Putnam was a tragic accident, Marshal."

The three soldiers started clamoring otherwise, taking up the first one's claim that Ace was responsible for the saloonkeeper's death. The others were starting to come around now, including Sergeant MacDonald, and as they staggered to their feet, they added their voices to the commotion even though they probably didn't know what they were agreeing to. But they stuck together and made Ace and Chance out to be the villains of the whole affair.

"All of you, shut your yaps!" the marshal roared after a moment. Nobody was going to argue with a man holding a shotgun, so silence fell on the barroom.

The lawman went on, "I'm gonna have to talk to the other men who were in here when the trouble started. Honey, you're gonna give me their names, as best you can remember. But until then, I'm lockin' up the whole lot of you!"

"You can't do that!" MacDonald said. "We're cavalry troopers. You got no authority over us!"

"You're wrong about that, Sergeant. My jurisdiction covers everybody in this settlement, army and civilian alike."

MacDonald's mouth twisted in a snarl that pulled the scar on his face even tighter. "There's eight of us and one of you, old man."

"Yeah, and at this range, more than likely I can only kill two or three of you with this Greener. But that'll give me time to get my Colt out and kill two or three more of you. You want to bet that you'll be one of the few left alive?"

Clearly, this veteran lawman still had plenty of bark on him, and none of the soldiers wanted to make that wager. The marshal took the shotgun in his left hand and drew the revolver on his hip with his right.

"Everybody put your hardware on the bar," he ordered. "Just look like you're thinkin' about doing anything foolish, and you'll get a slug for your trouble."

Ace and Chance exchanged a glance. Ace said, "Once he talks to the other witnesses, they'll clear us of any wrongdoing."

"You've got more faith in your fellow man than I do, Ace," Chance said sourly, "but I suppose we don't have much choice."

Other than a gun battle with a lawman—something neither of them wanted—that was true. Ace unbuckled the gunbelt around his hips and put it and the holstered Colt on the bar. Chance followed suit, removing the crossdraw rig he wore and the ivory-handled .38 caliber Smith & Wesson Second Model revolver in its holster.

As a noncommissioned officer, Sergeant MacDonald was the only one of the troopers to have a handgun. With a surly glare on his face, he placed it on the bar. The soldiers gathered up their forage caps while Ace picked up his brown Stetson and Chance found his cream-colored hat on the floor. Chance made a face as he brushed sawdust from it.

"Move," the marshal ordered. The ten prisoners filed out of the saloon with the lawman following.

"What about poor Mr. Putnam?" Honey called from behind them.

"I'll send the undertaker to collect him," the marshal replied. He chuckled dryly. "You boys ought to know what's comin' next. March!"

CHAPTER THREE

Ace and Chance Jensen were twins, although most folks wouldn't think so to look at them because they were fraternal twins, not identical. Ace, born a few minutes earlier, had dark hair and broader shoulders and preferred to dress in simple range clothes. Chance, slender and sandy-haired, had a fancier taste in his garb, running toward tan suits, stylish cravats, and stickpins.

Their taste in other things differed as well. Chance had more of an eye for a pretty girl, liked to spend most of his time playing cards in saloons, and could be reckless and impulsive. Ace sometimes worried that he was too level-headed and boring, but he supposed that he and Chance balanced each other out fairly well.

Well enough, at any rate, that they had survived several years of drifting around the frontier, working when they had to, and displaying an alarming tendency, as Ace had noted, of winding up in some sort of trouble.

The cell door clanged as Marshal Hank Glennon

slammed it shut behind them. Ace knew the lawman's name because he had spotted it on some correspondence on Glennon's desk as he goaded the prisoners through the marshal's office into the cell block.

At least Glennon hadn't locked them in the same cell as those troopers. There were four cells back here, two on either side of a short center aisle. The soldiers were in the cells across the way, four prisoners in each enclosure. Several of them, including Sergeant Vince MacDonald, gripped the bars and glared murderously at the Jensen brothers.

"You'll pay for what you done," MacDonald said. "You've ruined everything!"

"We were just looking for a peaceful drink, maybe a card game," Chance said. "Don't blame us for you being a hotheaded brute."

MacDonald snarled and looked like he wanted to rip the bars of the cell door apart.

"Don't waste your breath arguing with him," Ace told his brother. "You're not going to change anybody's mind. Let's just hope the marshal rounds up enough witnesses to clear us of any wrongdoing and lets us out of here."

"He's got to, because we *didn't* do anything wrong."

The cell had two bunks in it. Chance went over and sat down on one of them. He looked down at his suit and sighed. The breast pocket was ripped, and brown stains blotched the fabric here and there.

"I think a spittoon must have gotten knocked over during the fight," he said as he made a face.

"I wouldn't be a bit surprised."

Ace sat down on the other bunk. He and his brother had drifted west from Texas, and they'd made it all the way through New Mexico Territory without encountering any problems. That had been encouraging enough to make Ace hope that maybe their luck had changed. They were fiddlefooted sorts, never content to stay in any one place for too long, but it would be nice if they could indulge their wandering ways without having to fight all the time.

Now, on their first night in Arizona Territory, they had wound up behind bars. So much for a change of luck.

Marshal Glennon had left the heavy door between the office and the cell block open, but now he closed it, plunging the cell block into darkness except for what light came through a small, barred window in the door. A moment later, Ace heard the office's outer door close.

"He's going out to round up those witnesses now," Ace said. "We'll probably be stuck in here until tomorrow morning. The marshal will charge us with disturbing the peace, and the local judge will levy a fine against us and make us pay for some of the damages to the saloon."

"You predicting the future now, Ace?" Chance asked dryly.

"Well, it's not like we've never been through this sort of thing before." Ace stretched out on the bunk and put his hands behind his head, lacing the fingers together. "We might as well try to get some rest. And look on the bright side . . . we didn't have to pay for a hotel room."

On the other side of the aisle, the soldiers had gathered together on both sides of the bars that separated the two cells. They talked in low, urgent voices. Ace couldn't make out any of the words, but they sounded upset. More upset than spending a night in jail for disturbing the peace ought to make them, Ace thought with a frown. Maybe they were worried that Private Haygood would be charged with causing the death of Putnam, the saloonkeeper. Ace wasn't sure that would be fair. As he had told Marshal Glennon, Putnam's death had been a tragic accident. He was confident the witnesses would bear that out.

But *were* there any witnesses to that part of the fight? Or had they all fled from the saloon by that time, except for Honey? Ace wasn't sure about that. Maybe, as far as Glennon was concerned, the facts of the case *weren't* as cut-and-dried as they appeared to Ace. And *that* was a mite worrisome . . .

"You just keep looking on the bright side, Ace," Chance said into the gloom from the other bunk. "But me . . . I've got a bad feeling we may have wound up on the road to hell."

Eventually, the troopers in the other cells fell silent—until they started snoring. At times the racket seemed loud enough to rattle the iron bars in the windows. Ace and Chance dozed off, resigned to the fact that the marshal wasn't going to release them tonight, and slept some, but not well.

In the morning, as the gray light of a new day brightened the windows, MacDonald and the other soldiers were even more sullen, because now they were hung over as well as locked up. One of the men directed a low, monotous drone of obscenity at Ace and Chance. They ignored him as best they could.

The cell block door opened, and an old man in overalls and a battered straw hat limped in. He had a coffeepot in one hand, using a thick piece of leather to hold its handle, and a wicker basket with tin cups in it in the other hand. He held out the basket and the men reached through the bars and helped themselves to the cups. Then the old-timer began filling them from the coffeepot.

"Ain't we gonna get anything to eat, Turley?" a trooper asked.

The old-timer snorted and said in a wheezy voice, "It ain't the jailer's job to feed you varmints. That's up to the marshal, if'n he wants to, and I don't reckon he figures you boys are worth the trouble. You're lucky I was feelin' generous and brewed up this pot o' coffee."

MacDonald took a sip, grimaced, and said, "You used yesterday's grounds!"

Old Turley sneered through the bars. "Like I said, consider yourself lucky you're gettin' anything at all."

He turned to the cell on the other side of the aisle to let Ace and Chance claim the remaining two cups in the basket.

"We're much obliged to you, mister," Ace said as Turley poured the brown liquid in his cup. When he tasted it, it wasn't very good, but better than nothing, he supposed.

"You know when the marshal's going to let us out of here?" Chance asked.

"He don't tell me nothin' about that." Turley

cackled a laugh. "I wouldn't go gettin' your hopes up, though!"

Ace said, "What do you mean by that? We're prepared to pay a fine for disturbing the peace and our share of the damages to the saloon, but—"

"Don't bother me with all that," Turley said. "None o' my business. Now drink up, the lot o' ya, so's I can have them cups back."

The soldiers slurped the rest of their coffee and dropped the empty cups back in the basket. Ace and Chance finished theirs as well, and as Ace put his cup in the basket, he said, "You didn't seem worried about any of the prisoners trying to throw hot coffee in your face and escape."

"Why in tarnation would I worry about that? Scaldin' me wouldn't do nobody a durned bit o' good. I ain't got the keys to these cells. They're out in the office. And folks around here know that if you mess with me while you're locked up, I'll fetch my varmint gun and dust your britches with rock salt. I've blasted many a unruly critter right through them bars."

"Well, we're not going to give you any trouble," Ace said.

"That's right," Chance said. "We just want to put this mess behind us, along with this sorry settlement!"

Turley slapped his overalled thigh and whooped with laughter. "You just go on a-thinkin' that, son, you just go on a-thinkin' that!"

The old jailer was still laughing as he left the cell block, and Ace didn't like the sound of it at all. He and Chance exchanged a worried glance.

Ace didn't think it would do any good, but he went

to the cell door, looked across at the other prisoners, and asked, "Do you know what the old man was talking about? He seems to think we might be in some real trouble."

Sergeant MacDonald sneered at him. "Yeah, that's generally what happens when you kill a man."

"But we didn't kill him. Mr. Putnam's death was an accident. If anyone's to blame, it's—"

Ace stopped short. MacDonald and the others wouldn't want to hear anything about it being Private Haygood's fault that the saloonkeeper died. They would all swear it hadn't happened that way, and there were eight of them against the word of the two Jensen brothers.

His and Chance's fate might well be riding on the testimony of that saloon girl, Honey, Ace realized, and it was a sobering thought. He had no idea what the girl might do. She might be grateful because Chance had tried to help her, but she might be angry that the whole thing was going to cause her trouble, or too afraid of MacDonald and the others to tell the truth.

Half an hour dragged by, and then a key rattled again in the lock of the cell block door. It swung back and Marshal Glennon came in, shotgun tucked under his arm. Three men followed him, and each of them carried a Greener, too. Two went to the far end of the aisle and took up positions there, while the other man posted himself next to Glennon, who said over his shoulder, "All right, Turley, let them out."

Turley came in, grumbling. "That's right, send the old man to unlock the cells so if them varmints try to escape, he'll get mowed down right along with 'em.

You boys better behave yourselves, 'cause if I get killed on account o' you, I'll be waitin' right there at the Devil's right hand to torment you for all eternity when you get down yonder to the fiery pit!"

"Shut up, you old pelican," Glennon snapped. "Nobody's going to try anything with four shotguns pointed at them, not even this bunch. And not those two saddle tramps, either."

Turley unlocked the cells and scurried out with his crablike gait. Glennon motioned with his shotgun and ordered, "Come on. You fellas have all got a date with the judge."

CHAPTER FOUR

Packsaddle wasn't the county seat, so there was no courthouse. A town hall was located down the street from the marshal's office and jail, though, so that was where Glennon and his deputies herded the prisoners. Glennon led the way, with a man on either side of the group and one bringing up the rear. Surrounded by shotguns that way, the prisoners had no opportunity to try anything.

Quite a few townspeople watched from the boardwalks as the procession went by. Saloon brawls were nothing unusual, but a man had died in this one, a prominent local businessman, at that. Ace saw expressions of avid interest on the faces of those they passed.

No sympathy, though, except from one elderly, white-haired woman with a wrinkled face under a sunbonnet, who looked at the prisoners as if they were her wayward grandchildren.

The town hall was set up as a courtroom, with a table in the front of the big room for the judge and ladderback chairs arranged in rows facing it. Marshal Glennon motioned for the prisoners to arrange themselves along the front row of chairs and told them, "Stay on your feet. Judge Bannister will be here in a minute, so there ain't no point in you sittin' down."

Some of the townspeople filed into the hall behind them and filled the rest of the seats as spectators.

True to the marshal's prediction, a door in the back of the room opened a couple of minutes later and a portly figure with a round face and smooth brown hair came out. The man wore a black robe and carried a gavel and a Bible.

"All rise," Glennon intoned. The spectators got to their feet as the judge shuffled over to the table and put the gavel and Bible on it. He sat down and waved them back into their chairs, including the prisoners.

After a rap of the gavel, the judge said, "This court is now in session, Judge Horace Bannister presiding. That would be me. Marshal, what have we got here?"

Glennon had removed his hat. He stood at the end of the front row where the prisoners sat and said, "The following are here to answer to the charges of disturbing the peace and destruction of property, Your Honor."

He named the troopers, starting with Sergeant Vince MacDonald, but he didn't call the names of Ace and Chance Jensen. That omission deepened the frown that was already on Ace's face.

"And what about those two at the end?" Judge Bannister asked. "The two who aren't soldiers."

"They claim they're brothers. Ace and Chance Jensen are the names they gave me. They're also being charged with disturbing the peace and destruction of property . . ." Glennon paused, clearly for dramatic effect. "And murder."

Hearing it spoken that way was like a punch in the gut. Chance shot to his feet and exclaimed, "That's a lie!"

Ace couldn't stay seated, either. He stood up and forced himself to stay calm as he said, "That's not how it happened, Your Honor."

The deputies had already snapped their shotguns to their shoulders and trained the weapons on the Jensen brothers. Bannister glared at Ace and Chance and said, "Sit down! You'll have a chance to answer to the charges."

"But we didn't—" Chance began.

"Marshal!" Judge Bannister said. "If these two prisoners don't comport themselves with the dignity that should be accorded to these proceedings, I want you to have them restrained and gagged!"

Glennon looked like he would be more than happy to carry out that order. Ace put a hand on his brother's shoulder and told him quietly, "We'd better take it easy. We're liable to just make things worse if we argue right now."

"But . . . but . . ." Chance sighed. "All right."

Muttering, he sank back into his chair. Ace sat down beside him.

Bannister pointed the gavel at them and said, "I'm warning you two. No more foolishness like that." He nodded to Glennon. "Proceed, Marshal. I assume since we have no official prosecutor, you'll be handling that part of the proceedings as well?"

"That's right, Your Honor. The charges arise

from an altercation in Putnam's Saloon yesterday evening, an altercation provoked by Ace and Chance Jensen."

Chance leaned forward, ready to leap to his feet again and deny that accusation, but Ace caught his eye and gave a tiny shake of his head. Seething, Chance sat back again.

"A considerable amount of damage was done in that brawl," Glennon went on, "including broken furniture and more than a dozen broken bottles of whiskey, and that's why Sergeant MacDonald and the other troopers are charged with disturbing the peace and destruction of property. But the fight also resulted in the death of George Putnam, the owner of the establishment and a leading citizen of Packsaddle. Because the Jensen brothers started the fight, and because the actions of Ace Jensen, in particular, resulted in Mr. Putnam's death, they're being charged with murder as well."

Judge Bannister nodded solemnly and looked at Ace and Chance. "How do you plead?"

Ace started to get to his feet, then paused and glanced at Marshal Glennon, who nodded for him to go ahead. Ace straightened and said, "My brother and I plead not guilty, Your Honor."

"Which one are you?" Bannister asked.

"Ace Jensen, sir."

"Do you expect me to believe that your mother actually named the two of you Ace and Chance?"

"Well, uh . . . no, sir. My name is really William, and my brother is Benjamin. But we've always gone by the other names. You see, the man who raised us . . . he was a gambler—"

"Never mind," Bannister said. "I just wanted your real names to enter into the record. This is a court of law, not a gambling den." He looked at the soldiers. "What about the rest of you? How do you plead to the charges against you?"

Sergeant MacDonald stood up as the spokesman for the group and said, "Guilty, Your Honor." He looked and sounded surly about it but didn't hesitate. "We'll pay the fine and the damages."

"We'll get to that, we'll get to that. First there's the matter of determining the outcome of the other charges."

MacDonald took a step forward and said, "But we pled guilty. Just tell us how much the fine and the damages amount to, and we'll pay it."

An anxious edge in the three-striper's voice made Ace remember what Honey had said the night before about how the soldiers had seemed to be in a hurry when they first came into the saloon. MacDonald sounded impatient now, and the other troopers looked worried. Ace supposed they were eager to get back to the fort before they got in trouble for not being at their posts. He wasn't familiar with the forts in this area and didn't know how far away this one was from Packsaddle.

"All in due time, Sergeant," Bannister responded. "Justice will not be rushed." He nodded to Glennon. "Proceed with your case against William and Benjamin Jensen, Marshal."

"Yes, sir. I'd like to call Alice Winslow to testify."

A young woman with her hair pulled back from her face in a severe bun stood up and moved forward. With her hair like that, and wearing a plain gray dress, she didn't look much like the saloon girl called Honey, but Ace knew that's who she was. She gave him a glance as she went past. He saw sadness in her eyes, and that made his guts tighten.

He got to his feet again and said, "Your Honor, aren't defendants supposed to have a lawyer?"

Bannister smiled, but the expression didn't make Ace feel any better. "Son, if you can find another lawyer in Packsaddle besides myself, you're free to engage his services. But I don't believe you will. In the meantime, although it's somewhat irregular in most courts, I will allow you to represent your brother and yourself."

Ace swallowed. "Uh . . . thank you, Your Honor."

When he sat down, Chance leaned over to him and whispered, "We're in bad trouble, aren't we?"

"It's starting to look like it."

"Wish I could say I'm surprised . . . No, it really wouldn't make any difference if I was, would it?"

Ace didn't answer that. He watched as Judge Bannister instructed the witness to place her hand on the Bible and swear to tell the truth, the whole truth, and nothing but the truth, so help her God.

"I do," Alice Winslow said.

"Just take a seat there, in that chair at the end of the table, my dear."

Marshal Glennon said, "Miss Winslow, you work at Putnam's Saloon, is that right?"

"Yes, Marshal, you know I do."

"And you were there last night, when the fight started between those two strangers and the soldiers from the fort?"

"Yes, sir."

"Who started the fight?"

Alice—or Honey—bit her bottom lip for a second, and Ace hoped she would tell the truth. But then she said, "That man there, the one called Chance Jensen. He . . . he attacked Sergeant MacDonald."

Chance was on his feet too fast for Ace to stop him. "MacDonald threw the first punch! And all I did was try to get him to stop hurting this girl!"

"Sit down," Bannister grated. He looked at Alice. "Was the sergeant hurting you, Miss Winslow?"

"N-no, he was just . . . playing around, the way he always does."

Down the row of chairs, MacDonald leaned forward and smirked at Ace and Chance. His companions, though, still seemed bothered by the fact that they were sitting here in the town hall when clearly they would have preferred to be elsewhere.

"So Chance Jensen started all this trouble without any good reason, is that right?"

Alice swallowed and nodded.

"You'll have to speak up, Miss Winslow," the judge prodded. "It's your testimony that Chance Jensen acted without provocation in causing this altercation?"

"Y-yes, sir. That's what happened."

Chance whispered to Ace, "She's too scared to tell the truth." Ace just nodded.

"And after that?" Glennon said. "When Private Haygood climbed onto the bar to get away from the fight?"

Alice just looked down and didn't say anything. After a couple of seconds, Glennon went on harshly, "Ace Jensen pushed him off, didn't he? He caused Haygood to fall on George Putnam and break his neck?"

Alice's voice was so low Ace could barely hear it. "That . . . that's right." She didn't lift her head, as if she were afraid to let her eyes meet his.

Glennon looked at Bannister and said, "I reckon that's about the size of it, Judge."

Ace put his hands on his knees and pushed himself to his feet. "You said that I could represent myself and my brother, Your Honor. I'd like to question Miss Winslow."

"That is your right," Bannister said. "Proceed." When Ace started to step forward, Bannister lifted a hand and added, "From there will suffice."

"All right. Miss Winslow . . . Alice . . . are you sure things happened exactly the way you've told them?"

"I . . . I wouldn't lie in court," she said.

"I know you wouldn't want two innocent men to be convicted of such serious charges, so I'll ask you again. Is that the way it *really* happened in the saloon last night—"

Alice lifted her head and cried, "I told you! I said what happened! I don't know what else to say!" Then she put her hands over her face as she started to cry.

"That's enough," Bannister said. "The witness is excused."

Alice stood up and hurried past Ace and Chance. This time she didn't as much as glance in their direction. She went all the way out of the town hall and broke into a run as she went through the doors. Ace figured guilt and shame were making her flee—but they weren't enough to make her tell the truth.

Judge Bannister looked coldly at Ace and Chance. "Do you have anything else?"

"Your Honor, my brother and I are being railroaded. Everybody here knows that. I'm sorry about what happened to Mr. Putnam, but it wasn't our fault. I never laid a hand on the fella who knocked him down—"

"Do you have any witnesses to prove that?" Bannister snapped.

"No, sir. We've been locked up since it happened—"

"The legal system operates on the testimony of witnesses. Since you have none to testify on your behalf, I have no choice but to declare this trial concluded and render a verdict."

Ace couldn't hold in the reaction that boiled up inside him. "We're being railroaded! This wasn't a proper trial! There wasn't even a jury—"

Bannister leaned forward, gripping the gavel tightly, and his voice was cold as ice as he said, "Do you really believe a jury would have made any difference?"

It wouldn't have. Ace knew that. Just like he knew that the outcome had always been a foregone conclusion.

"You there," Bannister said. "The other one. You stand up, too."

Chance rose to his feet. His face was pale with strain under his permanent tan, and Ace imagined he looked the same way. Both of them knew what was coming.

"William Jensen and Benjamin Jensen, I find you guilty on the charge of murder in the death of George Putnam," Bannister said, "and I sentence you both to be hanged by the neck until dead."

The gavel came down on the table like the crack of doom.

CHAPTER FIVE

"No!" Chance took a threatening step toward the table. "We didn't do it, I tell you!"

Shotgun hammers cocked ominously as the three deputies pointed their weapons at the Jensen brothers. Marshal Glennon had leaned his shotgun in the corner, but he rested his hand on the butt of his revolver, ready to draw and fire if need be.

Ace caught hold of Chance's upper arm. He knew that if Chance rushed the judge, one or more of the deputies would blast him with a double load of buckshot.

As he held his brother back, Ace said, "Judge, I object. I'm asking for a fair trial in another town."

"You committed your crimes here, and you've had your trial here," Bannister said. "And it was fair, according to the laws of the territory. Both of you sit down while these proceedings continue, or else Marshal Glennon and his men will have no choice but to open fire on you."

A frightened murmur swept through the spectators. Some of them toward the back of the room

stood up and edged toward the entrance. If the
deputies cut loose with those Greeners in here, there
was no telling where all the buckshot might go.

Ace wasn't sure how the proceedings could continue when Bannister had already found them guilty
and sentenced them to death, but getting themselves
cut down by those shotguns wouldn't accomplish anything except to put them in an even earlier grave. So
he urged Chance back into his chair and then sat
down himself.

"That's more like it," Bannister said. "I'm glad to
see that you boys are going to be reasonable. Now,
as far as the other defendants go—"

"Just tell us how much we owe, Judge," Sergeant
MacDonald interrupted, drawing an angry glare
from Bannister.

"All right, I will, Sergeant," the judge snapped. "I
rule that fines and damages in the amount of five
thousand dollars will be paid to this court."

Now it was the turn of MacDonald and the other
troopers to leap to their feet and shout in stunned,
angry amazement. At Glennon's barked order, two of
the deputies swung their shotguns toward the soldiers
while the other man kept his weapon trained on Ace
and Chance. Adding to the commotion in the makeshift courtroom, Judge Bannister pounded on the
table with his gavel until the troopers finally quieted
down.

MacDonald said, "Judge, you know good and well
we can't pay five grand."

"In that case," Bannister said with a shrug, "I

sentence each of you to thirty days in jail. I know you're capable of doing *that*."

The troopers looked at each other with expressions of sheer desperation on their faces. For some reason, the jail sentence struck terror into their hearts. Ace couldn't see why it would unless they believed it would also get them in trouble with their superiors at the fort, which seemed entirely possible.

Ace wasn't sure why he was even pondering that question at such a time, unless he was trying to distract himself from being sentenced to death just a few minutes earlier. That was almost too much for him to grasp.

"Court is adjourned," Bannister announced. "Marshal, escort the prisoners back to jail."

"With pleasure," Glennon said. He raised his voice. "All you people, clear out! I want a clear path for these men when they go out of here."

The spectators who were left in the town hall departed rapidly. Once again, the marshal and his men ringed the prisoners so they would be in a crossfire if they tried anything, and then Glennon ordered them to get moving.

"We can't just let them take us back to jail," Chance said in a low, urgent voice. "They're going to hang us!"

"I know, but if we try to make a break for it, they'll gun us down," Ace argued. "You can tell by looking at Glennon, he'd like nothing better. Maybe if we cooperate, there'll be a better chance later—"

"Until they *hang* us!"

"Did you see a gallows anywhere in town?"

Chance frowned but didn't say anything, which was the same as agreeing that he hadn't.

"Well, that means they'll have to build one," Ace went on. "That gives us some time. Maybe that girl will change her mind and tell the truth. The way she rushed out of here, it seemed like lying under oath bothered her."

"You think that judge will pay any attention to her, even if she does?"

This time it was Ace who didn't have an answer. He had to admit, it seemed as if Judge Bannister had had his mind made up before he ever entered the courtroom—and not just where the verdict was concerned, but the sentence, as well.

What it all came down to was that there was very little room for argument with four shotguns. That amounted to eight barrels of buckshot, and even if all the prisoners rushed the lawmen at the same time, it was unlikely more than one or two of them would survive, if that many. They had to decide between slaughter and even the thinnest thread of hope—and hope won out.

The prisoners shuffled out of the town hall. The townspeople lined the boardwalks again to watch as they walked back down the street to the jail. And as they did, the bitter, sour taste of defeat was strong under Ace Jensen's tongue.

Back in the same cell, Ace and Chance sagged onto the bunks. They stared into space in front of them, and after a few minutes, Chance asked, "Do you think the marshal will bother feeding us? Or will he just consider that a waste of money and effort?"

"A lawman's got to feed his prisoners."

Suddenly, the sound of hammering somewhere in town drifted through the barred window. "You think so?" Chance said with a wry smile. "Sounds to me like they're already getting that gallows built for us. When you have several men working on the job, it doesn't take long to hammer one of those things together."

That was true. In fact, from the sound of it, the townspeople would have the gallows ready before the day was over.

Oddly enough, across the aisle in the other cells, the troopers were glum enough that anybody looking at them might think that *they* were facing death sentences.

After a while, the cell block door opened and the jailer, Turley, came in. He had someone with him, the old woman Ace had noticed earlier as they were being taken from the jail to the town hall for the so-called trial. Turley said, "You fellas got a visitor. Behave yourselves, or you'll plumb regret it."

The woman had a wicker basket with a cloth over it. She said, "I baked biscuits for you boys. Least I can do to make your time here pass a little easier."

She took the cloth off the basket and moved along the bars, letting the prisoners reach through to get biscuits.

When she turned to the Jensen brothers, Chance didn't get up from his bunk. "I don't have much of an appetite," he said with a surly expression on his face.

"Don't mind my brother, ma'am," Ace said as he

went to the bars and reached through to take a biscuit. "I surely do appreciate your kindness. If it's all right with you, I'll just go ahead and take a biscuit for him, too. I'm sure he'll eat it in a little while."

"You go right ahead, sonny," she said. "You boys remind me so much of my grandsons."

"Why thank you, ma'am."

The old woman smiled, bobbed her head, and moved on. After he had ushered her out, Turley pushed the cell block door up most of the way and looked back at Ace.

"Don't go thinkin' kind thoughts about that ol' gal," the jailer said. "Her grandsons were owlhoots, both of 'em. Plumb lowdown varmints, and rattlesnake mean. They wound up dancin' on air over at Yuma Territorial Prison, and considerin' everything they done, you could've hung 'em half a dozen more times and it would'a just started payin' for all of it. Ever since then, she's been comin' in here to bring food to the prisoners, but it never changes nothin'. They're still dead!"

Cackling, Turley went out of the cell block. Ace sat down and ate one of the biscuits, but it didn't taste as good as it might have otherwise.

The jail's thick stone walls kept some of the heat out, but even so, it grew stiflingly warm in the cell block as the day went on. Or maybe that was just desperation he was feeling. By the middle of the afternoon, when it had become obvious that the prisoners weren't going to get a midday meal, the hammering stopped.

"Executions are usually carried out at sunup, aren't

they?" Chance said. "Maybe they're going to change things up and hang us when the sun goes down."

Or maybe they wouldn't even wait that long, because a few minutes later, the cell block door opened again and Marshal Hank Glennon strode in, shotgun tucked under his arm. The trio of deputies followed him.

"All right, you Jensen boys, on your feet," he said. "You've got another date—and this time it's with the hangman."

CHAPTER SIX

Ace's heart seemed to fill his throat. He couldn't believe everything was going to end in this scruffy little Arizona Territory settlement. He didn't stand up, and neither did Chance.

Glennon drew his Colt. "All right, if that's the way you want it, I'll blast your kneecaps and we'll drag you to the gallows. Either way, you still wind up at the end of a rope."

The Jensen brothers looked at each other. Chance said, "If I've got to cross the divide, I want to be on my feet when I do it."

"Yeah, that's the way I feel, too."

They rose from the bunks at the same time. Glennon kept the gun trained on them as he said, "Let 'em out of there, Turley."

The old jailer crabbed along the aisle to the door and unlocked it, then got out of the way in a hurry. Glennon motioned with the Colt. Ace and Chance walked out and followed the marshal as he backed into the office, where the shotgun-toting deputies waited.

Sergeant MacDonald called from the cell block,

"You boys are gonna be shakin' hands with the Devil real soon now! Hope you enjoy it!"

Ace and Chance ignored the taunt. With the deputies surrounding them, they walked out of the marshal's office. Shotgun barrels prodded them toward the edge of town, where the gallows stood waiting. Just one rope dangled from the crossbar above the trapdoor.

"You're gonna have to take turns," Glennon said. "I'll let you decide who goes first. If you can't decide, I'll flip a coin."

"I was born first," Ace said. "Reckon I can leave first."

"Yeah, that's just like you," Chance said. "Always hogging the lead." The brave grin he gave his brother took any sting out of the words.

Not surprisingly, quite a crowd had turned out to watch the double hanging. A feeling of celebration hung in the hot air. There was nothing like an execution to spice up the monotony of day-to-day life in a frontier settlement.

As they trudged along the dusty street, Chance asked in a low voice, "Are we going to make a break for it?"

"We'll just get gunned down if we do."

"Yeah, but that's a better way to go than dancing on air, isn't it?"

Ace looked around at the townspeople gathered on the boardwalks and in the street. "It's just like in the courtroom," he said. "If any shooting starts, innocent folks are liable to get hurt."

Chance made a face. "And we can't have that. I

swear, Ace, sometimes I think you're just too blasted decent for your own good."

"If that was true, Fate ought to see to it that something happens to get us out of this mess. But it's not looking like that's going to happen."

Indeed, the brothers had reached the bottom of the thirteen steps leading up to the gallows platform. When they hesitated, Glennon said, "We can still shoot you and carry you up there, if that's what you want."

"We're going, we're going," Ace muttered.

"Up you go, then."

Ace headed up the stairs first, with Chance following him. Another deputy with a shotgun waited at the top, along with a scrawny man in a dusty black suit who clutched a small black book. Ace figured he was a preacher, there to share a last-minute prayer with the men about to be executed, if they so desired.

Glennon followed them to the platform, with Turley behind him. The marshal ordered, "Tie their hands behind their backs." Turley had a couple of short pieces of rope ready to carry out the order. He jerked the knots painfully tight, but from the looks of things, Ace and Chance weren't going to be uncomfortable for long.

The nervous-looking minister said, "If you boys would like to say anything, either to these folks or the Lord—"

Ace interrupted him. "Sorry, sir, but I reckon the Lord already knows what's in our hearts and minds."

"And we don't have anything to say to this bunch," Chance added as he cast a hostile glance over the assembled crowd eager to watch them swing.

"All right, then," Glennon said as he took the dangling noose and started to fit it over Ace's head and around his neck.

The old woman who had brought biscuits to the jail stood in the front ranks of the crowd. She cupped her hands around her mouth and shouted, "They're innocent! They didn't do it!"

"Hush," Glennon snapped at her. He tightened the noose around Ace's neck. Ace took as deep a breath as he could with the rope pressing against his throat and closed his eyes. The crowd was hushed in anticipation now.

That silence meant the sudden rattle of hoofbeats sounded even louder than it might have otherwise. Ace opened his eyes.

A cavalry patrol of two dozen men, led by an officer and trailed by a wagon drawn by a team of four mules, came down Packsaddle's main street from the west. They didn't stop when they reached the edge of the crowd, so the group was forced to part for them as the soldiers rode right up to the gallows.

The officer in charge was a lieutenant, Ace saw, a wiry, dark-haired man with a thin mustache. As he reined in, he held up his other hand in a signal for the rest of the detail to halt.

Glennon asked, "What do you want, Lieutenant?"

"I understand you're holding some men from Fort Gila in your jail, Marshal."

"How'd you know that?"

"It's the army's business to know what goes on," the lieutenant answered. "Is it true?"

"Yeah, I've got 'em locked up. They busted up a

saloon, and they can't pay the fine and damages. The judge sentenced them to thirty days behind bars."

"Well, that sentence will have to be set aside. The army has a prior claim on them."

"What in blazes are you talking about?"

"They're deserters," the lieutenant said. "We've come to take them back to the fort so that military justice can deal with them."

That explained why MacDonald and the other soldiers had been so anxious to put Packsaddle behind them this morning. They must have known that someone would be coming after them. They might have believed that their absence wouldn't be noticed for a while, and for that reason, they had delayed their escape long enough to stop in the settlement for a drink.

Of course, everything had gone awry for them after that. If they had been able to ride out early this morning, they might have still gotten away, but stewing in jail most of the day had given the lieutenant and his men time to catch up to them.

Those thoughts flashed through Ace's brain. This was an interesting development, but it wasn't going to do anything to save him and Chance.

Marshal Glennon began, "If you think you can just ride in here—"

"As a matter of fact, I do think that. I think I can ride in and do whatever is necessary to complete my mission, considering that I have the full weight of the United States Army behind me."

Glennon looked like he wanted to argue, but even though he had a handful of deputies to back any play he wanted to make—assuming that they would do so—they wouldn't be a match for two dozen hardbitten cavalry troops.

After a long moment, Glennon said, "I'll have to talk to Judge Bannister. If he agrees, I don't guess there's anything I can do about it."

"You do whatever you need to do, Marshal," the officer replied blandly, "as long as you release those ten prisoners into my custody." He smiled and nodded toward the gallows. "Then you can get on with your other business."

"All right, I suppose I can—Wait a minute. Did you say *ten* prisoners?"

"That's right. That's how many men deserted yesterday."

"There are only eight troopers locked up in my jail."

The lieutenant looked surprised and somewhat disbelieving. "That can't be," he insisted.

"Well, it's the truth, as you can see for yourself if you take a look in my cell block."

"What happened to the other two men?"

"How in blazes should I know? Maybe they split off from the rest of the bunch and ran away in some other direction."

The two men stared at each other for a few seconds, then the lieutenant jerked his head toward the marshal's office and said, "Come on. Send for the judge, and we'll get to the bottom of this."

Glennon stomped down the stairs from the gallows, paused to issue an order to one of his deputies, and then walked toward his office. The lieutenant dismounted and handed his reins to one of the troopers, then followed Glennon. Both of them disappeared into the sturdy stone building. The deputy Glennon had spoken to trotted off toward the town hall to fetch Judge Horace Bannister.

Quietly, Ace said, "Sort of wish the marshal had taken this noose off of me before he left. It's not the most comfortable feeling in the world, having a rope around your neck."

"As long as it's not too tight, I reckon you can put up with it," Chance said. "What do you think is going to happen?"

Ace shook his head. "Blamed if I know."

The judge emerged from the town hall, out of his black robe now and wearing a brown suit and hat. He went into the marshal's office, and after a while— which seemed a lot longer to Ace and Chance as they stood on the gallows waiting for their destiny to be revealed—Glennon and the lieutenant emerged from the marshal's office and came toward the edge of town where everyone waited tensely.

When they got there, Glennon didn't climb the steps. He just looked up at Turley on the platform and said, "Turn them loose. They're going with Lieutenant Olsen."

"What?" Ace and Chance exclaimed at the same time.

With a smug smile, the lieutenant said, "I was sent to bring ten men back to the fort. I'm going to deliver ten men, as ordered."

"But we're not deserters," Chance protested. "We're not even in the army!"

"That's what I pointed out," Glennon said, "but the lieutenant seems to think you'd prefer that to what you've got waiting for you here."

Chance looked at Ace, cocked his head to the side, and said, "He's got a point there."

Ace couldn't contain a sigh of relief as Turley lifted the noose from his neck. A second later, he felt the jailer cutting the bonds that held his hands behind his back. As the rope fell away, Ace pulled his arms in front of him and started rubbing some feeling back into his numb hands.

"I reckon we're in the army now," he said.

CHAPTER SEVEN

The Jensen brothers' horses had been put in the stable the night before when they were locked up.

"Ed Watson down at the livery was disappointed when he heard you boys wasn't gonna get your necks stretched after all," Turley informed Ace and Chance as they stood next to the army wagon. "He figured with you boys bein' dead, he'd get to sell these critters." The old-timer lowered his voice. "O' course, he'd'a had to split whatever he got for 'em with the marshal, but it still would'a been a nice little profit."

"What about our guns and the rest of our gear?" Ace asked.

"Where you're goin', you ain't gonna need it! Same as the horses. So Ed gets to sell it all anyway! Turns out it's a great day for him!"

That set Turley off in gales of laughter once again. He walked away guffawing.

"You know," Chance mused as he watched Turley, "I don't think I like that old codger."

They had traded guards. Now, instead of deputies with shotguns watching them, troopers with Springfield rifles stood nearby with the weapons held at the ready. Other soldiers escorted the prisoners out of the jail. Lieutenant Olsen and Marshal Glennon were on the boardwalk, watching as the deserters climbed awkwardly into the wagon. Ace and Chance were forced at gunpoint to join them. The soldiers had brought ten pairs of manacles and shackles with them, and soon those restraints were fastened around the prisoners' wrists and ankles.

"I wonder how far away this Fort Gila is," Ace said. "The lieutenant said MacDonald and the others deserted yesterday, so it can't be too far."

"Even if the patrol just left there this morning, it's too late in the day for us to get back there before dark. We'll have to spend a night on the trail."

"Are you thinking we might have a chance to get away?"

"The thought crossed my mind," Chance admitted as he made a face at the uncomfortable irons he wore.

"If we did that, we'd be fugitives, not only from the law but probably from the army as well. I'm not sure I want to be looking over my shoulder for the rest of my life."

"What's your idea, then?"

"Talk to the commanding officer when we get to the fort," Ace said. "He's bound to be a reasonable man. He won't punish us for deserting when we're not actually in the army."

"Yeah, but he's liable to send us back to Pack-saddle . . . where there's a gallows waiting for us, remember."

"Not if we can convince him we're telling the truth about what happened. Since MacDonald and the others are deserters, maybe he won't put too much stock in their version of the story."

Chance sighed. "You sure have a lot of faith in other folks' intelligence and decency, big brother. You just don't realize how stupid and venal most people are."

"I just like to give them the benefit of the doubt," Ace said.

"Well, in this case, I hope you're right and whoever's in charge at the fort will be reasonable."

The troopers mounted up. Lieutenant Olsen gave the order to move out. As they left Packsaddle behind them, Ace didn't look back. He hated to lose the things he and Chance were leaving behind, but he supposed the horses, guns, and other items were a small price to pay to escape the gallows.

Of course, as Chance had pointed out, they could only hope they weren't heading into something even worse . . .

This part of the territory was flat and semi-arid, for the most part, although some stretches were green with vegetation and there were occasional rolling hills. Low but rugged-looking mountain ranges loomed in the distance.

Ace and Chance had been in Arizona before, but not this particular area. Ace knew some isolated ranches were located here and there, and mining was also important in these parts, but mostly the region seemed to be pretty sparsely populated.

That probably had something to do with the Apaches who lurked in the mountains and came out to raid from time to time. The army had been engaged in hostilities with them for quite a while without seeming to make any real, long-term dent in the Indians' activities. From what Ace had read about the conflict, it was a war unlike any other the soldiers had fought before. The Apaches were able to strike and then disappear as if they had never been there.

Maybe that was one reason Sergeant MacDonald and the other troopers who had deserted with him looked so unhappy about going back. Not only would they have to endure whatever punishment was meted out to them, but they would have to go on dealing with the threat of the Apaches, too.

The group made camp that evening atop a small, lightly timbered ridge that swept down into a broad, dry valley. Lieutenant Olsen posted guards to watch the horses as well as the prisoners. The shackles were removed from their ankles so they could move around a little, but the manacles remained locked on their wrists. They all had to stay close together to make it easier for the sentries to watch them, so there was only a short distance between where Ace and Chance sat on the ground and the cluster of troopers led by MacDonald.

The scarred noncom glared at the Jensen brothers in the fading light and declared, "This is all your fault."

"How do you figure that?" Chance asked. "We didn't make you desert."

"If it wasn't for you two—especially you, pretty boy—we'd have had our drinks and ridden out of Packsaddle last night. We'd have been a long way off before they discovered this morning that we were gone. And they never would have caught us."

"If you were in that much of a hurry, you never should have stopped to get drunk and maul young women."

MacDonald let out a harsh laugh. "You're talkin' about Honey? She don't mind the fellas havin' a little fun. She likes it! Anyway, any gal who works in a saloon oughta be used to a little rough treatment. It ain't like they're delicate little flowers!"

"That's right, Sarge," another trooper said. He added a few obscene comments about Alice "Honey" Winslow to what MacDonald had just said.

Ace sensed his brother getting angry. "Take it easy," he advised quietly. "Another fight's not going to do our case with the commanding officer any good."

"Don't you ever just want to wallop somebody who's got it coming?"

"All the time," Ace said. "But if I did that, I wouldn't have much time to do anything else."

Chance grunted disdainfully, but he settled back down on the ground.

After a few minutes, Ace asked, "What happened to the other two men who were with you? Did they take off on their own like Marshal Glennon suggested?"

"That's exactly what they did, the sorry sons. I would've tried to stop them—we agreed to stick together—but they slipped off when I wasn't looking. Well, good riddance to them."

"Yeah, good riddance," another man said dryly.

"We're goin' back to hell, and who knows where they are?"

"Going back to hell?" Chance repeated.

"Shut up," MacDonald snapped sullenly at the other troopers. They fell silent, obviously unwilling to cross him.

Later, when the men were trying to go to sleep, Chance whispered to Ace, "You heard how he described the place we're going as hell. Still think the commanding officer there is going to listen to reason?"

"There's not much else we can hope for, is there?"

Ace lay there thinking, and after more time had passed, he whispered, "Something's not right about this."

"Wha . . . ?" Chance responded sleepily. "What are you talking about? Of course it's not right! We got railroaded for murder, and now we've been thrown in with a bunch of army deserters!"

"Marshal Glennon gave in too easily when the lieutenant said he wanted to take us. There was no legal basis for that, and yet the marshal went along with it. Evidently the judge agreed, too. There has to be a reason they did that."

Chance sounded more awake now as he said, "You mean it was some sort of . . . I don't know. A scheme of some kind? Something crooked?"

"If it is, the marshal and the judge have to be in on it, and the lieutenant must be, too. I wonder if we're the first civilians who have been taken back to Fort Gila as deserters."

"I don't know, Ace. That seems like a real stretch to me. Why would anybody do such a thing?"

"That's what I can't figure out," Ace admitted. "And I'm not sure we'll get any answers until we get to the fort."

"Your little theory doesn't make me feel any better. Now I'm more worried than I was before."

"But at least we didn't hang," Ace pointed out, then said, "I wonder if we were ever really supposed to, or if they were just trying to scare us into cooperating and being glad for the army to take us into custody."

"If they were, they did a pretty good job of it!"

Ace remembered how it had felt, standing on that gallows with a noose around his neck, and said, "Yeah, they sure did."

CHAPTER EIGHT

The night passed quietly—but that wasn't destined to last.

Ace woke to the smells of coffee brewing and bacon frying. The prisoners had been fed cold, meager rations the night before and had passed around a canteen of water because Lieutenant Olsen didn't want to build a campfire. As far as Ace knew, there had been no recent reports of Apaches raiding in the area, but he supposed the lieutenant wanted to be cautious.

This morning, though, they would have a hot breakfast before continuing on to Fort Gila. The trooper in charge of it filled plates and coffee cups.

"Blast it, how do you expect us to eat with these chains on?" MacDonald complained.

"You can manage or not, I don't care," the trooper said. "The lieutenant didn't tell me to take 'em off of you, so I don't reckon I ought to."

MacDonald raised his voice. "Lieutenant Olsen, these cuffs are mighty tight, and they make it hard to eat. Considerin' what we're goin' back to, you oughta have a little pity on us!"

Olsen walked over and smirked at the prisoners. "No one forced you to enlist, Sergeant. You knew what you were getting into."

A few yards away, Ace and Chance exchanged a glance. MacDonald's comment didn't make them feel any better about what they were facing. If the brutal, hardnosed three-striper was dreading whatever waited at Fort Gila, it had to be pretty bad.

Bacon, a biscuit, and a cup of hot, strong coffee made them feel a little better. While a couple of the soldiers were hitching the mules to the wagon, MacDonald said to Olsen, "We got to take care of personal business before we set out again, Lieutenant."

Olsen waved a hand at the landscape. "There you go, Sergeant. Anywhere you please."

"Blast it, at least let us go behind those trees over there!" MacDonald pointed with his manacled hands.

Olsen grinned and asked, "What, are you worried about your delicate sensibilities being offended, Sergeant? Fine, go behind the trees. One at a time, though, and with a guard."

MacDonald rattled his chains. "And we got to have these things off."

Olsen lost his grin and said, "Don't push your luck, mister."

Grumbling, MacDonald shrugged and struggled to his feet. He trudged off behind the trees with a rifle-carrying trooper following him. When he came back, the others took their turns, one by one. Ace and Chance would be last.

When the final member of the party of deserters had gone off behind the trees with the guard, Chance said quietly, "This might be our best chance to make a break. And our *last* chance."

"We talked about this," Ace said. "We don't want to be fugitives for the rest of our lives."

"From the sound of it, that might be better than what's waiting for us at that fort."

The worst part of it, Ace thought, was that Chance might be right. The way MacDonald and the others were acting about being taken back to Fort Gila made him think twice about everything he had said to his brother. He supposed they had to at least consider the idea of trying to escape . . .

An alarmed yell, followed instantly by the blast of a shot, interrupted those thoughts. The sounds came from the trees where the last of the deserters had gone, accompanied by a guard. Immediately, the camp was in an uproar as the men turned toward the commotion, cursed, and shouted questions.

A figure burst into view, dashing down the slope. That was the prisoner, Ace realized. He was making a break for it, just as the Jensen brothers had discussed doing, and based on the speed with which he was moving, the shot fired by the guard hadn't hit him. He certainly didn't seem to be injured as he sprinted down the ridge.

Several of the troopers lifted their rifles, but Lieutenant Olsen called, "Hold your fire!"

They stopped what they were doing and looked at him in surprise. Meanwhile, the escaping prisoner was getting farther away with every passing second and each lunging stride.

Olsen held out his right hand and snapped his

fingers. "Private Franklin," he said to one of the troopers near him, "your rifle, please."

"Sir?" the soldier said in obvious confusion.

Olsen just snapped his fingers again, and Private Franklin handed him the Springfield rifle he held. The lieutenant checked the weapon, then lifted it to his shoulder and aimed down the slope toward the fleeing man. Olsen laid his cheek against the smooth wood of the stock and peered over the sights for a long moment before stroking the trigger.

The crack of the shot made several of the men flinch. The fleeing man flung both arms straight out. Momentum kept him running down the slope for several more steps before he finally tripped and lost his balance. He plunged forward, landing face first, and skidded a few more feet. When he came to a stop, a little cloud of dust swirled around his sprawled figure for a moment, then dispersed in the gentle, early morning breeze.

Echoes from the shot rolled away, leaving silence in their wake. Most of the men, troopers and prisoners alike, stared down the slope at the would-be escapee's body.

Not Sergeant MacDonald, though. He was looking at the lieutenant, Ace noted, and hatred burned in the noncom's gaze.

With a look of smug satisfaction, Olsen tossed the rifle back to Private Franklin, who caught it rather awkwardly. "You need to check the sights on that rifle, Private," Olsen said. "I think they're a hair off. I may have gotten Bleeker through the left lung rather than the heart. A couple of you go down there and make sure he's dead."

"You didn't have to kill him," MacDonald grated. "He wasn't much more'n a kid. Green and scared. He would've stopped if you'd fired over his head."

"Not likely. The guard who was with him had already fired a shot, and Bleeker didn't even slow down. So I made *certain* he stopped, didn't I?"

Chance said, "I thought you brought me and my brother along because you were so determined to go back to the fort with ten prisoners."

Olsen looked annoyed for a second, but he shrugged and said, "Bleeker gave me no choice. By trying to escape, he was attempting to desert again, and deserters can be shot." He looked around. "Where in blazes is Private Figueroa? He was supposed to be guarding Bleeker."

One of the troopers approached nervously. "I'm sorry, Lieutenant," he said. "Bleeker just panicked and took off running. I yelled for him to stop, and then I fired a warning shot at him."

Olsen looked at MacDonald. "There's your warning shot, just as I said."

The sergeant just glared and made no reply.

Olsen turned back to the frightened private and went on, "If you ever find yourself in that situation while you're under my command, no warning shots. You shoot to kill, do you understand?"

Figueroa swallowed hard and nodded. "Yes, sir."

Olsen raised his voice. "That goes for all of you in this detail. These prisoners are deserters. That means they're criminals. The lowest of the low. If you have to fire a shot, make sure it's meant to be a fatal one."

The men Olsen had sent down the ridge to check

on Bleeker came trudging back up. One of them saluted and reported, "Private Bleeker is dead, sir."

"Could you tell if I got him through the heart?"

"Uh, no, sir, not for sure. Looked like you might have, but I reckon it'd take the post surgeon to tell you that."

"Very well. We'll stop as we go by and put him in the back of the wagon. It may be a little crowded back there since Bleeker won't be able to sit up anymore, but you prisoners will just have to make do." Olsen looked around at his men. "And I want the shackles back on their ankles, too! Get to it."

The soldiers hustled to carry out Olsen's orders while he stood there looking pleased with himself.

MacDonald didn't look pleased, though. Ace thought the sergeant looked like if he could get his hands around Olsen's neck, he would gladly squeeze the life right out of the lieutenant.

Olsen was right: it was more crowded with a corpse in the back of the wagon, and certainly the rest of the trip to Fort Gila was even more unpleasant than the first part had been.

Ace found himself sitting across from MacDonald at the rear of the wagon bed as the vehicle rocked along, surrounded by mounted troopers. Keeping his voice low so maybe the driver and guard up on the seat wouldn't be as likely to hear him over the thudding hoofbeats from the mules and the creaking wheels, Ace said, "You've had run-ins with Lieutenant Olsen before, haven't you, Sergeant?"

MacDonald turned his head and spat over the

sideboards. "I never met an officer I liked," he said, "but Olsen is worse than most." He added an obscenity, then, "He'll hurt people, just for the fun of it."

From where he sat beside Ace, Chance said, "That's rich, coming from you, MacDonald. If you hadn't been hurting that girl in the saloon, none of us would be here."

"No, if you'd kept your nose where it belonged, none of us would be here!"

"Take it easy," Ace told both of them. "We're in enough trouble without the two of you locking horns again." He paused. "Just what's waiting for us at the fort, MacDonald?"

The sergeant glared at him for a second, then let out an ugly laugh. "You'll find out when you get there," he said. "And knowing that I'll get to watch is the only thing that makes this whole mess bearable."

He folded his arms over his chest, glared at the Jensen brothers, and refused to say anything else. Knowing how the others in the group took their lead from MacDonald, Ace didn't bother trying to ask them what it was like at Fort Gila. He knew they wouldn't give him any information, either.

The temperature had risen steadily along with the sun. Ace and Chance's hats had been left back in Packsaddle with the rest of their gear, so they had nothing to protect their heads from the scorching rays. By midday, it was miserably hot in the back of the wagon, and the shirts of all the men were dark with sweat.

The little procession was headed toward one of the low mountain ranges that dotted the landscape. The slopes were grayish green, with a few stunted trees growing in what was mostly bare stone. Ace wondered if any bands of Apache were hiding in there. That was unlikely, he decided, since the mountains seemed to be their destination.

The journey came to an end before the wagon and the riders reached those peaks, however. They topped a small rise, and Ace saw Fort Gila about half a mile ahead of them, in a small, shallow valley watered by a tiny stream that threaded through it. The fort consisted of a dozen adobe buildings arranged around a dusty parade ground. The American flag on a pole at one end of the parade ground hung limp and still, since the stifling air was completely motionless now.

A low adobe wall, barely higher than a man's head, surrounded the compound. It wasn't laid out in a perfect square but, rather, jutted out at one of the rear corners to enclose a corral. A small garden patch was located in the other rear corner, behind one of the buildings. Ace had been around enough frontier forts to have a pretty good idea what functions the buildings served: the office of the post commander and other administrative offices; a sutler's store; officers' quarters; enlisted men's barracks; an infirmary; an armory, and other storage areas. One of the buildings was probably the guardhouse where prisoners would be locked up. Prisoners such as the deserters . . .

And Ace and Chance Jensen.

CHAPTER NINE

Lookouts inside the fort must have seen them coming, because a pair of heavy wooden gates in the adobe wall swung back as the group approached. Lieutenant Olsen was in the lead, of course, and if a man could strut while on horseback, the lieutenant was strutting.

The trail led past something Ace hadn't noticed until they got closer to it. A small cemetery with perhaps a dozen graves in it was laid out to the left, outside the fort's adobe wall although a short picket fence surrounded it. No grass grew inside it, but a few patches of hardy cactus had taken root in the dirt and gravel. It was a desolate spot, made more so by the fact that the markers on nearly all the graves were simple wooden crosses bleached by the sun and weathered by the elements. Winding up lying for all eternity in such a miserable place would be a terrible fate.

Only one of the graves had an actual headstone. Set at the rear of the cemetery, it also contained the only spot of color in the graveyard, a small vase of flowers that must have come from that garden. Ace's keen eyes made out the name chiseled into the stone.

AMELIA SUGHRUE

A few words, a sentiment of some sort, more than likely, were below the name, but Ace couldn't make them out. He was able to read the year of birth, though—1838—and the date of death, fourteen months ago.

Ace was surprised to see that a woman was buried here at this lonely frontier outpost. Considering that she had been in her mid-forties when she passed away, probably she had been the commanding officer's wife. No one else would have been allowed to bring a family member to such a small garrison.

Ace nudged his brother and nodded toward the cemetery as they went past, but Chance just nodded and said, "Yeah, we'll probably be there soon enough." If he had noticed the tombstone, he gave no sign of it.

Sentries stood at attention just inside the gates as the procession moved in. Olsen rode toward a fairly large building that Ace took to be the headquarters of this garrison. This guess was confirmed when another officer emerged from the building onto the porch and came down the two steps, then walked crisply to meet the newcomers.

This man was tall and well-built, but his shoulders sagged slightly, as if weighed down by some burden. Despite the heat, he was in full uniform. His hat had the crossed sabers insignia of the cavalry on it, and the shoulder boards on his jacket indicated that he was a major. A corporal, probably his aide, trailed him, as did a private carrying a rifle.

Olsen reined in, swung down from the saddle, and snapped a crisp salute to the major, who returned it and said, "At ease, Lieutenant. Was your mission successful?"

"Yes, sir, for the most part, Major." Olsen moved his left hand toward the wagon, which had also come to a stop. "As you can see, I've brought back Sergeant MacDonald and the other men who deserted."

The major frowned at the prisoners in the back of the wagon and said, "I count only nine men . . . and two of them appear to be civilians."

"Private Bleeker was killed trying to escape, sir. And those two had already changed into civilian garb."

"Wait just a blasted minute!" Chance exclaimed. He started to stand up. "We *are* civilians! We're not in the—"

At a curt nod from Olsen, one of the troopers brought his horse alongside the wagon and slammed the barrel of his rifle down on Chance's shoulder. Chance cried out in pain and slumped back down on the bench seat built along that side of the wagon.

"What was that man trying to say?" the major asked.

"Don't pay any attention to him, sir," Olsen answered without missing a beat. "You know men like that will say or do anything to get out of the proper punishment that's coming to them."

"A firing squad, you mean? When we were marching through Georgia, you know, back during the war, any man who tried to desert was given a swift court-martial and executed." The major's pale, bushy eyebrows drew down in a glowering frown. "Sometimes, in the interest of expediency and because of battlefield conditions, the court-martial and the, ah, sentence were carried out concurrently."

"So I've heard, Major, and entirely proper under the circumstances, in my opinion. But you told me when you gave me my orders and sent me after these men that they weren't to be killed unless it was unavoidable, as it was in the case of Private Bleeker."

"I did?" The major sounded puzzled, even maybe a little confused.

"Yes, sir. These men are going to be sentenced to the work detail."

That answer seemed to clear up the major's confusion. He nodded and said, "Ah, yes, the work detail. Of course. We're engaged in a very important mission here, Lieutenant, as you well know. Nothing must jeopardize it."

"I'm sure nothing will, sir, as long as you're in command."

In the wagon, Chance leaned closer to Ace and whispered through teeth still clenched against the pain in his shoulder, "That major's not right in the head."

"I think you may be right," Ace said. "How's your shoulder?"

"Not broken, I can tell that much. But when that trooper walloped me, my whole arm went numb. It's not back to normal yet, but I think it will be."

Ace nodded but didn't say anything else, because at that moment, the major gave the order for the prisoners to climb out of the wagon and line up.

They did so, under the watchful eyes of the soldiers. Chance's arm and shoulder were still giving him trouble, so Ace had to help him from the wagon to the ground. Chance's independent streak meant that he didn't like that, but he didn't want to fall on his face, either.

Once the nine men were lined up, the major clasped his hands together behind his back and stalked up and down in front of them as he spoke.

"There is no greater crime in this man's army than desertion," he proclaimed. "To desert means that you are abandoning your fellow soldiers, the men who need you the most, the men who would never abandon you if your positions were reversed. Because desertion is a perverse abomination and a rejection of the very concepts of duty and honor, it is only right and just that a man who commits such a crime shall receive the most stringent punishment." The major flung out an arm and pointed at the adobe wall around the outside of the compound. "Under other circumstances, I would have you men against that wall, facing a firing squad!"

The officer's tone and the self-righteous anger turning his beefy face an even darker shade of red reminded Ace of some hellfire-and-brimstone preachers he had seen and listened to in the past. This major was every bit as fervent as they had been.

"But because we are engaged in a vital endeavor that will require the full effort of each and every one of us assigned to this post, you men will be spared that punishment. Instead, you will be sentenced to . . ."

The major looked at Olsen, who said, "I believe one year would be appropriate, Major."

"Very well." The major cleared his throat. "You men are hereby sentenced to one year on work detail.

When not working, you will be confined to the guardhouse. That is all."

A couple of the prisoners groaned quietly in dismay. The major ignored the sounds.

Instead he looked again at Olsen, as if he needed the lieutenant's confirmation. Olsen nodded.

Satisfied, the major said, "Carry on, Lieutenant."

"Yes, sir." Olsen gave him another salute, which the major returned, then the senior officer turned smartly and strode toward the building he had come out of earlier.

"Ace, look," Chance breathed. "At the window in that cottage beside the headquarters building."

Ace wasn't sure an adobe house like that ought to be called a cottage, but he knew what his brother meant. He looked quickly at the window Chance had mentioned and caught just a glimpse of a face there before the curtain inside the window dropped back into place.

"Was that a girl looking out at us?"

"It was," Chance said. "And a good-looking one, too, from what I could tell."

Even under these perilous circumstances, Ace wasn't surprised. If there was a pretty girl within a hundred miles, Chance Jensen would find her. It seemed to be a law of nature. And even with the danger hanging over their heads, he would notice her, too.

"The major's daughter, you reckon?" Chance asked.

"Could be. I spotted a gravestone out there in that cemetery with a woman's name on it. More than likely, she was the major's wife, so the gal you saw must be their daughter."

Chance nodded and was about to say something else, but he didn't get the opportunity. Instead, Lieutenant Olsen undid the flap on his holster, pulled out the army revolver, and ordered the prisoners, "All right, you men! Over to the guardhouse, now! March!"

The guardhouse was a squat adobe building with no windows except for high, slotted openings too narrow for a human being to get through. As the prisoners headed toward it, Chance said, "They're going to lock us up in there with MacDonald and the others. That's not going to be good, Ace. What happened to telling the commanding officer what's really going on?"

"You saw the major," Ace said. "Olsen's got him under his thumb. I don't think he would have believed a thing we told him."

"Maybe we should have made a run for it, too," Chance muttered.

"If we had, we probably would have wound up like Private Bleeker." Ace glanced toward the gates, which were closed now, blocking his view of the little cemetery. "And wound up in the same place he's going, too . . ."

CHAPTER TEN

In addition to the nine new prisoners herded into the guardhouse at rifle point, a dozen men were already locked up there, all wearing gray trousers and shirts. The prison was just a single large room with a dirt floor and a couple of buckets in one corner for human waste. The stiflingly hot air took Ace's breath away, and the foul stench made him gag and wish he didn't have to breathe. The narrow windows let in very little fresh air or light.

When the heavy wooden door closed behind the newcomers and the guards dropped the bar across it, the sound had an ominous finality, even though Ace knew that eventually they would be let out again. They couldn't work while they were locked up in here, after all.

The prisoners already in the guardhouse sat with their backs propped against the thick adobe walls. One of them got up and sauntered toward the newcomers. He was short, stocky, and swarthy, with thick black hair and a pugnacious jaw that he thrust out as he said, "I didn't expect to see you back here, MacDonald. I heard the guards talking about how you and your cronies had deserted. What did you do to get caught, stop somewhere and get drunk? That seems like something you'd be stupid enough to do."

"Get away from me, Costello," MacDonald snapped. "It's bad enough I have to be locked up in here and smell your stink. I don't have to talk to you."

"Well, that's just too bad," the prisoner called Costello said with a sneer, "because I heard what Sughrue told you. We're all gonna be prisoners to- gether for a long time."

One of the other men muttered, "We'll all die in here, or up in those blasted hills."

"Yeah," another prisoner put in. "With our brains roasting over some Apache torture fire, more than likely."

Costello turned his head and said, "Shut up, Nolan. You, too, Howell. Talk like that doesn't help anything."

Ace could tell that Costello was a leader of sorts here in the guardhouse. The stocky man turned toward him and Chance and asked, "Who in blazes are you two?"

"Finally," Chance said, "somebody willing to listen."

"Yeah," MacDonald said. "Somebody who can't do you a bit of good."

"I'm Chance Jensen," Chance went on, ignoring the sergeant. "This is my brother Ace. We're civil- ians. We were arrested in Packsaddle and sentenced to hang."

"Hang for what?" Costello wanted to know.

Ace said, "That's a long story, and it doesn't really matter right now. The important thing is that we're in- nocent, but that didn't stop us from being railroaded.

Then Lieutenant Olsen showed up with his detail and took us away from the sheriff. He brought us back in place of two deserters who actually got away and then told the major we were those men instead of who we really are."

"And Sughrue believed him, I'll bet," Costello said, nodding slowly.

"That's right, he did."

"That's because Major Flint Sughrue is loco, and Olsen's taken advantage of that."

"But if he's not right in the head," Chance said, "why is he still in command here?"

"He's not, not really. Olsen's calling the shots. Sughrue's just a figurehead. He has been ever since his mind started slipping, not long after his wife passed away from a fever. As soon as he saw his chance, Olsen wormed his way into the major's brain. He convinced him that I was betraying him and intended to relieve him of command."

Chance said, "Wait a minute. You're an officer, too?"

"I was a lieutenant, like Olsen. Second in command here at Fort Gila, actually. But Olsen persuaded the major to have me arrested and thrown in here, and then they held a court-martial that was nothing more than a kangaroo court and busted me back down to private, as well as sentencing me to a year at hard labor on the work detail."

Ace said, "We know all about kangaroo courts. We were the victims of one in Packsaddle."

"Well, I'm sorry about that, kid. But we've got our own problems here . . . like staying alive."

"What is this so-called work detail doing, anyway?"

Costello looked at MacDonald. "You didn't tell them anything about what's going on here or what they've gotten themselves into, did you?"

"Why should I?" MacDonald answered in a surly voice. "It's because of them we got caught!"

"That's a lie," Chance responded instantly.

Costello held up a hand and said wearily, "You can tell me all about it later, if you want to. But to answer your . . . brother, was it? . . . To answer his question, we're building a road." The former lieutenant chuckled, but there was no real humor in the sound. "A road to hell, I reckon you might call it."

"Like I said, it started a little over a year ago when the major's wife died," Costello said when they had all sat down next to the wall. Ace and Chance were beside him, while MacDonald and the other deserters had moved away as much as they could.

MacDonald still cast murderous glares toward the Jensen brothers now and then. It was only a matter of time, Ace thought, before MacDonald tried to settle what he regarded as a score between them.

"Actually, though, I suppose it started before that, when an old prospector stumbled across some gold in the mountains just west of here. The Prophets, they're called. Don't ask me why. They had the name long before the army had a post here."

"So there's gold in the mountains," Ace said. "That's not the first time I've heard about gold being discovered here in Arizona Territory."

"Yeah, there have been several strikes. This was a

small one, not enough to cause a real boom. The vein seems to begin and end on the same claim, but the thing is, it extends pretty deep. The man who owns that claim is going to get good and rich by the time it plays out."

"That old prospector, you mean," Chance said.

Costello shook his head. "No, that desert rat went down to Tucson, got drunk, and gambled the claim away to some slick Englishman. Then he got his throat cut in an alley later that same night. If you ask me, the Englishman might've had something to do with that, too."

"So now this Englishman owns the mine."

Costello nodded. "Eugene Howden-Smyth is the man's name. Like I said, he's slick. Which means he's the perfect sort to team up with a sorry specimen like Frank Olsen."

"Wait a minute," Ace said. "Olsen and this fella Howden-Smyth are partners? Are prisoners being forced to work in the mine?"

"No, Howden-Smyth brought in his own men for that, and a pretty tough lot they are, too. The problem is that the terrain's so rugged up there, the hardest job is getting the ore out. They have to pack it out on mules, and there's only so much they can carry. The operation would go a lot faster and be a lot more lucrative if Howden-Smyth could use wagons to transport the gold . . . so, we're building him a road."

"The army shouldn't be used for something like that," Ace protested.

"That's right. And that's why Olsen's a blasted crook. I don't know all the details, of course, but I'm guessing that once Olsen saw what sort of state the major was in after his wife died and figured out that he could take over, he got in touch with Howden-Smyth and struck a deal to provide free labor to build the road. In return for a share of the mine's profits, of course."

Chance said in obvious amazement, "Everybody in the fort *knows* about this?"

"We didn't at first," Costello said. "But then more and more, Olsen started taking over, and more men wound up being thrown in here for the least little infraction of the regulations. Sometimes they were sentenced to the work detail when they hadn't done anything wrong at all! I started asking questions, and then I suggested to Major Sughrue that he get in touch with the War Department. I even offered to take a telegram to the telegraph office in Packsaddle." The former lieutenant shook his head. "I guess Olsen found out about it and decided that I had to be gotten out of the way. It was only a few hours later that he and some of his cronies came to arrest me."

"This is outrageous," Ace said. "Surely not every soldier posted here was willing to go along with Olsen's scheme."

"Yeah, and you can see what happened to those of us who weren't." Costello nodded to their fellow prisoners. "You might've noticed the cemetery just outside the fort, too. There are some pretty fresh graves in it."

Ace leaned his head against the wall and closed his eyes. The situation was worse than he had ever dreamed it might be. Frank Olsen was more outlaw than soldier, and apparently he had most of the garrison at his command. Some of the troopers were bound to have figured out what was going on, but they were willing to cooperate in the hope that some of the payoff from the lieutenant's scheme would find its way to them. Others probably knew what they were doing was wrong, but they were scared to buck Olsen—and evidently for very good reason, if what Costello had been saying was true.

Ace lifted his head and opened his eyes. "Major Sughrue doesn't have any idea what's going on? Olsen's completely fooled him?"

"Sughrue knows we're building a road, but Olsen has convinced him there's a military reason for it and that the War Department has ordered us to carry out the task. He even faked some telegrams to make it look like that. And he's the one responsible for sending all the major's reports on the project to Washington, so for all Sughrue knows, the whole thing is legitimate. Those reports never make it any farther than the fireplace in Olsen's quarters, of course." Costello sighed. "It's a shame things have come to this for the major. Flint Sughrue was a hero during the war. He served under General Sherman and had a distinguished career. Somewhere along the way, though, he got crosswise with somebody and kept getting passed over for promotions. And then he was sent out here to take over this hellhole and never realized that he had the Devil himself in his command. If he had known what Olsen is really like, he might not have brought his wife and daughter with him."

"His daughter," Chance repeated. "*She's* the one I want to hear about."

Chapter Eleven

Costello stared at Chance in apparent disbelief for several seconds, then let out a harsh bark of laughter.

"All the trouble that you boys are in, and you're interested in a *girl*?"

"That's my brother, Lieutenant," Ace said with a wry, faint smile.

"Like I told you, I'm not an officer anymore. Legal or not, I got busted down to private when they threw me in here."

"What's her name?" Chance asked.

"You're determined, aren't you? Her name is Evelyn. You sounded like you knew she was here, even before I mentioned her."

"We caught a glimpse of her looking out the window in the major's house when we first got here," Ace explained.

"And from what I could tell, she's really pretty," Chance added.

Costello nodded and said, "You're right about that. Very likely the prettiest girl who's ever set foot in this part of the territory. But that's not going to do *you* any good. You're a prisoner, and before you know it, you'll be worn out and filthy and broken down like the rest of us. You won't be thinking about Evelyn Sughrue anymore."

"I wouldn't count on that." Chance leaned forward. "But is there any chance she might help us? Does she know how Olsen is taking advantage of her father?"

"I don't see how she could help but know."

Ace said, "Does she want to stop him? Does she care what Olsen's doing?"

"Evelyn's a good, decent girl," Costello replied with a little heat in his voice. "Of course she cares. But she's just one girl. What can she do against somebody like that?"

From where he sat against one of the other walls, MacDonald laughed. He said, "Hearin' you say that don't surprise me the least bit, Costello. You're sweet on the gal yourself. I bet if you ever got the chance, you'd like to—"

"Shut your filthy mouth, MacDonald," Costello interrupted. "I'm old enough to be that girl's father, and you know it."

"That don't make any difference. Not when she's the only female this side of Packsaddle who ain't an Apache."

"Don't pay any attention to him," Costello told the Jensen brothers. "He's just a brute, and not a very smart one, at that. If he was, once he got away from here, he never would have slowed down until he had put at least fifty miles behind him."

MacDonald got to his feet. "You're not an officer anymore, Costello. Until the major busts me and makes it official, *I* outrank *you* now. So I don't have to put up with your guff." He balled his hands into fists. "Let's settle this . . . and once that's done, I've got a score to settle with those Jensen boys, as well!"

He jerked his rock of a chin toward Ace and Chance.

Costello put his hand on the ground to brace himself and then pushed upright. "Why don't you let it alone, MacDonald?" he said. "We're all locked up in here together, so we might as well try to get along."

MacDonald shook his head. "I'm not interested in getting along with the likes of you."

With that, he rushed through the gloom with a fist cocked back to throw a punch at Costello.

As MacDonald's fist shot forward, Costello ducked under the blow. Considerably shorter than MacDonald to start with, the former lieutenant had no trouble avoiding the blow. He stepped in and hooked a right and a left into MacDonald's belly, the same strategy Chance had used when he clashed with MacDonald back in Packsaddle.

Despite his weight and strength, Costello had the same lack of success Chance had had. MacDonald bellowed and wrapped both hands around Costello's head. He held Costello off and started to squeeze, as if he were trying to pop Costello's skull like a melon.

Costello grabbed MacDonald's arms and tried to loosen his grip. MacDonald turned, pulling Costello along with him, and threw the former lieutenant against the wall. Costello bounced off, and when he did, MacDonald was waiting to land a roundhouse right that crashed into Costello's jaw with such force that it sent him flying through the air. He slammed into the wall again and dropped loose-limbed to the ground, evidently out cold.

"Now," MacDonald growled as he swung around to glare at Ace and Chance. He took a step toward them.

Costello wasn't unconscious after all. He raised a somewhat shaky hand and clamped it around MacDonald's ankle. He yanked, but he wasn't strong enough to pull MacDonald's leg out from under him.

In fact, MacDonald just stopped, looked down at Costello, and laughed. "Stubborn, ain't you?" he said. "Well, I guess I'll just go ahead and stomp you good and proper."

"Wait a minute," Ace said as he scrambled to his feet. "If you kill him, that'll make Olsen mad. He needs every available man to work on the road to the mine, doesn't he?"

"One man won't make a difference," MacDonald said, baring his teeth at Ace. "He'll just throw somebody else in here on trumped-up charges and put him to work with the rest of us. You think I haven't seen how Olsen operates over the past year? Everybody in this fort is doomed! He'll sacrifice all of us if he has to, to get his share of that gold. The men who have thrown in with him just don't realize that yet." He started to turn back toward Costello. "So it won't matter if I stomp this good-for-nothing little polecat to pieces!"

Over and above his code of common decency, Ace sensed that he couldn't stand by and allow MacDonald to murder Costello. The former lieutenant might be the only true ally he and Chance would have here at Fort Gila. So Ace did the only thing he could.

He tackled the brawny three-striper from behind.

If MacDonald had been expecting the attack and braced his legs and feet, Ace might not have done any good. But he took MacDonald by surprise, and the sergeant stumbled forward a couple of steps. Chance had started moving the same time Ace did. He threw himself at MacDonald's legs and knocked them out from under the man. Ace, Chance, and MacDonald all fell to the hard-packed dirt floor.

MacDonald roared in anger and twisted around. His long arms and big hands reached for Ace, who was the closest to him. Ace tried to fend him off, but MacDonald got a hand around his throat and started to squeeze with those thick, sausage-like fingers.

Chance levered himself up, lunged at MacDonald, and rammed his knee into the sergeant's groin. MacDonald groaned in pain and let go of Ace.

"We gotta help the sarge!" one of the deserters yelled. Several of them started to dive into the melee.

"Help . . . the Jensens!" Costello gasped to the men who had been locked up with him.

Some of them held back, unwilling to get mixed up in this brawl, but half a dozen charged into battle, meeting MacDonald's friends with a flurry of fists. Punches rained back and forth, accompanied by grunts of effort and pain and the thudding of fists against flesh.

Ace scrambled to his feet and came upright at the same instant as MacDonald. The sergeant threw wild, roundhouse blows that Ace ducked and weaved away from. He knew it wouldn't do any good to go after

MacDonald's body, so he watched for his opportunity and then seized it, shooting a hard, straight right that landed squarely on MacDonald's nose. That was a weak spot on many a big man.

Evidently not Sergeant Vince MacDonald, though. The force of the blow rocked MacDonald's head back for a second and caused blood to flow from his nostrils, but he recovered almost instantly and caught hold of Ace's arm with a flashing sweep of his big left paw.

MacDonald reached down with his right hand and grabbed Ace's thigh. Before Ace could do anything to stop him, MacDonald hoisted him into the air above his head. Ace knew that the burly noncom was about to smash him into the adobe wall of the guardhouse. Such an impact would break bones and pulzerize flesh.

Before MacDonald could do that, Costello heaved himself up from the ground and rammed his shoulder into MacDonald's knees from behind. The sergeant's knees buckled, and he couldn't hold Ace over his head anymore. He and Ace both fell, collapsing in a heap on top of Costello.

MacDonald shrieked in pain as they all writhed around on the hard-packed dirt. Costello must have bitten him, or else gotten hold in a tender place and twisted. In a tangle of arms and legs like this, there was no room for throwing punches. Dirty fighting was the only kind of fighting there was.

Ace spotted an opening and drove his elbow into MacDonald's throat. Such a blow might crush a man's windpipe and prove fatal, but Ace wasn't worrying about that now. His survival, and that of his brother, was the only thing that really mattered to him.

MacDonald gagged and thrashed, then heaved up from the ground and threw Ace off like a bucking bronco. He was still lying on top of Costello, who wrapped both arms around MacDonald's throat and hung on, squeezing harder and harder. Beside them, Chance reared up on his knees, clubbed his hands together, and brought them down on MacDonald's face. More blood spurted from the sergeant's nose. He bucked a couple more times, then went still as unconsciousness claimed him.

Ace had rolled against the wall and wound up on his stomach. He raised his head and shoulders and propped himself up on his elbows. Men were down all over the guardhouse floor, whaling away at each other in struggling knots of humanity. It was impossible to tell which side was winning, if indeed either was.

How things might have turned out would never be determined. The heavy door swung open with a creaking of hinges and spilled light into the room. Ace squinted against the sudden glare and saw troopers rushing into the guardhouse with Springfield rifles held ready. A pair of them sprang into action, raising their rifles and slamming the butts down against the heads of brawling men. It took only a few seconds of that before the fight was over. The men who hadn't been knocked cold scrambled away from the guards.

"Stop it!" Costello yelled at the troopers. "There's no need to hurt anybody else."

The guards pulled back and kept their rifles leveled now, in case they needed to open fire. Through a gap in their number strode Lieutenant Frank Olsen. For a long moment, he regarded the combatants with a cold, murderous glare, but then a vicious smile broke out across his face.

"I had thought I'd give all you men the rest of the day off and start fresh on our mission in the morning, but I suppose this is what I get for trying to be nice," the lieutenant said. "Very well. If you have this much energy, you might as well be accomplishing something. Corporal!" he barked at one of the guards. "Get these men up and out of here and put them to work!"

CHAPTER TWELVE

Chance helped Ace up, and then both of them assisted Costello to his feet. Prodded by the rifle-toting guards, the men who hadn't been knocked out picked up the ones who had and shook and slapped them back to consciousness. It took three of MacDonald's deserter friends to get him back on his feet. As he shuffled out, he glared at Ace and Chance with a roaring fire of anger and hatred in his gaze.

"MacDonald sure doesn't like you boys," Costello muttered.

"The feeling's mutual," Chance said.

"You'd better keep an eye on him any time he's around. If he sees a chance to kill you, he'll take it. And they give us picks and shovels when we're out there working on the road, so it's not like he'll be unarmed."

Ace said, "If you have tools you can use as weapons, why haven't you overthrown the guards and taken command back from Olsen?"

"Like I said, there are fresh graves out in that cemetery," Costello said as the three of them filed out of the guardhouse after the others. "Olsen makes sure that the men guarding us are ones who won't mind shooting to kill, and those are the orders he gives them. Anybody makes the slightest move that a guard might regard as a threat, he gets a bullet in the head." Costello shrugged. "After you've seen a few of your friends gunned down like that, you get to where you'd rather take a chance on being worked to death. Although that's happened, too, a few times . . ."

Once all the prisoners were outside, the guards herded them into a group and kept them there, under the threat of the rifles, until a pair of mule-drawn wagons could be brought up. Then, again at gunpoint, they climbed into the wagons, which lurched into motion and headed for the mountains to the west.

"I wish we were going past the major's house again," Chance said quietly as he sat between Ace and Costello in the back of the lead wagon.

"So maybe you could get another look at Miss Evelyn?" Costello asked. He shook his head. "Your brother's right. You really do have an eye for a pretty girl, don't you?"

Chance grinned. "Nothing wrong with that, is there?"

"I didn't say there was. It's just that not many men would be thinking about such a thing if they were in a fix like you're in."

"As long as we're alive, we don't give up hope that we'll get out of trouble, no matter how bad it is," Chance said. "Something in the blood, I guess."

"I guess . . . Anyway, we'll see how interested you

are in pretty girls once you've spent a few days hacking a road out of those mountains."

The Prophets weren't towering, snowcapped peaks but rather gray, razor-backed folds in the landscape, twisting back and forth in a mad pattern that made no sense to anyone except—maybe—the Apaches. It took the wagons the better part of an hour of following a rutted trail to reach the foothills. As they approached, Ace was able to make out the beginning of the road that had been cut through the rugged terrain.

Interested in spite of the trouble they were in, he asked Costello, "How deep in the mountains is the mine?"

"About five miles," the former lieutenant replied. "We have almost a mile of road built."

"In a year?" Chance said. "You mean it'll take four more years to finish the job?"

"Actually, we've only been working on it for a little over six months. It took a while after the major's wife passed for Olsen to establish a strong enough hold over Sughrue to get away with what he wanted."

Ace said, "Even so, at that rate it'll still take several more years to build the rest of the road."

"Yeah. When the Central Pacific had to put their railroad through the Sierra Nevadas, they had a whole horde of Chinamen to work on it. We've got part of a small garrison of troopers. So even though this job isn't anywhere near as difficult as that one was, it'll still take us longer . . . assuming we live to finish it." Costello grunted. "That's a pretty big assumption."

"Then it may never be completed," Ace mused, "and everything Olsen has done will all be for nothing."

"Not for nothing," Costello said. "He's already collecting from Howden-Smyth. The real jackpot's still a good ways off, but Olsen's making sure he gets something out of the deal all along."

The two wagons full of prisoners, followed by a smaller cart carrying the tools and drawn by a single mule, started up the road into the foothills. Ace could tell that it had been constructed by breaking up any rocky outcroppings that were in the way and then leveling the path with shovels. No wonder progress had been slow, especially with the limited number of men available to work on the project.

"Have you had to use dynamite to blast any of the rocks out of the way?" he asked Costello.

"Yeah . . . but if you're thinking about what you might be able to do if you got your hands on any of the stuff, you can forget about it. Olsen doesn't let the prisoners get near any explosives. He handles it himself, or gets one of his more trusted men to do it."

Ace shrugged. "It was just an idle thought."

"Trust me, if it involves getting out of this mess or turning the tables on Olsen, I've considered it. I just haven't come up with anything yet that wouldn't get innocent men killed."

Chance was looking around, studying the surrounding foothills and the slopes rising above them. As his eyes narrowed, he said, "Have you had any trouble with the Apaches around here?"

"Not really. When the fort was first established about five years ago, there were some skirmishes in the area. I wasn't here then, I hadn't been posted to

Fort Gila yet, but I've heard about them. Our patrols have spotted some Indians from time to time in recent months, but they always shy away and don't seem to be looking for trouble."

"What about the mine?" Ace asked. "Have they attacked it?"

"Not that I know of. Like I said, Howden-Smyth has a pretty salty crew up there, including some men who do nothing but guard the place, and they're all good with guns. Why do you ask?"

"We just like to know what's going on," Ace said.

"This time it's more than that," Chance said. He nodded toward one of the low, rounded peaks looming ahead of them. "Look up there."

Ace turned his head to see what his brother was talking about. Instantly, he spotted the trio of riders perched up high, looking down at the new road snaking its way through the foothills. Although they were too far away for him to be able to make out any details about the watchers, he had no doubt who they were.

Apparently, neither did Costello, who said in a quiet voice, "Yeah, those are Apaches, all right."

"What do you reckon they want?" Chance asked.

"Maybe they're just curious. They probably don't think it's a good thing, white men building a road into a domain they consider to belong to them."

Ace said, "Wouldn't they feel the same way about the mine? It's an intrusion into their land, too."

"Mines come and go," Costello said. "Maybe they're hoping the vein will play out and the white men will go away. But a road . . . that's different. Any time there's a road, whether it's one like this or a railroad, it usually means that more and more white men will be coming, until there are so many of them that they never leave. If you think back on it, opening up some sort of new route has nearly always been what started Indian trouble."

Ace nodded. The former officer was right. "Maybe they're watching to see whether or not the road keeps getting built. Maybe they're hoping it'll be too hard and Olsen will give it up."

"They don't know Frank Olsen," Costello said. "He's never going to give up on something that he believes will put a lot of money in his pocket."

Chance said, "Then sooner or later, the Apaches will get tired of watching and hoping and decide they need to put a stop to the road themselves."

"I don't doubt that you're right. Question is, how long will it take them to get fed up and do something about it?"

"If we keep working on this road," Ace said, "I expect we'll find out."

Chapter Thirteen

A short time later, the wagons reached their destination. The Apaches who had been watching from the heights had wheeled their ponies around and disappeared, and Ace and Chance hadn't caught sight of them again.

The troopers handling the mule teams hauled back on their reins, and the guards on horseback halted their mounts. With Springfield rifles covering them, Ace, Chance, Costello, MacDonald, and the other prisoners clambered down from the wagons and lined up to receive picks and shovels from the soldier manning the equipment cart.

Once they had the tools, the soldier in charge of the work detail pointed to the cluster of small boulders that sat directly in the way at the point where the road stopped.

"Bust up those rocks and get 'em out of there," he ordered. "We've only got a few hours of daylight left. I want those boulders gone by the time we start back to the fort."

As they started toward the boulders, Costello said with a note of bleak humor in his voice, "Making little rocks out of bigger rocks. That's the fate of prisoners since the beginning of time." He looked over at Ace and Chance. "Have you boys ever done work like this before?"

"As a matter of fact, we haven't," Ace replied. "We've, ah, found ourselves behind bars a few times, but it was always a misunderstanding, like the one back in Packsaddle."

Chance said, "That little misunderstanding could've gotten our necks stretched. I'll take busting rocks over that, any day."

"You say that now . . ." Costello told him, again with a faint smile.

Soon, the ringing blows of pickaxes smashing into boulders echoed across the foothills. Ace and Chance both wielded picks, their young, sinewy muscles swinging the tools high and then bringing them down on the rocks with as much force as they could muster. As the boulders cracked into smaller pieces, other men picked up those chunks, carried them off to the sides, and tossed them out of the way. Men with shovels scooped up gravel and dirt and slung those loads away from where the road would be. They also scraped the ground to smooth out rough spots.

All of it was hard, tedious work, and it didn't take long for Ace's muscles to start protesting, especially those in his shoulders and back. When he glanced over at his brother, he could tell that Chance was suffering the same sort of aches and pains. The late afternoon sun beating down on their bare heads didn't help matters.

"Maybe Costello was right," Chance muttered after a while. "Maybe getting our necks stretched *would* have been better. At least it would have been over with a lot quicker."

"We don't give up as long as we're still alive, remember?" Ace reminded him.

"Tell that to my hands," Chance said as he paused to show Ace the blisters forming on his palms.

"Get back to work, you two!" one of the guards yelled at them. The Jensen brothers sighed and started swinging their picks again.

The lowering sun turned the landscape red as it neared the horizon. When it dipped below that line, shadows closed in quickly, as they tended to do in this high-desert country. The guards called a halt to the work. Most of the prisoners leaned wearily on their picks and shovels for a moment before they started trudging back to the wagons.

"If this was just part of a day," Chance said, "what's it going to be like when we're out here for a whole day?"

"There's a reason they call it *hard* labor," Ace said. "I guess we'll have to be tough enough to stand it, at least for a while."

Chance glanced over at him. "What *are* we going to do? We don't deserve to be here, Ace. We have to find a way to escape."

"I'm not sure any of these men deserve to be here. What we really need to do is figure out a way to get word to the proper authorities about what's going on at Fort Gila."

"Not that sheriff and judge at Packsaddle," Chance said. "They're as crooked as Olsen, I'll bet."

"You're probably right about that," Ace agreed. They stopped their muttered conversation as they reached the tool cart and handed over the pickaxes. Nobody else needed to know what they were talking about.

They climbed into one of the wagons, trying not to groan from exhaustion and pain as they did so. Costello lowered himself onto the bench seat beside Ace and asked, "How are you boys holding up?"

"We're alive," Ace said, "but it's just going to get worse, isn't it?"

"More than likely," Costello said. He had wielded one of the shovels during the afternoon. "Try not to do the same job every day. That'll help . . . a little."

Once all the picks and shovels had been returned and the prisoners had clambered into the wagons, the vehicles started back to the fort. Full night had fallen, but millions of stars popped into view overhead and cast enough silvery light for the drivers to follow the rutted trail.

"Do the prisoners normally work until after dark like this?" Ace asked Costello.

"No, usually we head back in time to reach the fort about dusk," the former lieutenant replied. "Even though there hasn't been any trouble with the Apaches lately, traveling at night like this probably isn't a good idea. Some people will tell you that Indians won't attack at night, but in my experience, that's not true. They'll attack whenever the odds favor them, or just when the mood strikes them, and nobody's harder to predict than an Indian."

Ace remembered the watchers Chance had spotted earlier. He wasn't the sort to get antsy, but his nerves crawled a mite during the group's unhurried return to Fort Gila. When the lights of the fort finally appeared up ahead, it was a relief.

The gates were open when they got there. The wagons pulled up in front of the guardhouse, where several troopers waited to cover the prisoners with their rifles as they climbed out of the vehicles.

Lieutenant Frank Olsen was waiting, too. He said to the soldier who had headed up the detail, "Did you get those rocks moved, Parnell?"

"Yes, sir," the man replied. He had dismounted and stood there holding his horse's reins. "I knew you wanted it done today, so I kept the men at it until they finished, even though we'd be getting back later than usual."

Olsen nodded. "Very good. I want that stretch smoothed in the morning, and then you can move on from there."

"Yes, sir," the trooper called Parnell said again. "We'll—" He stopped short, then quickly took off his forage cap and went on, "Evening, miss."

Ace and Chance had just dropped from the wagon's tailgate to the ground when they heard that. Chance turned quickly. Ace didn't react quite as fast, but he was curious, too, and looked in the same direction as Parnell was.

A blob of yellow light from a lantern approached. As it came closer, Ace saw the pale glow wash over the face of the young woman holding the lantern out at the same level as her head. She had a shawl around her shoulders to ward off the night's chill, but her head was bare. Thick waves of red hair fell around her rather thin face.

Olsen took off his hat as well and smiled as he said,

"Good evening, Miss Sughrue. What brings you out after dark like this?"

"I heard the wagons coming in," Evelyn Sughrue said. "I wanted to make sure these men get some supper, even though it's later than usual."

Olsen's voice was still cordial enough, but Ace thought he heard an undertone of annoyance and tension in it as the lieutenant said, "I've told you before, Evelyn, you concern yourself too much with these men. They're not worth being worried about by a young lady such as yourself."

"They're not animals, Lieutenant. Prisoners or not, they're still human beings."

"Of course," Olsen said. "And they'll be given their normal rations, I assure you."

"Well, I'm glad to hear it. If there's anything I can do to help . . ."

"There's not. You've done more than enough."

There was more than one way that comment could be taken. But she just said, "All right, thank you, Lieutenant."

"Bid your father a pleasant good evening for me, if you would."

"Of course." Evelyn turned and walked back toward the quarters she shared with her father, the major, carrying the lantern with her.

Ace could still see Olsen well enough in the starlight to tell that the lieutenant wanted to say something else, but whatever it was, Olsen kept it to himself. He jerked a hand toward the prisoners and ordered, "Get them locked up, and then see to it that they have their rations."

"Yes, sir, Lieutenant," Parnell replied. He put his cap back on and tugged it down.

Still holding his hat in his hand, Olsen stalked off toward the row of officers' quarters.

With the ready Springfields of the guards aimed in their general direction, the prisoners marched into the darkened guardhouse. They all slumped tiredly to the ground and leaned back against the walls. As they did, Ace asked, "Do snakes and scorpions ever get in here?"

"Sure they do," Costello replied. "That's why it's a good idea to shuffle your feet while you're moving around. That's not a guarantee you won't get bit or stung, but at least it improves the odds that you won't. A little bit."

"That was nice of Miss Sughrue to come out and check on us like that," Chance said. "We might not have gotten any supper otherwise."

"Oh, they'd have fed us," Costello said. "You can't get enough work out of a man if you don't feed him. Mind you, you don't have to feed him a lot, and the rations don't have to be particularly good, but you have to give him *something*."

As if to prove his point, the bar on the outside of the guardhouse door rattled as it was taken down, and then the door swung open. Light from another lantern preceded rifle-toting troopers who moved the prisoners back against the rear wall. Another soldier placed jugs of water on the ground, along with large bowls containing hunks of bread and pieces of salt pork. The man with the lantern stood by so the prisoners would have light as they helped themselves to the water and food. The rifle-carrying guards stood watch over them, as well.

The prisoners reminded Ace a little of a pack of dogs as they swarmed around the food. Luckily, there was no snapping and snarling, and no fights broke out. The men were too tired and hungry for that.

The bread was stale but not weevily, the pork hard on the teeth but not too bad. There wasn't really enough to go around and leave everyone satisfied, but at least it was better than nothing. When everything was gone, the guards collected the bowls and jugs and withdrew, letting the darkness claim the place again as the door was closed and the bar dropped into place.

As they sat with their backs propped against the wall again, Chance murmured, "If Miss Sughrue is really sympathetic to the prisoners, maybe *she* could get the word out about what's really going on here."

"How did she take it when her mother passed away?" Ace asked Costello.

"It was rough on her, of course," Costello said, "but the major took it even harder, and I guess you could say that taking care of him was a welcome distraction for Evelyn. She's devoted to him, and even more so since Mrs. Sughrue passed."

"That could make her *less* likely to help us, then. Because if the truth ever comes out, the major's going to look pretty bad, no matter how it happened."

Costello said, "I wouldn't put it past Olsen to try to claim the whole thing was the major's idea, if the law or the War Department ever caught up to him. I've thought about trying to catch Evelyn alone sometime—although I don't really see how I'd do that—and appealing to her for help, but I worried that it might backfire. We could wind up worse off than we already are."

"It's something to think about, though," Chance said. "I just can't believe that a girl who looks like that would stand for something as shady as what Olsen's pulling."

Costello chuckled and said, "Well, there's your mistake, thinking that just because a girl is pretty, she can be trusted. It doesn't always work out that way."

"But—"

"Why don't we all just try to get some sleep?" Costello suggested. "Morning's going to be here a lot sooner than you expect, and all those rocks out there in the foothills will still be waiting for us."

CHAPTER FOURTEEN

Costello was right about the first part of his statement. It seemed to Ace like he had barely closed his eyes when the bugle blew the next morning and the guardhouse door opened to admit troopers bringing a breakfast of coffee, bacon, and beans. The coffee was watery, the beans and bacon underdone. Nobody complained, though, not even Vince MacDonald. After the meal, the prisoners filed out into the gray dawn and loaded up on the wagons to head for the foothills and the day's work.

Muscles had stiffened up overnight and protested mightily this morning when the wagons reached their destination and Ace and Chance went back to swinging the pickaxes. Costello had advised working on a different job today, but the soldier in charge of the tools handed picks to them and didn't look inclined to discuss the matter.

After a while, blisters burst and slickened the tools' handles, so the Jensen brothers had to be extra careful not to let the picks slip out of their grasp and fly off dangerously. The morning passed in pure misery, and the short breaks that the guards allowed didn't help much.

The prisoners got to take a longer break at midday and were given bread, water, and jerky. Then it was back to work in the hellish heat and sun of an afternoon that seemed to last an eternity.

By the end of the day, Ace had become one giant, throbbing bundle of pain, and his brain was stunned into submission. When coherent thoughts began to form again once the prisoners were in the wagon and headed back to Fort Gila, he could see why some men just gave up and surrendered to despair when they were in situations such as this. Mere survival, making it to the end of the day, became all that mattered.

On the other hand, he could also understand why some men *never* gave up and were driven to escape, no matter what dangers they might face in doing so. That was the way he and Chance would be, he hoped. They had never admitted defeat before, and he didn't want to start now.

"Do you hurt too much to ever move again?" Chance asked as they rocked back and forth slightly in the swaying wagon.

"It won't last," Ace said. "I hope."

Costello, who was sitting next to him, said, "It won't. I'm not saying you'll ever get used to it, but it gets better."

Ace wasn't sure if he believed that or not, but he didn't have time to ponder it. At that moment, one of the troopers called out to Corporal Parnell, who was in charge of the detail again today. Parnell reined in and turned his horse so he could look where the other soldier was pointing.

Ace looked, too, and saw what had caught the trooper's attention. A single rider sat on top of a knob about five hundred yards away. The only detail Ace could make out was a spot of bright blue where the man's head was.

Costello saw the same thing. He said, "See that blue? That's the bandanna he's got tied around his head. The Apaches really like red or blue bandannas, and they'll wear bright-colored sashes around their waist, too. That's generally the only color you'll see them sporting."

"Don't they realize that makes them easier to spot . . . and aim at?" Chance asked.

"I reckon they do. They're too good as fighting men *not* to know it. But the Apaches make war the same way they do everything else, according to their own lights, and they don't care what anybody else does or thinks about it."

Corporal Parnell called for the wagons to halt and waved the outriders in. As the mounted troopers gathered around the wagons and stared anxiously into the distance at the Indian who was just sitting there, Ace quietly asked Costello, "Do you think they're going to attack us?"

Costello licked his lips and said, "No way to know. If they *are* bound on starting some mischief, we may not know it until it's too late. Apaches can blend into the landscape so well that one of them can be a stone's throw away from you, or even closer, without you having any idea he's there. Parnell and the others know that. That's why they're nervous."

Chance said, "Shouldn't we keep moving and try to find a place to fort up if we have to?"

Costello didn't have time to answer the question before the lone Apache suddenly whirled around and disappeared. Parnell heaved a sigh of relief and said, "Thank goodness he's gone."

Speaking with the voice of experience, Costello said, "Just because you can't see him anymore doesn't mean he's gone, Corporal. Maybe it would be a good idea for us to get moving again and get on back to the fort. Tonight probably isn't a good night for us to be out after dark."

Parnell looked like he wanted to dismiss Costello's comments, but maybe he remembered that the former lieutenant had been out here longer and knew more about the Apaches than he did. After a second, he jerked his head in a nod and waved the drivers ahead. The work detail got underway again.

"The worst part about it," Costello said quietly to Ace and Chance, "is that there aren't enough weapons to go around for all of us. If the Apaches do jump us, we'll have to rely on those guards to fight them off. I don't like that idea at all. If somebody's trying to kill me, I want to be trying just as hard to kill them."

"Amen to that," Chance muttered.

No one jumped the wagons and the troopers on their way back to Fort Gila. They didn't spot any more Apaches—but that didn't stop Ace from feeling like eyes were watching them the entire way.

Two more days followed that were very similar in most respects—pure hell for Ace and Chance, in other words. Fortunately for them, their drifting ways had toughened them up and accustomed them to hardships, although seldom any as extreme as what they were enduring now.

One difference was that no one caught sight of any Indians during the journey from the fort to the hills on those days. Maybe the Apaches had decided to stop keeping an eye on them . . . although Ace remembered quite well former lieutenant Costello's advice that just because you couldn't see the Apaches, it didn't mean they weren't there.

The next morning, the guards didn't come to wake them before dawn, and when Ace opened his eyes and saw sunlight coming through the high, narrow slits on the eastern side of the guardhouse, he realized immediately that something was different.

He reached over and shook Chance awake. Chance started to sit up quickly, saying, "Wha—" but Ace's hand on his shoulder stopped him.

"Something's wrong," Ace whispered. "The sun's up."

From where he was lying on his side a few feet away, his head pillowed on his arms, Costello said quietly, "Nothing's wrong, you idiots. It's Sunday. We don't work today."

"Oh," Ace said, feeling as foolish as Costello accused him of being. Since they had been here, every day had seemed the same, like an endless string of miserable days that never changed, and it hadn't occurred to him to think about what day it actually was. "I'm surprised Olsen doesn't work us seven days a week."

"He probably would if he thought he could get away with it. But Major Sughrue wouldn't stand for that. His wife always made sure we had a little church service in the mess hall. We don't do that anymore, but the major still says no work on Sunday except for essential duties." Costello rolled over and added over his shoulder, "Now shut up and let the rest of us sleep."

Ace and Chance tried to doze off again, but they still hurt too much for sleep to come easily. They sat up and leaned against the wall, talking in whispers.

"Have you thought of any way we can get out of here?" Chance asked.

"Not yet. How about you?"

"Not a blasted thing. You agree, though, that we ought to try to escape if we can."

Ace sighed. "Yeah. We can't hope for any help from somewhere else. I don't like the idea of being a fugitive, but if we can get away, maybe we can locate some authorities who'll actually listen and get to the bottom of what's happening here."

"Where do you plan on finding someone like that?"

"Smoke is friends with the governor of Colorado. He's bound to know somebody in Washington."

"Smoke . . ." Chance repeated. Smoke Jensen, the famous gunfighter and now a highly successful and respected rancher, was their uncle, and they had fought side by side with him against various enemies, numerous times in the past. "You're right. If we can ever get to a telegraph and get in touch with Smoke,

Olsen's liable to feel like all hell's blown up in his face." That prospect made a grin stretch across Chance's face, and Ace liked the idea, too.

The guards didn't bring breakfast, but at midday, after all the prisoners were awake, they showed up with fried chicken, potatoes, greens, canned tomatoes, and buttermilk. Simple fare, but a veritable feast compared to what the prisoners had been eating. They were allowed to sit outside against the guard-house wall while they enjoyed the food.

"Don't wolf it down," Costello advised the Jensen brothers. "You'll regret it later if you do."

"We've been hungry before," Ace told him.

"Although maybe never this hungry *and* tired," Chance added.

"*And* sore."

"But we know what you're talking about," Chance said as he gnawed another bit of meat off a chicken bone.

When the meal was over, a soldier Ace hadn't seen before appeared at the guardhouse. He was older than most of the troopers, somewhere in his thirties, and wore a pair of spectacles perched on his hawk-like nose.

"That's Lieutenant Driscoll," Costello told Ace and Chance. "The post surgeon."

One of the guards said, "All right, anybody who needs medical attention, come on up and we'll see whether you need to go to the infirmary with the lieutenant. But no shamming. You know what'll happen if you say you're sick or hurt and there's nothin' wrong with you."

Chance leaned over to Costello and whispered, "What happens in that case?"

"Forty-eight hours in the box."

Ace didn't know what the box was, but it didn't sound like anything good.

"Unless you're in really bad shape, you don't want that quack doctoring you anyway," Costello added.

The Jensen brothers probably would have left it at that and not requested any medical attention, but then both of them caught sight of red hair flashing in the sun behind Lieutenant Driscoll.

Chance instantly shot to his feet.

CHAPTER FIFTEEN

"Blast it, Chance," Ace said under his breath. He reached for his brother's arm but was too late. Chance was already striding forward.

Chance held out his hands so that the blisters on his palms were visible. "How about these, Doc?" he asked. "Is this bad enough to need your attention?" Then, as if noticing Evelyn for the first time, he smiled and went on, "Hello, Miss Sughrue. I didn't see you there."

Several guards had lifted their rifles to their shoulders and aimed them at Chance as he walked toward Evelyn and Lieutenant Driscoll. The one who'd been giving the orders barked, "Hold it right there! You ask permission before you do anything like that, prisoner."

"But you told us to come up," Chance protested. "How do I know whether I need to go to the infirmary unless the doc takes a look at me?"

Evelyn stepped around Driscoll and said, "It's all right, Private. With all you guards around, I don't think these men are going to try anything. Lieutenant, would you take a look at this man's hands?"

"Certainly," Driscoll said. He stepped forward, took hold of Chance's wrists, and studied the young man's palms. After only a few seconds of cursory examination, he dropped Chance's hands and said, "Just typical blisters. I see them all the time. These are already starting to heal."

The spokesman for the guards glared at Chance. "I warned you, mister—"

"This man is new," Evelyn said. "I don't believe he should be punished for not knowing exactly how things are done here at Fort Gila."

"But I told them—" The trooper stopped short, grimaced slightly, and took a breath. "Yes, miss, that's fine." He jerked the barrel of his rifle at Chance. "You there, consider yourself lucky Miss Sughrue spoke up for you. Now go back and sit down with the others."

Chance did so, but not before smiling at Evelyn Sughrue again. The smile she gave him in return was weak and tentative, but it was there, Ace noted.

When Chance sank down crosslegged on the ground beside him, Ace whispered, "You reckon flirting with her is going to gain us anything?"

"We won't know unless we try, will we?" Chance replied. "Besides, I got a smile out of her, and that's worth something by itself."

Maybe it was worth something to Chance, but Ace didn't see how it really helped his brother, or any of the rest of the prisoners.

One of the other men had gouged his leg with a missed pickax swing the day before. That was the only injury the surgeon deemed serious enough to take the man to the infirmary. As they walked off, Evelyn lingered. Ace thought Chance might try to say something to her again, but before he had time to do that, the gates in the wall at the other end of the fort swung open and a man rode in, followed by a buggy pulled by a fine-looking black horse. Several more men trailed behind the buggy.

Ace recognized the rider in the lead as Lieutenant Frank Olsen. He hadn't known that Olsen had left the fort, but the lieutenant didn't keep Ace or any other prisoner apprised of his comings and goings. The other men all appeared to be civilians. The riders trailing the buggy wore range clothes and struck Ace as a hardbitten bunch.

The man in the buggy itself was a different story. He drove the vehicle over to the major's quarters and smoothly brought it to a halt. Olsen reined in beside him. The lieutenant swung down from the saddle while the visitor climbed out of the buggy. He wore a tan suit and white hat, both of which looked expensive even from a distance. As the coat swung back a little, sunlight winked on the grips of a pearl-handled revolver hostered on his right hip.

Evelyn hurried in that direction. As she did, her father appeared from the house and shook hands with the well-dressed newcomer. They exchanged words, but Ace was too far away to catch anything they said. Then the man turned to greet Evelyn, taking off his hat as he did so. That revealed a well-barbered head of crisp, dark hair. He smiled as he reached out to clasp Evelyn's hand.

"Let me guess," Ace said quietly to Costello. "That's Eugene Howden-Smyth."

"It sure is," Costello said. "He visits from time to time."

With a frown, Chance said, "I don't like the way

he's smiling at Miss Sughrue, and he's hanging on to her hand a lot longer than he needs to."

"He's got his eye on her, that's for sure. It wouldn't surprise me a bit if he intends to marry her one of these days." Costello laughed humorlessly. "That would make his grip on the major even stronger. He'd never be able to cross Olsen and Howden-Smyth if that happened."

Chance leaned forward. "Somebody needs to do something about that."

"Sure, but who and what? We don't exactly have a lot of options here."

Costello was right about that. Ace kept coming up against stone walls when he tried to think of a way out of their predicament. Even though he worried about his brother's tendency to fall for pretty girls and get in trouble because of it, he had to admit that appealing to Evelyn Sughrue might be their best chance of putting an end to the villainy going on at Fort Gila.

He saw now, though, that that was probably hopeless. With Major Sughrue deeply implicated in the scheme hatched by Olsen and Howden-Smyth, Evelyn wouldn't risk crossing them. She was too devoted to her father for that. And Olsen was too smart to allow such an opportunity, anyway.

This day of rest was welcome, but Ace knew it would be over all too soon—and then it would be back to hell for the prisoners of Fort Gila.

Lieutenant Frank Olsen, who had some surveying experience, had laid out the route for the road to Eugene Howden-Smyth's mine in the Prophet Mountains. Costello had explained this to the Jensen brothers during the first few days of their captivity. Olsen maybe wasn't as good a surveyor as he thought he was, though, because the next day the route reached a solid wall of rock well before noon.

"It would take a year to get through that with pickaxes," Corporal Parnell declared as he stared disgustedly at the barrier. He looked around at the troopers guarding the work detail and went on, "Somebody's going to have to ride back to the fort and let Lieutenant Olsen know what we've run into. He'll need to blast that rock out of the way." He paused. "Any volunteers?"

None of the troopers said anything or moved, except for a couple who nervously shuffled their feet.

"All right, then," Parnell said impatiently. "Higgins, you've got the job."

"Aw, Corporal, why me?" the trooper said. "You know how them redskins like to catch a man out on his own."

"We haven't spotted any Apaches for several days now."

"Maybe not, but they could still be watchin' us. If they see me ridin' off by myself, there ain't no tellin' what those savages might do."

"Then you'd better not dawdle around and waste any time getting back to the fort," Parnell snapped. "If you start now, you can get to the fort and back here with Lieutenant Olsen in time for us to get rid of this big rock today."

Higgins whined and delayed a few minutes longer,

until Parnell threatened him with being put on the work detail himself. Despite his fear and reluctance, Higgins didn't want that, so he mounted up. As Higgins rode off to the east, toward Fort Gila, Ace saw the trooper's head swiveling back and forth quickly. Higgins was already searching for any signs of the Apaches.

If they *were* out there, there was a good chance Higgins would never know about it until it was too late.

Parnell faced the prisoners and said, "Put those picks and shovels back on the cart. As much as it pains me to say this, there's nothing we can do until the lieutenant gets back with some dynamite and blows up that rock wall. You men might as well hunt some shade and sit down."

The prisoners weren't going to argue with that. They did as Parnell said. Shade was in short supply, but in this heat-blasted landscape, even a sliver of it was welcome. Ace and Chance found some by sitting against a smaller boulder and leaning their heads back. Former lieutenant Costello joined them.

Ace already had his eyes closed, but when he heard someone else sit down nearby, he opened them to slits and glanced in that direction. His eyes opened wider and he sat up straighter as he recognized the brutal, bullet-headed Vince MacDonald.

Costello sounded as surprised as Ace felt as he said, "What in blazes do you want, MacDonald?"

"Take it easy," the big three-striper said. As far as Ace knew, none of the people running things at Fort Gila had bothered with the formality of a court-martial, so technically, MacDonald was still a sergeant. "I'm not looking for trouble, Costello. I just want to talk to you and these two new friends of yours."

"I've never known you to say anything I was interested in hearing."

MacDonald ran a big hand over his sunburned head. "How about this? My boys and I are going to get out of here."

"Oh? How do you plan to do that?"

In spite of his dislike for MacDonald, Ace was interested to hear what the noncom was going to say.

Costello went on, "We outnumber the guards, but not by much, and they have guns while we don't. Even if you jump them and manage to overpower them, most of you will die in the process. I don't think you can sell that to anybody as an escape plan."

"We're not gonna try anything out here," MacDonald replied. "The key to everything is back at the fort."

"Where there are even *more* soldiers to shoot you down like a dog," Costello pointed out.

"That's not all that's there," MacDonald replied with a smug smirk.

"Talk plain, blast it."

MacDonald shook his head. "Not yet. I'm not gonna spill my guts and have you sell us out to Olsen. What I want to know, Costello, is whether you and your bunch are willing to throw in with us."

"What makes you think I have a bunch?"

"Don't give me that," MacDonald scoffed. "I know how most of those poor varmints look to you to do their thinkin' for them. I'm not askin' you for a decision right now. You go ahead and mull it over . . . But don't take too long, because we're not gonna suffer in this hellhole any longer than we have to."

He shoved himself to his feet and ambled off. The guards watched him but didn't appear to think anything of the fact that he'd just been having a conversation with one of his enemies.

"What in the world is he up to?" Ace asked as they watched MacDonald walk away.

"I don't know, but you can count on a couple of things," Costello said. "First, anything he does is going to be good for Vince MacDonald, and second, he's not going to care who gets hurt . . . or even killed . . . along the way."

Chapter Sixteen

Private Higgins didn't run into any Apaches on his way back to the fort. That became obvious when he returned to the foothills with Lieutenant Olsen by the middle of the afternoon. A ten-man patrol rode with the lieutenant, just in case they encountered any hostiles on the way.

Olsen also had a pack mule with him, and that mule was carrying a small wooden crate. Ace had a hunch the crate contained dynamite, and when Olsen removed the lid and revealed several red, greasy-looking cylinders cradled in wool packing, he knew he was right.

"Sorry to have to bother you, sir," Corporal Parnell said after he had saluted the lieutenant. "But I knew it would take a long time to get through that slab without blasting."

"You did the right thing, Corporal. Move the men back."

Parnell turned to the work detail and waved an arm. "You heard the lieutenant! Get back away from here."

MacDonald said, "Don't worry, I don't want to be anywhere near that stuff." He and his friends retreated, and the other group of prisoners followed suit, although they stood a little apart from MacDonald's bunch.

"Ever been around dynamite?" Costello asked the Jensen brothers.

"A little," Ace said.

"I don't like it much," Chance said. "It goes off too easy."

"It's not as bad as nitroglycerine," Costello said. "I've heard plenty of stories about how the men who worked with it while the railroad was being built were all the time blowing off hands or arms . . . or getting themselves killed. As long as a man knows what he's doing, dynamite isn't as touchy." The former officer shrugged. "He may be a no-good skunk who's a disgrace to the uniform, but Olsen's pretty good at handling dynamite, I'll give him credit for that."

Olsen took two of the cylinders from the crate and carried them over to the rock face, along with a drill. He placed the dynamite on a smaller rock and went to work with the drill, boring two holes in the rock after studying it for a few minutes to decide on the right location for them. When he was satisfied with that part of the task, he molded two blasting caps with long rolls of fuse attached to them to the ends of the dynamite and slipped the cylinders into the holes.

Turning to look at the work detail and the guards, Olsen waved at them. "Get back farther, you idiots! Do you have any idea how far rock is going to fly when this blast goes off? Get down behind something if you can."

The men retreated even more while Olsen unrolled the long fuses attached to the dynamite. It would take several minutes for fuses of that length to burn down, Ace knew, which would give the lieutenant enough time to put sufficient distance between himself and the explosion.

"I don't know about you, but I'm going to find a place to hunker down," Costello muttered. He put that plan into action by kneeling behind a rock. It didn't shield him completely, but at least it provided some cover.

Ace and Chance looked around for cover of their own. Not finding much, they stretched out on their bellies so they would be smaller targets if any debris from the blast flew this far. From where they were, they could look straight along the road that had been hacked from the rugged terrain to the place where Lieutenant Olsen now stood, holding the ends of the two fuses clasped together in his left hand while his right took a match from his shirt pocket. He snapped the lucifer to life with his thumbnail and held it to the ends of the fuses, which sputtered for a second and then caught.

At that instant, a flicker of movement caught Ace's eye. He raised his head a little more and looked at one of the knobs commanding a view of the road from just beyond the huge rock slab Olsen was about to blast.

An Apache warrior stood there, a red bandanna tied around his forehead to keep his long black hair back. A breechcloth, high-topped boots, and a sheathed knife slung at his waist were the only other things he wore.

He held a Winchester snugged against his shoulder as he aimed the rifle squarely at Olsen, who had just dropped the sparking, flaring fuse ends to the ground.

"Lieu—" Ace started to shout, but that was all he got out before the rifle cracked and Olsen dropped like a poleaxed steer as his hat flew off his head.

"Get that redskin!" Corporal Parnell shouted as he flung his rifle up. He fired, as did several of the other troopers, but the Apache who had ambushed Lieutenant Olsen was diving back out of sight already.

The shooting continued, though, with echoes racketing across the foothills as other hidden riflemen opened up. Some of the soldiers cried out as bullets found them.

Ace stared at Olsen's sprawled figure as the fuses continued to burn, the trail of sparks inching its way toward the rock wall where the dynamite waited. The Indians hadn't directed any more shots toward Olsen, probably because he had looked dead as he crumpled to the ground, but as Ace watched, he saw the lieutenant's arm move.

Olsen wasn't dead after all—but where he was lying, the flying rocks from the explosion might finish him off if the Apaches didn't.

As bullets whined through the air and kicked up dust all around the work detail and the patrol, Ace pushed himself onto hands and knees.

"Ace!" Chance cried. "Where are you going?"

Ace didn't take the time to answer. He surged to

his feet and dashed along the newly smoothed trail toward Olsen.

If he'd been forced to put his motivation into words, he might have said that he couldn't just stand by and watch any defenseless person lie there and be killed, even a sorry specimen such as Lieutenant Frank Olsen. He didn't waste any mental effort thinking about it, though. Instead he concentrated on zigzagging back and forth as Apache lead kicked up dust and gravel near his feet and whined past his head.

Behind him, Chance saw one of the troopers slump to the ground nearby. The man's rifle fell within reach. Chance picked it up and raised himself onto one knee as he brought the weapon to his shoulder. He knew he was making himself more of a target, but his Jensen fighting blood was up. When he saw an Apache try to dart from one rock to another, he was ready.

The Springfield cracked and bucked against Chance's shoulder. The slug it spat interrupted the Apache's dash and flipped him over backward as it ripped through his chest.

The rifle was a single-shot weapon, but by this time Costello had crawled over to the fallen soldier and grabbed his ammuntion box. "Give me that rifle!" he called to Chance. "I know how to use it!"

Chance thought he had done pretty well with his one shot, but he knew that Costello had a lot more experience with the Springfield and could reload and fire swifter and more efficiently than he could. So he passed the rifle over to the former lieutenant and looked along the road to see how his brother was doing.

Ace's mad dash had reached Olsen's side without the young man getting hit. He saw a bloody streak along the side of Olsen's head, then glanced at the fuses and saw that half their length had burned. Maybe a little more than half . . .

He didn't waste any time as he grabbed Olsen and lifted him. With a huge grunt of effort, Ace draped the unconscious lieutenant over his shoulder and then started back the way he had come in a half-run, half-stagger. More bullets from the ambushers whipped around him.

Ace didn't think about what he was doing. He just kept his legs moving. His chest heaved from the effort of carrying Olsen. He knew that if he fell or even stopped moving, the Apaches would have time to draw a good bead on him, as well as the lieutenant.

Panting roughly, he didn't know how long he had been running when he glanced up and spotted his brother waving frantically at him. It took Ace a couple of seconds to figure out that Chance was motioning for him to get down.

The dynamite . . .

Ace flung himself and Olsen forward even as that thought cracked through his mind. At that same instant, a huge explosion bloomed behind them in a ball of flame, smoke, and dust. The high banks along the sides of the road funneled the force of the blast along it, and Ace would have been knocked off his feet even if he hadn't already dived to the ground. As it was, rocks pelted him painfully, but luckily none of them were large enough to do any real damage. They hurt like blazes, though.

The blast had hurt his ears, too, like two giant hands clapping over them, but the ringing it left behind subsided fairly quickly. As he lifted his head, blinking his eyes rapidly to clear some of the dust from them, he heard the sharp barking of rifle shots nearby, then, slightly muffled, the voice of his brother shouting, "Ace! Ace, get out of there!"

Then, as Ace's vision cleared even more, he saw the reason for Chance's alarm.

All around them, bounding down out of the hills, were dozens of Apache warriors bent on slaughter.

CHAPTER SEVENTEEN

Ace located Olsen lying on the ground a few feet away, still out cold. But the lieutenant's army revolver was on the hip closest to Ace, in a holster with the flap still closed. Ace lunged for the weapon, tore the flap open, and yanked the gun free.

He rolled onto his other side in time to see one of the Apaches looming over him with a rifle poised to dash his brains out with the butt. Ace fired before the blow could fall. The bullet caught the Apache under the chin, bored up through his brain, and blasted the top of his head off in a grisly, grayish pink spray of blood, bone shards, and brain matter. The dead warrior went over backward as a good-sized chunk of skull with some brain still clinging to it plopped to the ground beside Ace.

He ignored the feeling of sickness that welled up inside him at that gruesome sight and twisted around as a bullet zinged past his ear. The Apache who had fired it was about ten yards away, levering his Winchester for another try. Ace thumbed back the revolver's hammer and fired first. His bullet tore into the

Apache's guts and doubled him over. The warrior managed to pull the trigger again before he collapsed, but the slug went harmlessly into the ground right in front of him.

Pounding footsteps made Ace roll back the other way. As he came around, he saw an Apache leaping at him and got a flash of a knife in the man's hand. Metal clashed against metal as Ace used the revolver's barrel to fend off the blade. That gave him a chance to grab the Apache's wrist with his left hand and keep the knife away from him.

At the same time, he tried to bring the gun to bear, but the warrior grabbed *his* wrist. They were locked in a standoff, rolling back and forth on the ground as each of them struggled to strike first.

They came to a stop with Ace on the bottom, the Apache's knee digging painfully into his belly and pinning him to the ground. With grimacing faces only inches apart, each man strained to use the weapon he held while fighting equally hard to prevent the other man from doing that. Whoever slipped first, even the least bit, likely would die . . .

Suddenly, the Apache's eyes opened wide with shock and pain. His strength deserted him like water spilling on the ground. The shocked eyes glazed over in death. As the man's head fell forward limply on Ace's shoulder, Ace looked up past him and saw Chance standing there, withdrawing the cavalry saber he had just plunged into the warrior's back. Ace rolled the corpse off himself and reached up to grasp the hand his brother extended to him.

"Where'd you get the saber?" Ace asked, although he could think of only one reasonable answer.

"It's Olsen's," Chance replied. "He took it off and hung it on his saddle before he started getting ready to blast that rock. I saw it and grabbed it."

He didn't get to say anything else because at that moment, Ace threw a shoulder into him and knocked him down, dropping to a knee beside him. A bullet whistled through empty air where Chance's head had been a split second earlier. Firing from his kneeling stance, Ace punched a bullet into the chest of the Apache warrior who had almost killed his brother.

Chance scrambled up and swung the saber at another warrior closing in with a knife. The extra reach the saber gave him allowed Chance to slash the man's arm and make him drop the knife, and then a back-handed swipe of the long, curved blade opened a crimson-spurting gash in the Apache's throat. Gagging and choking on his own blood, the man clutched at the wound but couldn't stem the fatal tide. He pitched to the ground and writhed out his last few seconds on earth.

With that, the Jensen brothers stood back to back and waited for the next attack. Chance was armed only with the saber, but he had wielded it to deadly effect so far. Ace wasn't sure if he had one or two bullets left in the revolver, but however many there were, he would make the shots count.

He didn't have to, because the members of the patrol Olsen had brought back with him had launched a counterattack of their own, and as a result, the corpses of Apache ambushers littered the ground along the sides of the newly built road. The rest of the warriors were fleeing into the hills. The troopers sent

.45-70 Springfield rounds after them to hurry them in their retreat.

The Apaches hadn't suffered the only losses, though. Ace saw several blue-clad soldiers sprawled on the ground, along with a couple of the work detail in their gray uniforms.

Ace wasn't given to profanity, but he had to bite back a curse as he saw that one of the prisoners lying on the ground was Costello. A large circle of blood stained the front of the former lieutenant's shirt. Chance saw him at the same time and exclaimed, "Is he—"

"Yeah," Ace said as he saw how Costello's wide-open eyes stared sightlessly. He hoped that whatever the man was looking at now, it was a prettier sight than this Arizona Territory hellhole.

Costello had been their only real friend at Fort Gila, Ace mused. His death was going to make it more difficult for the Jensen brothers to escape . . . or even to survive their captivity. Ace was pragmatic enough to recognize that.

As if to emphasize that, Corporal Parnell came running up to them and brandished his rifle. "Drop that gun!" he yelled at Ace. "Drop it now, or I'll shoot!"

"Take it easy," Ace told him. Carefully, he bent over and placed the revolver on the ground, then stepped back away from it. As keyed up as Parnell appeared to be, he wouldn't need much of an excuse to shoot.

Parnell jerked the rifle toward Chance and went on, "You, too, Jensen! Put that saber down, now! Where did you get it?"

"It belongs to Lieutenant Olsen," Chance replied. "But he wasn't using it, so I figured I might as well."

"And he saved my life by doing it," Ace added. "That pistol I was using is the lieutenant's, as well."

"It's against the rules for prisoners to have weapons—"

Vince MacDonald stood nearby with some of his friends. He spat on the ground and then broke into the corporal's rant by saying disgustedly, "Not even you can be that stupid, Parnell. Those two were just defendin' themselves . . . and killin' more than their share of Apaches, too, from what I saw."

The fact that MacDonald would defend them surprised Ace. Maybe MacDonald disliked Parnell even more than he did the Jensen brothers. Right now, Ace and Chance didn't pose any real threat to MacDonald or his plans.

Parnell scowled at MacDonald, then turned to Ace and Chance again and snapped at them, "Just don't try anything funny, you two."

"We don't intend to," Ace said.

With Olsen still unconscious, Parnell was in charge. He told the Jensen brothers to move over with the other prisoners and ordered several troopers to guard the entire group. Other men were posted as lookouts, in case the Apaches tried to sneak back and ambush them again.

With that done, Parnell went to Olsen's side and knelt by the lieutenant. He placed his rifle on the ground and pushed his forage cap to the back of his head as he frowned and obviously struggled with trying to figure out what to do next.

From what Ace could see, Olsen's wound hadn't

bled much. Head wounds, even the ones that weren't serious, normally bled like a stuck pig, so the lack of gore told Ace the bullet must have barely nicked Olsen. The impact had been enough to knock him out cold, though.

"I don't think he's hurt bad," Ace said to Parnell. "Maybe if you get some water into him, that might bring him around."

"I didn't ask for your advice," Parnell snapped. Despite that, he followed it, telling one of the men to bring over a canteen. Carefully, Parnell lifted Olsen's head and shoulders, rested them on his leg, and tilted the canteen to his mouth. He let only a little water dribble into the lieutenant's mouth, and even that was enough to choke Olsen. He coughed and sputtered and shook, but as Ace had predicted, he came to. He looked disoriented for a moment, but then as he began to realize that he was lying there with his head in Corporal Parnell's lap, anger and embarrassment replaced the confusion.

"Blast it, stop that, Corporal," Olsen said as he batted aside the canteen when Parnell tried to give him another drink. "Let me up."

"Yes, sir." Parnell helped Olsen to a sitting position, where the lieutenant promptly began swaying as if the whole world were spinning wrong around him.

After a minute or two, Olsen's head seemed to settle down. He ordered Parnell to help him to his feet. Parnell and another trooper did so. Olsen looked around at the bodies and asked, "What about the rest of the Apaches?"

"They fled, Lieutenant. I took precautions in

case they doubled back, but we haven't seen any sign of them."

"And our men? How many casualties?"

"I, uh, don't know for sure, sir. There hasn't been time to check—"

"Then check now, and report."

"Yes, sir."

While Parnell was doing that, Olsen looked along the road toward the rock wall in which he had placed the dynamite. The rock had a gaping hole in it now, so obviously the blast had gone off, but Olsen would have no memory of it.

He frowned again at the bodies of the slain Apaches and said, apparently to no one in particular, "What happened here? The last thing I remember is lighting the fuses for that dynamite."

"I'll tell you what happened," MacDonald spoke up. "Ace Jensen there saved your life."

Again, Ace was surprised that MacDonald would give him credit for anything. Olsen looked shocked, too. He peered at Ace and asked, "Is that true?"

Ace shrugged. "I saw you moving a little after you were hit and knew that bullet to your head had just knocked you out instead of killing you. I wasn't going to let you just lie there and get killed by the blast or by the Apaches."

"So you came and got me."

Chance said, "And we both fought to keep the Indians off of you, too. That has to count for something, doesn't it, Lieutenant?"

"Count for what?" Olsen asked sharply. "You think that out of gratitude to you and your brother, I'll turn you loose? You can forget about that. It's not going to happen. That's not the way things work around here."

Chance looked like he was going to argue more, but Ace caught his eye and shook his head. It would be a waste of time and energy, he knew. Olsen wasn't going to let a little thing like Ace saving his life interfere with his plan to wind up with his hands on a big share of whatever fortune Eugene Howden-Smyth took out of that mine.

Parnell came up and reported, "Two members of the work detail were killed, Lieutenant, and one member of the patrol you brought back here with you. Four more men are wounded, but maybe not too seriously."

"Good. Load everyone back up in the wagons, Corporal, including our men who were killed. We're going back to the fort so the wounded men can get medical attention and the ones who were killed can receive a proper burial."

"Yes, sir." Parnell hesitated. "What about the Apaches who were killed?"

"Leave them where they fell," Olsen said coldly. "Either the other savages will come back for them later, or the scavengers will take care of them. Either way, these particular filthy redskins are no longer any of our concern."

CHAPTER EIGHTEEN

Because of the bullet burn on his head, Lieutenant Olsen wasn't able to put his hat on. Ace didn't think the wound would require stitches, but when they got back to the fort, the surgeon, Lieutenant Driscoll, could clean it and decide about any further treatment.

It was a sober bunch that headed to Fort Gila. Costello's body was placed in one of the wagon beds, along with those of the other two dead troopers, and then some of the men covered them with blankets. Ace knew it would be a while before he forgot the sightless stare in the former lieutenant's eyes.

A couple of the wounded men were hurt badly enough that they had to ride in the wagons, as well, so that meant the vehicles were crowded as they rocked along through the semidesert country toward the fort. The journey was a solemn one.

When they reached Fort Gila in the late afternoon, one of the guards at the gates saw the blanket-shrouded forms and took off at a run toward the headquarters building. By the time the wagons came to a stop at the infirmary so that the wounded men could be unloaded and seen to, Major Flint Sughrue was striding briskly in that direction.

"What's happened here?" he asked as he came up to them, then exclaimed, "Lieutenant, you're injured!"

"It doesn't amount to anything, sir," Olsen said. He made a vague gesture toward the bloody welt on the side of his head. "Just a little bullet graze."

Lieutenant Driscoll emerged from the infirmary building in time to hear the comment. He said, "Any head injury is nothing to take lightly, Frank. You'd better come on inside and let me take a look at that."

MacDonald protested, "There are other wounded men, Doc."

"And I'll get to all of them," Driscoll said with an annoyed frown. "But I'm going to tend to Lieutenant Olsen first."

Driscoll ushered Olsen into the building, and Major Sughrue followed them. MacDonald muttered, "Reckon the doc intends to carve himself off a chunk of however much loot Olsen winds up with, so he don't want anything happening to him."

"Shut up, MacDonald," Corporal Parnell snapped from where he still sat his horse beside the lead wagon. "What officers do is none of your business . . . or mine."

MacDonald looked across at Ace and said, "It ain't hardly fair. Olsen likely wouldn't even be alive if it wasn't for you, Jensen. The Apaches would've gotten him if that explosion didn't."

Ace's puzzlement grew. MacDonald acted almost like he wanted to be their friend now, after all the trouble he had caused for the Jensen brothers in the first place.

Then a possible explanation occurred to him. MacDonald had approached Costello, as well as Ace and Chance, while they were all in the guardhouse and tried to talk them into throwing in with him on an escape attempt. They had turned him down at the time, but maybe now, with Costello dead, MacDonald believed the Jensen brothers would be more likely to back his play, whatever it was. It would be an audacious move, but MacDonald clearly didn't lack for gall.

Drawn by the work detail's arrival and the resulting commotion, Evelyn Sughrue hurried from the major's quarters. As she approached Parnell, she said, "Corporal, do you have wounded—Oh!"

Evelyn put a hand to her mouth as she stared over the wagon's sideboards at the blanket-covered bodies.

"Miss, you should go back inside," Parnell told her.

"Are those . . . are those . . ."

"Yes, miss," Parnell said. "We ran into some Apaches and suffered some casualties. Actually, it wasn't so much a matter of running into them as it was of them jumping us."

"Who . . . ?"

"Costello, Ryerson, and Larch. And we have some other men who are hurt."

"Where is Lieutenant Driscoll?"

"Tending to Lieutenant Olsen. He's got a head wound."

That sounded a lot worse than it really was, Ace thought as he watched Evelyn Sughrue bite her lip anxiously. He wanted to tell her that Olsen's injury wasn't serious. He had never seen any sign that Evelyn was fond of Olsen—just the opposite, in fact—but the fact that the Apaches had dared to attack a good-sized detail like that might have spooked her.

He didn't say anything to her, however. Evelyn had to have a pretty good idea that Olsen was taking advantage of her father's mental state but hadn't done a blasted thing about it. Maybe she was afraid that trying to expose Olsen would backfire on her and harm Major Sughrue, as the Jensen brothers had discussed with Costello.

Whatever the motivation for Evelyn's actions—or lack of action—the important thing was that Ace knew he and Chance couldn't count on any help from her.

As much as he hated to admit it, their best chance of getting out of here and alerting the authorities to Olsen's scheming, just might be to cooperate with Vince MacDonald . . .

A burial detail was formed, and the three men who had been killed in the ambush were laid to rest in the little cemetery outside the post walls that evening, not long before the sun went down. The service was a short one. There was no chaplain at Fort Gila, but Major Flint Sughrue read from the Scriptures and said a prayer over the graves.

Less than a dozen mourners were on hand. Olsen had said, "Those bloodthirsty savages might be looking to catch all of us outside the fort proper. We're not going to play into their hands."

Olsen posted lookouts all along the walls. The

gates were left open, so those outside could get back in quickly if they needed to. Since two prisoners from the work detail had been killed, Sughrue declared that anyone from that group who wanted to attend the burial would be allowed to. Olsen didn't look happy about that, but he didn't try to change the major's mind. Probably figured it wasn't worth the time and effort, Ace thought.

He and Chance walked out to the cemetery with a few other men from the work detail, but not MacDonald or any of his cronies. Corporal Parnell and some of the troopers were there as well. But not Evelyn Sughrue. Her father had forbidden her from attending.

"You stay in the fort where it's safe, dear," he told her.

With her face showing the strain she was under, Evelyn had said, "Is anywhere out here in this wilderness truly safe, Father?"

"It will be, someday," Sughrue had replied gruffly. "Someday the frontier will be tamed, and folks can live in peace."

Ace thought that was an admirable sentiment, but then Sughrue added, "And that's the reason we have to finish that road to Eugene's mine! That's one more link in the chain it'll take to bring civilization out here!"

Olsen couldn't keep a faint smirk off his face when the major said that. Sughrue was completely under his spell, and Olsen knew it. The lieutenant brought that reaction under control quickly, but not quickly enough that Ace failed to catch it.

The burial went off without a hitch. Following
the service, Sughrue walked over to his wife's grave,
removed his hat again, and stood there solemnly for
a long moment. Out of respect for him, none of the
other men moved while he was doing that. They
didn't start back to the fort until he turned away and
clapped his hat back on his head.

As the men were walking back, Sughrue said to
Olsen, "There's something I don't understand, Lieutenant. Corporal Parnell reported that Apache scouts
had been sighted watching the work detail several
times during the past week."

Ace and Chance were close enough to overhear
this conversation as guards herded them along at
riflepoint.

"That's true, Major," Olsen admitted.

"Yet they didn't attack any of those times. They
waited until our force in the field was larger, so they had
less chance of overpowering it. What sort of enemy
passes up better odds only to attack when the odds
are worse later?"

That was actually pretty shrewd reasoning on the
major's part, Ace thought. Costello had mentioned
that Flint Sughrue had been a well-respected officer,
even a hero of sorts, during the Civil War. The man's
heart and soul might have been overwhelmed by the
grief he felt at his wife's passing, but he still had
the mind of a military man, at least at times.

"I can only hazard a guess, Major," Olsen said.
"The first shot they fired was directed at me, so my
theory is that they were waiting to get a crack at an
officer. They wanted to kill either you or me, because

they know that Fort Gila can't get along without either of us."

"I suppose you're right. How are you feeling, Frank?"

"I'm all right, sir." Lightly, Olsen touched the bandage the surgeon had wrapped around his head. "I have a bit of a headache, but that's to be expected. Lieutenant Driscoll said I should be fine."

"Good, good," Sughrue said, nodding as he walked along with his hands clasped behind his back. "You know how much I depend on you in these troubled times, Lieutenant. I . . . I don't think I could get along without you."

"It's an honor to hear you say that, sir. Don't worry, nothing's going to happen to me. I'll see to that."

I'll just bet you will, Ace thought from where he trudged along behind them. *You'll always look out for Frank Olsen before anybody else.*

The solemn atmosphere continued that night in the guardhouse as darkness closed in. The men hadn't done much actual work today, since they'd had to wait for Olsen to show up and dynamite that rock wall, and then after that they'd been occupied with the Apache ambush. So they weren't as numb with exhaustion as they usually were and didn't fall into sodden slumber right away after they'd eaten.

Ace and Chance were sitting up, leaning against the wall, when someone sat down beside them. The familiar harsh tones of Vince MacDonald said, "Jensen."

"Which one?" Chance asked with a hint of a chuckle.

"Both of you, blast it. You boys need to listen to me."

"I don't know why we would do that," Ace said. "If we hadn't had that run-in with you in Packsaddle, my brother and I wouldn't even be here."

"I wouldn't be so sure about that. You two weren't the first drifters who got railroaded on phony charges and brought out here. That marshal and judge in Packsaddle have themselves a pretty good operation. They provide workers nobody would ever miss for Olsen and get a cut of what he makes."

"I thought maybe something like that was happening," Ace said.

Chance asked, "What happened to all the other civilians?"

An ugly laugh came from MacDonald in the darkness. "When they get worked to death, they wind up in unmarked graves out in the desert, and it was like they were never here. Only actual soldiers unlucky enough to get on Olsen's bad side and wind up on the work detail get places in the cemetery when they're done. One of those unmarked graves is where you boys are bound for. I'll bet they won't even dig two holes. They'll just dump you in the same one." MacDonald paused. "Unless you get smart and throw in with me. You never should've listened to Costello. He was holdin' you back from your only real chance outta here."

"Why would you want to help us?" Ace asked. "The trouble you and your friends had with us in town is part of the reason you didn't get away."

"Because I've seen plenty of evidence now what sort of fightin' men you are," MacDonald said. Despite

Ace's wariness and dislike of the burly noncom, he realized that the words had the ring of truth to them. "I need good men for what I've got in mind."

"You've never said what that is," Chance pointed out.

"And I won't say any more until I have your word that you're bustin' out of here with us."

"I don't trust you, MacDonald," Chance said. "We're going to have to think about this."

"Don't think about it too long," MacDonald warned as he pushed himself to his feet, "because we're not gonna be waitin' around here forever. You just remember what I said about that unmarked grave. The desert's a big, lonely place. Nobody'll ever even know you're there."

CHAPTER NINETEEN

The feeling of apprehension was like a physical thing in the air as the work detail set out from the fort the next morning. This time a larger force of guards rode with the wagons and the supply cart. Every man in the group spent a lot of time looking around, but they all knew in the backs of their minds that if their number was up, more than likely they would never see the Apache who killed them. The fatal bullet or arrow would come seemingly out of nowhere.

That knowledge didn't stop anyone from peering around nervously at the rolling, dusty landscape.

MacDonald made sure he sat next to Ace and Chance. When they were well away from the fort, he asked quietly, "Have you boys given any thought to what I said last night?"

"We have," Ace replied. As a matter of fact, he and Chance had discussed the matter in whispers after MacDonald left them alone. They agreed that neither of them trusted the burly noncom as far as they could throw him. "We're not going to promise we'll go along with any plan until we know what it is."

MacDonald glared, clearly displeased by that answer. "I don't like anybody layin' down the law to me."

"Then you probably shouldn't have enlisted in the army," Chance pointed out. "Taking orders is the main thing you have to do."

"Not exactly. Fightin' and killin' come first."

The relish in MacDonald's voice testified that he liked those things.

Ace said, "I'll be honest with you, MacDonald. We don't like the idea of throwing in with you. But we're not going to keep working on this road until we drop dead, either. So if you've got an idea how we can get away, we're willing to listen to it, but that's all we'll promise."

"You idiots don't know when somebody's tryin' to help you," MacDonald snapped. "Well, you can just stay here and rot, for all I care."

He moved to a different spot in the wagon, making another member of the work detail move over and give him room. He kept sending murderous glares toward Ace and Chance, who did their best to ignore him.

When they reached the spot where the ambush had taken place the day before, all the bodies of the dead Apaches were gone. That didn't surprise Ace. The surviving warriors had returned later for their fallen comrades.

The man in charge of the detail today was a corporal named Cochran. Parnell had remained behind at Fort Gila. Cochran got the men unloaded and the tools passed out while guards took up their posts on both sides of the road, which was still littered with debris from the explosion the day before.

"Get all those chunks of rock cleaned up," Cochran ordered. "Once that's done, you can get started widening the gap in that wall. The blast should've cracked it enough that the picks will chip it apart."

"You sound like you know something about a chore like that, Corporal," Ace commented as he shouldered the pick he had been given.

"I used to be a hard-rock miner before I joined the army. Get busy, mister. No time for talk. We've got a road to build."

It took a while for the tension the men felt to ease, but hard, grueling work had a way of distracting just about anybody. Swing the picks, lift the shovels, force already tiring muscles to continue working . . . It was hard to worry too much about Apaches when you were just trying to keep going.

Even so, the men glanced toward the hills fairly frequently and searched for any sign of movement, any lurking threat.

Nothing happened during the day except hard work, and plenty of it. The same was true the next day and the day after that. The gap in the rock wall was widened sufficiently and the work detail pushed on through the rugged terrain, clearing and leveling the route that gradually sloped upward toward the mountains. The Indian attack wasn't forgotten, but it faded in the minds of the men. The guards remained alert, however.

By the time Sunday approached, everyone was looking forward to a break from the routine, a chance to stay inside the fort, rest, and not worry that a horde of Apaches might sweep down out of nowhere and massacre all of them.

Evelyn Sughrue was mending clothes in the parlor of the little adobe house she shared with her father when she heard the rattle of buggy wheels outside along with the hoofbeats of a horse. The windows were open to let in whatever vagrant breezes might blow through and lessen the stifling Arizona Territory heat. They let in those troubling sounds as well.

Evelyn sighed and set her mending aside. She stood up from the rocking chair where she'd been sitting. She knew it would be only a matter of moments before the knock came on the door. When it did, she was not the least bit surprised.

She opened the door to find Eugene Howden-Smyth standing there, hat in hand, a smile on his face. No one else would have come here in a buggy.

"Good day to you, Miss Sughrue," he said in that cultured British accent many women no doubt found quite appealing.

Evelyn did not.

"Hello, Mr. Howden-Smyth," she said. "My father should be over at the headquarters building, if you're looking for him."

"I'm always glad to visit with your esteemed father, but actually, today it's you I've come to see."

"Oh?" Evelyn said, sounding surprised even though she really wasn't. "What can I do for you?"

He gestured vaguely with the hat. "Perhaps we could continue our conversation inside, out of this infernal sun?"

Evelyn thought about pointing out that it wouldn't be proper for the two of them to be alone together in the house, but she decided not to waste the time and energy doing so. It wouldn't do any good. Better to go ahead and find out what the Englishman wanted, she told herself.

She already had a pretty good idea what that was. He had made it clear enough through his veiled comments and the way he looked at her.

She moved aside and gestured. "Come in." She could be genteel and polite, as her mother had taught her to be—although she was doing precious little these days to honor the memory of Amelia Sughrue, she thought, the way she stood by and watched as Frank Olsen plotted and schemed and took advantage of her father.

She took Howden-Smyth's hat as he entered the house. She set it on a small table and asked him, "Would you like something to drink?"

"Some cool water would be lovely after that long, hot ride from the mine."

She poured water from a pitcher into a glass and handed it to him. "You were going to tell me what I can do for you," she reminded him.

"Of course," he said after he had taken a drink. "You can come spend the day and have dinner with me Sunday. I find myself in the need of some charming company, and there is no one in the entire territory more charming than you, Evelyn . . . if I may be so bold as to call you that."

He was bold, all right. At least, his eyes were as they roamed freely over her body in the dark green dress she wore.

Eugene Howden-Smyth was twice as old as she was. True, the touches of silver at the temples in his thick dark hair gave him a distinguished air, and it was obvious from looking at him that he was still a strong, vital man. Many girls Evelyn's age would be delighted to have someone like him take an interest in them. And in addition to being handsome, the man owned a gold mine! Some women would consider him incredibly desirable just for that reason alone.

Unfortunately, he was connected with Frank Olsen—and the lieutenant made Evelyn's skin crawl. That had been true from the first moment she had met Olsen and felt as if she were looking at a venomous snake. Maybe it wasn't fair to judge someone guilty by association, but that was the way she felt about Eugene Howden-Smyth. Because he was working with Olsen, *he* made her skin crawl, too, and she couldn't do anything about it.

She managed to smile, though—somehow—and say, "I'm honored by the invitation, Mr. Howden-Smyth, but I really couldn't."

He took another drink of the water and then asked, "Why not? I confess that my cook is accustomed to throwing together simple meals for a crew of hungry miners, but I assure you he's capable of more."

"Sunday is the day Lieutenant Driscoll tends to the men who need medical attention, and I often assist him in the infirmary. Also, my father and I usually visit my mother's grave on that day."

"I'm certain the post surgeon could manage to do without your services for one day."

"I don't know. He has several patients, men who

were wounded in that battle with the Apaches the other day. Have you heard about that?"

"I have," Howden-Smyth said. "Lieutenant Olsen sent word to me about it. He also assured me that it wouldn't slow down construction on the road."

"Well, I'd hate to leave Lieutenant Driscoll on his own . . ."

"I'll speak to the lieutenant," Howden-Smyth said briskly. "As for your father and your, ah, visit to your mother's resting place, perhaps you could do that early enough in the morning that I could pick you up later and we'd still get back to the mine in time for dinner."

"I don't know . . . all the way to the mine and back over those rough trails . . ."

"It *is* an arduous journey at times. It will be much better once that road the army is building is finished. Perhaps you'd be interested in seeing how the work is progressing along the way."

He wasn't going to give up, Evelyn thought. She would have to be blunt with him, perhaps even hurt his feelings . . .

The door opened and her father came in, followed by Lieutenant Frank Olsen. "There you are, Eugene," Major Sughrue said. "Frank told me you were visiting the fort today."

"I would have been by to pay my respects shortly, Major," Howden-Smyth responded. "I was just inviting your daughter on a bit of an outing first. I'd like for her to come up to the mine with me on Sunday so she can have a look at it—she's never been there, you know—and then have dinner with me."

"Well, that sounds like an excellent idea," Sughrue

said with a nod. He looked at Evelyn. "We'll go out and put flowers on your mother's grave early enough that it won't interfere with your plans, my dear."

Evelyn kept smiling and bit back a frustrated response. She saw the hastily concealed smirk on Olsen's face and knew the lieutenant had somehow gotten in her father's ear about this, too. Hardly anything went on at Fort Gila without Frank Olsen pulling the strings. And Olsen and Howden-Smyth worked together closely enough the lieutenant probably knew what had really brought the Englishman here today.

Frank Olsen was perfectly willing to push her into Howden-Smyth's arms if doing so would make their partnership run more smoothly. And Howden-Smyth, the oily scoundrel, was perfectly capable of demanding such a thing.

Howden-Smyth turned back to Evelyn and said, "Since your father has no objection . . ."

He let the words trail off and gave her a hopeful smile.

She was beaten, and she knew it.

She remembered how, not long after she and her mother and father had come here to Fort Gila, one of the soldiers had discovered a den of rattlesnakes in the rocks not far from the fort. Evelyn hadn't seen the creatures herself, but she had heard the men talking about them, how the coils of their scaly bodies had looped and entwined with each other as the ominous buzzing from their tails filled the air and their little tongues flicked in and out of their mouths as they readied themselves to strike. The description had been vivid and disturbing enough that nightmares about

snakes had cropped up frequently in Evelyn's dreams
for days afterward.

She felt now as if she were about to step into a
similar den of serpents, but she forced herself to nod
and say, "Of course I'll accept your invitation, Mr.
Howden-Smyth."

"Eugene," he prompted her.

"Eugene," she said, and in the back of her mind
she seemed to hear that rattling . . .

CHAPTER TWENTY

They had been here for more than a week now, Ace reminded himself on Saturday as he and Chance toted large but manageable chunks of rock to the side of the new road and tossed them out of the trail. In a way, it was hard to believe that that many days had passed.

At the same time, it seemed as if they had been in this predicament forever, either locked up in the guardhouse at Fort Gila or out here sweltering in the hot sun and busting up rocks at gunpoint.

Chance paused to sleeve sweat from his forehead. "I'm glad tomorrow's Sunday," he said. "Another day of this and I'd be ready to make a break for it just so they'd shoot me and put me out of my misery."

"Don't feel like that," Ace said. "We'll come up with a way to get out of here sooner or later."

"If it's much later, Ace . . . it's going to be too late."

Ace hated to admit it, but his brother was right. Their bodies were young and still strong, and they were getting enough to eat, so they weren't growing weaker at this point. The work had just hardened them that much more.

However, it was the condition of their minds that was worrisome, not that of their bodies. Much more of this and they would give up, Ace knew. The last vestiges of hope would evaporate, soaked up by despair like the thirsty desert sands sucked up water. Once that happened, they would continue to labor on mindlessly until the inevitable physical breakdown began.

And once they were no longer able to work—well, if they didn't simply drop dead while swinging a pick or shovel, Ace wouldn't put it past Frank Olsen to put bullets in their heads just to get rid of two mouths to feed. Those lost graves in the desert beckoned them . . .

A sudden screech of pain, followed by an outburst of vehement cursing, broke into Ace's bleak reverie.

He looked around and saw one of the prisoners hopping back and forth on one foot and trying to clutch the other foot he had lifted into the air. Curses poured out of the man's mouth. Nearby, MacDonald stood staring at the man and asked, "What in blazes did you do, Brunner?"

The man took one hand off his obviously injured foot and waved at a chunk of rock a little bigger than a man's head. An incoherent babble came out of his mouth. He lost his balance and sat down hard on the ground, which set off a new round of yelling and cursing.

"I think he must have dropped that rock on his foot," Chance said to Ace.

"Yeah, and a rock that size weighs enough it could have done some damage."

"And hurt like blazes," Chance added.

More men were gathering around Brunner now.

He was one of MacDonald's cronies, Ace recalled, and the sergeant was one of those who congregated. The commotion drew the attention of several guards, who bustled up brandishing their rifles.

"Break it up, break it up," one of the troopers ordered. "What happened here?"

Brunner was finally able to say something besides curses. "I broke my foot!" he yelled.

"Your foot ain't broke," the guard scoffed. "What'd you do, drop a rock on it?"

"That's exactly what he did," MacDonald said. He pointed. "And that's it right there. It's big enough he sure might've broke his foot with it."

The guard frowned and looked at the other troopers who had come up with him. One of them shrugged and said, "Well, don't look at me like I can tell you what to do. How should I know? Want me to go get Parnell?"

Corporal Parnell had taken over the guard detail again after a few days of being relieved from that task. He was already on his way, having noticed the other soldiers clustered together.

"Stand back," Parnell ordered as he came up to the group. "What's wrong?"

"Brunner broke his foot," MacDonald said.

"Dropped that big rock on it," Brunner added through teeth gritted against the pain.

"Let's have a look," Parnell said. "Get your boot off."

"I . . . I don't know if I can."

"Then get up and get back to work," Parnell said without any sympathy in his voice.

"Hang on, hang on," Brunner muttered. He began

trying to tug his boot off, grimacing in pain as he did so.

"Hurry up," Parnell snapped.

MacDonald dropped to a knee beside Brunner and said, "Lemme give you a hand." He caught hold of Brunner's boot and hauled on it. Brunner howled as the boot came off.

"What're you doin'?" he yelled at MacDonald. "Are you loco?"

MacDonald dropped the boot on the ground and spread his hands. "I'm just tryin' to help."

"Move back, MacDonald," Parnell said. He handed his rifle to one of the other guards. "Brunner, let me see that foot."

He knelt beside Brunner and took the man's ankle in one hand while he looked at the injured member. From where Ace stood, he could see what looked like a bloodstain on Brunner's sock.

"Take the sock off," Parnell said.

Gingerly, Brunner did so, revealing a pale foot that had a cut on the top of it and was starting to show some bruising.

"Yeah, you hurt it, all right, but I don't think it's broken," Parnell said.

MacDonald leaned over them and said, "Looks like it to me. See how it's swellin' there?"

He reached down and poked a finger hard against Brunner's foot. Brunner howled again and flopped over backward.

"Get that crazy man away from me!"

"Blast it, MacDonald, step back and stay there!" Parnell said. He put Brunner's foot back on the ground. "All right, get some of your friends to help you and you can go sit in the back of one of the wagons."

"You'd better send me back to the fort so the surgeon can take a look at it—"

"Tomorrow's Sunday," Parnell interrupted. "Lieutenant Driscoll can look at it then. Just be glad I'm not making you keep working, Brunner."

He straightened, shook his head, took his rifle back, and walked away. Brunner left his boot and sock off while MacDonald and another member of the work detail took hold of his arms and hauled him upright. With them helping him, he hobbled toward the wagons, not putting any weight on the injured foot.

"Lucky son of a gun," Chance muttered.

"Lucky how?" Ace asked. "His foot may be broken."

"Yeah, but he doesn't have to work the rest of the day. And if it really *is* broken, he probably won't have to work next week, either."

"And then it'll heal up and he'll be right back where he started."

Chance shrugged. "Yeah, I guess so."

Before they could say anything else, one of the guards told all the prisoners to get back to work.

Brunner complained most of the way back to Fort Gila, until Parnell threatened to make him walk the rest of the way, broken foot or no broken foot, or else sit down and wait until the Apaches found him. Brunner shut up after that, although he still wore a surly frown on his face.

When they got to the fort, MacDonald suggested,

"Why don't you go ahead and take the poor fella to see the doc, Corporal?"

"He can wait for the usual chance to see Lieutenant Driscoll tomorrow morning, like everybody else," Parnell said. "Anyway, by then the swelling probably will have gone down some, and the lieutenant can tell better just how bad the foot's really hurt."

"If you say so," Brunner responded through gritted teeth.

"That's how it's gonna be. Some of you men help him into the guardhouse now. Supper will be along after a while."

Brunner complained constantly, but at least he kept it at a fairly low volume, and Ace and Chance were able to ignore it for the most part. The injured man finally subsided and went to sleep after he had eaten his supper. Most of the other prisoners dozed off as well, and the sound of snoring filled the guardhouse.

Ace didn't doze off right away. Something nagged at his brain, just enough to keep him awake, but whatever the stray thought was, he couldn't grasp it well enough to pull it out into the open where he could take a look at it.

Beside him, Chance's deep, regular breathing indicated that he was asleep. Ace lay there on the hard-packed dirt, staring into the darkness as he waited for slumber to come to him, too.

Because he was awake, he heard two of the prisoners whispering, even though he couldn't make out the words. Whatever they were talking about, it wasn't any of his business, he told himself.

But then he recognized Vince MacDonald's harsh rumble, even though the noncom was trying to keep it down. The other voice, Ace thought, belonged to Brunner, who was awake again. That stirred Ace's interest. Some instinct prompted him to want to know what they were talking about.

Moving so slowly that he didn't make any noise, he eased across the ground toward the two men. He was careful not to bump into any of the sleeping prisoners, because that would probably wake them up and cause a commotion, and then MacDonald and Brunner would stop talking.

Ace began picking up a few words. ". . . didn't have to . . . so hard . . . hurt like . . ."

Those bits and pieces came from Brunner. MacDonald's response came equally sporadically to Ace's ears.

". . . make it look bad . . . not really that bad . . . infirmary . . . only chance . . ."

Ace stopped where he was, rather than trying to get closer. He had heard enough to piece together an idea. Brunner's tone sounded peevish and angry, as if MacDonald had done something he didn't like. The biggest thing that had happened to Brunner today—or any other day recently, for that matter—was dropping that rock on his foot and hurting himself.

What if he *hadn't* hurt himself? That question formed abruptly in Ace's mind. What if Brunner hadn't dropped the rock at all? MacDonald had been close to him. MacDonald could have done it—and it might not have been an accident, either.

A few days earlier, MacDonald had indicated to

Ace and Chance that he and his friends wouldn't wait long before making another escape attempt. He had also hinted that such an attempt would take place here at the fort, not out in the foothills where the road was being built.

Maybe the plan involved the infirmary somehow. One way for MacDonald to get inside there without being injured himself was if he was helping someone else who was hurt. Maybe he had in mind taking Lieutenant Driscoll as a hostage . . .

Or Evelyn Sughrue. Sometimes she helped the lieutenant in the infirmary.

Ace's breath caught in his throat as that thought came to him. His heart began slugging harder in his chest. MacDonald might believe that Major Sughrue and Lieutenant Olsen wouldn't come after him and his friends if Evelyn's life was in their hands. He might well be right about that, too. The major's continued cooperation was too important to Olsen's plan to risk letting anything happen to his daughter. He might have to allow MacDonald and whoever threw in with him to escape and hope that they would release Evelyn unharmed later.

Or Olsen might react entirely differently. Ace didn't know. He didn't know if this wild theory he had sketched together had any truth to it—even though his gut told him that he was right to suspect that Brunner's injury was part of Vince MacDonald's plan.

He was certain that he didn't want any harm coming to Evelyn Sughrue, though, and he knew Chance wouldn't want that, either. As Ace began slipping back to where he had been lying beside his brother, he told himself there was really only one way to make sure nothing happened to Evelyn.

If MacDonald made his attempt to escape from Fort Gila tomorrow, the Jensen brothers had to be part of it.

CHAPTER TWENTY-ONE

Early the next morning, before the guards showed up with breakfast, Ace got a chance to talk quietly and privately with Chance and tell him what he had overheard the night before.

Chance frowned and said, "You really think MacDonald busted Brunner's foot?"

"I think he could have," Ace replied. "And I think Brunner knew it was going to happen. MacDonald either persuaded him to go along with the plan, or threatened him into cooperating. Either way, from what I overheard, I don't think Brunner was expecting it to be quite so bad."

"But MacDonald wanted to make it look good," Chance breathed.

"Yeah, that's my theory. He didn't want to take a chance on Brunner not getting into the infirmary. And when the time comes, I'll bet a hat MacDonald is the one giving him a hand to get there."

Chance grunted. "No bet. It sounds to me like you've figured it out, Ace . . . but what's the point? What does MacDonald gain out of it?"

"A hostage, maybe."

"Lieutenant Driscoll?"

"Or worse. Driscoll . . . and Evelyn Sughrue."

Chance grimaced. "We can't let that happen. I hate to think of Miss Sughrue winding up in the hands of a man like that."

"I don't believe he'd hurt her," Ace said. "She would be too valuable to him as a hostage for that." He shook his head slightly. "But you can't ever tell, and I don't want to run the risk."

"Neither do I." Chance frowned. "Do you think we should tell somebody what we suspect?"

"Who? Olsen? I don't think he'd believe us."

"Major Sughrue might. I mean, we're talking about the safety of his daughter."

Ace considered that and nodded. "True, but it's not likely Olsen would ever let us get near enough to have a word with the major in private. Any time Sughrue is out among the men, Olsen is always right beside him, controlling everything he sees and hears. That way he can be sure of keeping the major under his control."

Chance rubbed his chin and frowned in thought. "If Sughrue comes around after we've eaten, when it's time for anybody who needs medical attention to go to the infirmary, maybe we could speak up then, instead of trying to tell him in private." Before Ace could reply, Chance held up a hand and shook his head. "No, that won't work. MacDonald could just deny the whole thing, and Brunner's bound to back him up. Then we'd look loco, and we'd give MacDonald one more grudge against us."

"I think the only way anybody's going to believe us is if MacDonald gets caught in the act."

"The act of kidnapping Miss Sughrue?" Chance sounded alarmed about that.

"Or whatever he's got in mind. But maybe . . . if MacDonald thinks he's going to get away with it and puts his plan into action, but somebody's there who's expecting trouble and can put a stop to it before anybody gets hurt . . ."

"Somebody like us, you mean?" Chance said.

"I don't see anybody else around here who's going to do it," Ace said.

As on the previous Sunday, the morning meal was brought to the guardhouse later than usual but also was more substantial and the men were allowed to go outside to eat. When they were done, the men who requested it were given the makings and rolled cigarettes for themselves. Most were relaxed and happy that they weren't going to have to toil in the hot sun all day.

Not Vince MacDonald, though. Ace could tell that MacDonald was trying not to show it, but the big man was keyed up about something—and Ace had a pretty good idea what it was.

MacDonald and Brunner sat together, leaning against the guardhouse wall. Brunner's injured foot was stuck out in front of him, wrapped in a spare shirt instead of having a boot and sock on it. The two men were talking together quietly but fell silent as Ace and Chance approached.

"What do you two want?" MacDonald asked them in a surly voice.

The Jensen brothers sat down next to the other

two men without waiting for an invitation. Keeping his voice quiet, Ace said, "You've been talking a lot the past few days, MacDonald, about getting out of here. Chance and I have come to the conclusion that you're right."

"I don't know what the devil you're talkin' about," MacDonald snapped.

"Look, you were the one who approached us more than once," Chance said. "There's no point in denying it now."

MacDonald glared at them. Brunner just looked nervous, as if he wished he had never gotten involved in this—whatever *this* was. Finally, MacDonald said, "How do I know I can trust you?"

"Because we want out of here as bad as you do," Ace said.

As the words left his mouth, he wondered if the simple statement contained some actual truth. He and Chance *did* want out of here. MacDonald's plan might work. And yet they were trying to convince MacDonald to include them so they could *stop* his plan, rather than going along with it and maybe escaping. For a split second, Ace wondered if they would be better off if they truly did throw in with MacDonald.

Then he discarded the idea. That would mean putting innocents in danger, most likely including Evelyn Sughrue. Ace knew that he and his brother could never do such a thing deliberately.

For a long moment, MacDonald sat there scowling. Then he appeared to come to a decision.

"In a little while, I'll be takin' Brunner here over

to the infirmary so the doc can take a look at his foot. You two figure out a way to get over there once Brunner and I have been inside for a few minutes. When you do, you're liable to hear a commotion inside. You jump the guards that'll be outside and get rid of them. Grab their guns when you do."

"You want us to kill them?" Chance said.

"I don't care if they're dead or not, as long as they can't interfere with my plan," MacDonald said. "Brunner and I will be comin' out of there in a hurry, and I'd just as soon not have to deal with guards as soon as we step out of the door."

"What are you going to do in the infirmary?" Ace asked.

MacDonald sneered and said, "You'll see when the time comes. I'm still not sure I completely trust you boys. I've told you what you need to do, and that's enough for now."

"All right," Ace said, "but you'd better not try to double-cross us."

MacDonald let out a curt laugh. "I was thinkin' it's the other way around. And you know what happens to anybody who tries to double-cross *me*. They don't live very long."

Ace let that veiled threat hang in the air for a moment, then asked, "How much time do we give you, once you're in the infirmary?"

"Five minutes ought to do it. It ain't like I got a watch in my pocket, though, so just don't be late. I want those guards taken care of."

Ace and Chance both nodded. "They will be," Chance said.

MacDonald grunted. "Now move on. Ain't no need to make anybody suspicious by the two of you havin' a long conversation with me."

The Jensen brothers stood up and moved away from MacDonald and Brunner, strolling casually as if they weren't doing anything except stretching their legs. As they walked, Chance said from the side of his mouth, "I was thinking, Ace . . . Maybe we ought to go along with what MacDonald wants until we're out of here . . ."

"Earlier, I thought the same thing," Ace admitted. "But that would mean putting Lieutenant Driscoll's life in danger, and probably Evelyn's, as well. I don't see how we can do that."

Chance sighed and nodded. "You're right. But say we stop the escape. Olsen's still not going to let us go."

"No, but if we save the life of the major's daughter, he's bound to be more willing to listen to us. Convincing him of what's really going on here is a longshot, but it may be our only play."

A minute or so later, Lieutenant Driscoll, accompanied by two troopers, walked up to the men gathered in front of the guardhouse and announced, "Anyone who requires medical attention, please step forward."

There was no sign of Major Sughrue, Lieutenant Olsen, or Evelyn this Sunday. That was a little surprising.

None of the prisoners got to their feet except MacDonald. He reached down, took hold of Brunner's arm, and helped the injured man up.

"This man's foot needs to be looked at," MacDonald said. "It should've been done yesterday."

"Well, I doubt that he's done much more damage to it in the meantime," Driscoll said. "Can you walk on your own, Brunner?"

"No, sir, not really," Brunner said. "I need help."

"Very well." Driscoll nodded curtly to MacDonald. "Bring him along." He looked around. "Anyone else?"

No one responded. Most of the men looked at the ground. Ace wondered if MacDonald had instructed them to do that.

"All right." Driscoll motioned to MacDonald and Brunner. "Come along."

The surgeon led the way, with MacDonald and Brunner coming along behind him, followed by the two troopers. Ace and Chance watched them go. So far, everything was proceeding according to MacDonald's plan. Driscoll, MacDonald, and Brunner disappeared inside the adobe building that housed the infirmary. The two soldiers took up posts on the porch right outside the door.

Ace still hadn't seen Evelyn. Of course, it was possible she was already inside the infirmary. They wouldn't know about that until things played out some more.

In hurried whispers, the Jensen brothers talked about their next move. They had to get over to the infirmary without attracting too much attention or suspicion, and Ace could think of only one way to do that.

"I'll handle it," Chance whispered. "I'm a better actor than you."

"I don't know about—" Ace began, but he didn't get any further than that before Chance abruptly dropped to his knees, clutched his midsection, and unleashed a breathless, quavering cry of agony that sounded like his entire innards were being ripped out.

CHAPTER TWENTY-TWO

Chance's actions came so quickly that the look of surprise on Ace's face wasn't totally an act. Maybe that was a good thing, because his reaction looked and sounded totally genuine as he cried, "Chance! What's wrong?"

Chance doubled over as he pressed his hands against his belly. "It's like . . . a knife . . . in my guts!" he gasped. He lifted his head, stared wide-eyed at his brother. "I think I'm dying!"

The first wail had attracted the trio of guards who'd been watching over the prisoners. Two of the troopers waved their rifles at the prisoners to keep them back while the third man came up to Ace and Chance and demanded, "What in blazes is goin' on here?"

"My brother's sick," Ace said as he bent over and took hold of Chance's upper right arm. "You can see that for yourself. He needs to see the surgeon."

"No, he had his chance for that a few minutes ago," the trooper said. "Sick call's over."

"But he wasn't sick then," Ace argued. "He's had spells like this before. They come on him sudden-like,

and he never knows when they're going to happen."
He embellished the lie a little more. "He was really
sick like this when he was a kid and almost died. Ever
since then, he's been fighting it. It's been a while since
he had a bout of it, so we hoped maybe it was finally
over . . ."

"Well, if he never died from it before, he's not
gonna die from it this time," the trooper insisted.

"That's loco! If it had happened five minutes ago,
you would've let him see the doc."

Chance groaned again, with even more misery in
the sound this time.

"I'm not gonna let a couple of prisoners wander
off half the length of the fort by themselves."

"You could go with us," Ace said. "It wouldn't take
but a couple of minutes, and then you could come
right back here."

One of the other guards said, "I don't want nobody
dyin' on my watch, Benjy."

"Oh, all right," the first trooper said disgustedly.
"Come on, but don't lollygag around."

"Thanks, Private," Ace said as he helped Chance to
his feet. Chance acted a lot shakier than he really was,
as they started stumbling toward the infirmary with
the reluctant trooper following them.

They weren't there yet when Ace saw Major
Sughrue and Evelyn come through the fort's open
gates, walking arm in arm. They appeared to be
headed toward the infirmary. Ace could think of only
one place outside the fort where they might have
been on a Sunday morning. That thought, and the
solemn expressions on the faces of both, told him
that they had been visiting Amelia Sughrue's grave.

Ace was a little surprised that Frank Olsen wasn't with them, but he supposed there were some parts of the major's life that Olsen hadn't been able to worm his way into.

Sughrue and Evelyn parted company at the infirmary. The major left his daughter on the porch and turned to start across the parade ground toward the headquarters building. Evelyn paused on the porch and watched as Ace and Chance, still about fifty feet away, continued heading in that direction.

"Blast it," Ace muttered under his breath. "I was hoping Evelyn wasn't anywhere around the infirmary this morning."

"My goodness," Evelyn said as they reached the pair of steps leading up to the porch. She wore a long, dark green skirt and a white, long-sleeved blouse with frills on the bosom. A gold brooch with an ivory silhouette of a woman set on it was pinned at her throat. "What's wrong with your brother, Mr. Jensen?"

"Just an old stomach ailment, miss," Ace said. He began helping Chance up the steps. The two troopers who had accompanied Lieutenant Driscoll on sick call stood to the left, obviously curious about why Ace and Chance were there but not particularly wary.

Ace and Chance had just reached the porch when the infirmary door burst open and Vince MacDonald charged out. "There you are!" he cried as he lunged at Evelyn.

Chance straightened from his bent-over hobble and threw himself at the two guards on the porch, hoping to occupy them while Ace dealt with the trooper who had followed them over here. The Jensen brothers hadn't worked out this strategy in advance. They just *knew* what to do when trouble erupted.

Ace whirled and dived back down the steps at the soldier. He crashed into the man and drove him backward off his feet. Taken completely by surprise, the trooper hadn't even had time to raise his rifle.

Ace got both hands on the Springfield and trapped it between them, using it to press the soldier's body into the ground while he lifted a knee into the man's groin. That made the man let go of the rifle.

Ace rolled away and sprang lithely to his feet, taking the Springfield with him. He saw that MacDonald had wrapped both brawny arms around Evelyn Sughrue and lifted her off the porch, so that both her feet kicked wildly as she struggled to free herself. She screamed as she struck at MacDonald with small, clenched fists, but he ignored the blows.

Behind him, Brunner had emerged from the infirmary as well. He had his left arm clamped around Lieutenant Driscoll's throat as he forced the surgeon along in front of him. The scalpel in his right hand flashed in the morning sunlight as he pressed it to the side of Driscoll's throat. Not much force would be required for Brunner to open the surgeon's throat from ear to ear.

To the left on the porch, Chance's surprise attack had knocked both guards off their feet. Chance had sprawled onto the planks with them, but he recovered faster and was up in time to kick one of the men in the jaw and lay him out, unconscious. Ace had seen that from the corner of his eye as he was surging back to his feet.

Chance scooped up the rifle dropped by the man who was out cold and backed away swiftly as he aimed at the other man lying on the porch, who seemed disoriented and unsure what to do.

"Throw your rifle away!" Chance shouted at him.

The trooper hesitated a second, then tossed his Springfield off the porch.

Shouts filled the air above the parade ground as men heard the commotion and ran to find out what was happening. Ace knew that he and Chance had to act quickly before they were swarmed. He aimed the rifle in his hands at MacDonald and ordered in a loud, clear voice, "Let go of Miss Sughrue, MacDonald!"

Chance leveled the Springfield he had grabbed at Brunner and barked, "Drop that scalpel and step away from the doc!"

MacDonald's face contorted and turned dark with rage as he stared at the brothers in disbelief. Obscenities began to spew from his mouth. "You're double-crossing me!" he roared. "You're really double-crossing me!"

"We never intended to let you get away with hurting innocent people," Ace said. "Now release Miss Sughrue and Lieutenant Driscoll. You can't get out of here."

"You could've gotten away—"

"We're not criminals," Ace said. "That's what we've been trying to tell people all along." He looked hard at Evelyn, who had fallen silent and stopped fighting in MacDonald's grip. "We just need someone to listen to us and make sure the truth gets out. That's why we pretended to go along with your plan."

Ace saw understanding in Evelyn's green eyes. She knew why he and Chance had done what they'd done. And maybe . . . just maybe . . . she could get through to her father and persuade him to listen to reason instead of allowing Frank Olsen to manipulate him. Maybe she could open Sughrue's eyes to the way Olsen was using him . . .

A hard ring of metal pressed against the back of Ace's neck, and a harsh voice grated, "Drop that rifle, Jensen, or I'll blow your head off."

Ace recognized the voice and couldn't stop himself from exclaiming, "Corporal Parnell?"

An ugly grin spread across MacDonald's face. "That's right," he told Ace. "It's not just the fellas who deserted with me before that have decided they want out of here today."

Ace glanced over his shoulder. He couldn't see Parnell except as a blur in the corner of his eye, but he saw three more troopers armed with Springfields forming a semicircle around the infirmary's front porch as they pointed the weapons *outward*, toward the men approaching on the parade ground. These three, along with Parnell, must have been waiting close by for MacDonald to make his move, since they had arrived on the scene first and taken up what were obviously planned positions.

Major Sughrue was close enough now to see MacDonald holding his daughter. "Evelyn!" Sughrue cried as he came to a stop. "MacDonald, put her down! Now!"

"With all due respect, Major"—MacDonald's mocking tone made it clear he didn't mean any respect at all—"you don't give me orders anymore, and the young lady's not goin' anywhere except with me."

"No!" Evelyn said. She started kicking and fighting again. MacDonald's arms tightened brutally until she couldn't do anything except gasp for breath.

Sughrue lifted a shaking hand. "Don't hurt her!"

"Well, that's gonna depend on you, Major." MacDonald glanced at Ace and Chance. "And on those Jensen boys. You two gonna drop those rifles or not?"

"Ace . . . ?" Chance said.

"I don't see that we have any choice," Ace said, even though the words were bitter and sour enough that they tasted like gall under his tongue. He lowered the rifle he'd been pointing at MacDonald, rested the butt on the ground, and let it topple over.

Up on the porch, Chance placed his rifle on the boards at his feet. MacDonald ordered, "Slide it over to me." Chance did so, pushing the Springfield with his foot. MacDonald kept his left arm clasped tight around Evelyn while he reached down with his right hand and caught hold of the rifle. He lifted and aimed the heavy weapon one-handed. It took a big, strong man to do such a thing, but MacDonald managed with apparent ease.

Quite a crowd of troopers had gathered around the infirmary by now and milled around in confusion. If they were to rush the place, they would overwhelm MacDonald and his handful of allies with ease, although likely not without suffering a few casualties.

What held them back was the threat to the lives of Evelyn Sughrue and Lieutenant Driscoll. Because of that, MacDonald held the upper hand right now, and he knew it.

Ace glanced around the crowd, surprised that he still didn't spot Lieutenant Frank Olsen anywhere. Clearly, Olsen wasn't even on the post this morning, or else he would have heard the commotion and come to see what it was about.

"Let these men through from the guardhouse." MacDonald called out three names. Ace recognized them as three of the men who had deserted from Fort Gila with the sergeant before, part of the group that had wound up getting caught in Packsaddle. Ace wasn't sure why the others apparently weren't involved in this escape attempt, unless they had decided they didn't want to risk getting even deeper into trouble.

Some of the other troopers had realized what was going on. The ones who had brought their rifles with them held the weapons ready, but most of the soldiers had been off duty and were unarmed. Some were dressed only in uniform trousers and their long-handled underwear.

The ones who were armed looked to Major Sughrue for orders. Sughrue glared at MacDonald for a long moment that grew more tense as it stretched out. But then the major sighed and made a vague gesture with one hand.

"Let them through," he said in a dull voice. "As long as he . . . as long as he has Evelyn, we have to cooperate with him."

"That's right, Major," MacDonald said, smirking. "You sure do."

The other men who were taking part in the escape

hurried along the edge of the parade ground and joined MacDonald and the rest of the bunch at the infirmary. Ace and Chance were still inside that circle of guns, and Ace realized with a shock that with the way things had played out, he and his brother might be considered hostages now, too.

The difference was, their lives weren't worth a blasted thing in the eyes of the United States Cavalry.

"Now," MacDonald said, "I want a dozen horses, each of them with a bag of supplies. And eight handguns and plenty of rounds of ammunition, too."

Those numbers were telling. Eight men were making this escape attempt, which explained the guns, and four more horses meant four hostages—including Ace and Chance.

Sughrue hesitated, and MacDonald barked, "Give the order, Major!"

He squeezed Evelyn hard enough to make her let out a little yelp.

Sughrue flapped both hands this time. "Get the horses. Give him whatever he wants, I tell you!"

Some of the troopers looked like they wanted to argue, but they couldn't very well do that. Sughrue was still their commanding officer. After a few seconds, men broke away from the crowd and hurried to carry out the orders.

Sughrue stared at Parnell and asked, "Corporal, how can you do this? You're a good man, been in the army a long time—"

"That's right, Major," Parnell interrupted. "I've been in the army a long time, and you just said it yourself. I'm still a corporal, ain't I?"

"But . . . but to desert! To help prisoners escape and threaten an innocent young woman—"

"How about you shut up, Major?" Parnell snapped. "You may still give orders to those other fellas, but not to me."

On the porch, Chance said to MacDonald, "Why are you taking Ace and me with you? We're not worth anything."

MacDonald chuckled. "You're sure as blazes not. Can't believe I started to trust you little varmints, even a little bit. But I can still get some use out of you." His smile was an ugly leer. "If we happen to run into any Apaches out in those badlands, why, we'll just leave you two boys as a little present for 'em. I figure they'll be too busy havin' fun with you to bother comin' after us!"

CHAPTER TWENTY-THREE

The saddled horses were brought to the infirmary, along with the supplies, the handguns, and the ammunition. MacDonald demanded that enough of the troopers turn over their rifles so that he and all his men had Springfields, too, and ammunition for the rifles was added to the supplies that were gathered. Major Sughrue ordered the rest of the soldiers to stack their rifles and withdraw to the far end of the parade ground, where they were to stay in sight. That was MacDonald's idea, as well.

"Nobody's gonna get in our way when we ride outta here, Major," he said. "You understand that?"

"I understand," Sughrue replied. He appeared furious beyond belief and terrified out of his mind at the same time, the latter emotion caused by the fear he felt for Evelyn.

MacDonald still had an arm around her, holding her close, although he had set her feet back on the ground. She had stopped fighting, and her head sagged forward in apparent despair. Every now and then, the sound of a soft sob came from her.

"I don't want anybody comin' after us, either,"

MacDonald said. "If they do, I'm liable to leave pieces of Driscoll along the trail for them to find. But if you do like I tell you, I'll let Driscoll go tomorrow and he can ride back here."

"Alone?" Driscoll exclaimed. He was white as milk. "I'd never get back by myself. The Apaches would find me!"

"Well, you'll just have to hope you're lucky and get through all right, Doc. Anyway, if your friends here at the fort don't do exactly like they're told, you won't have to worry about that."

Driscoll swallowed hard at the ominous implication of those words.

"What about my daughter?" Sughrue demanded. "Will you let her go tomorrow, too?"

"She'll be staying with us a mite longer than that," MacDonald answered. "There's a settlement on the other side of the Prophets called Moss City. If no one's bothered us by the time we get there, that's where you can find her in a week or so."

Sughrue's jaw clenched so hard a little muscle began jumping in it. "Moss City is a cesspool," he said. "No decent young woman will be safe there."

"You'd better hope you're wrong about that, Major. But if *we* don't make it to Moss City without any trouble, neither does little Evelyn here."

Sughrue was breathing hard as he visibly struggled to control himself. "If you harm her, if you hurt one hair on her head," he said, "I'll kill you, MacDonald. I'll kill you myself, with my bare hands, you brute!"

"Shut up, Major," MacDonald said. "I've listened to all your bluster I care to. And once we ride out of here, I'll never have to listen to it again."

Ace and Chance stood there listening to all this and seething because of their inability to do anything to prevent Vince MacDonald from carrying out his plans. MacDonald had told Corporal Parnell to keep an especially close eye on the Jensen brothers.

"They're insurance, that's all," MacDonald had said to Parnell. "So if either of them even looks like he's thinking about trying something, don't hesitate to blow his brains out."

"It'll be a pleasure, Vince," Parnell had said.

As soon as the horses were lined up, MacDonald's men quickly took charge of them, and the soldiers who had brought them from the stable had to go back to the other end of the parade ground with the others. Major Sughrue was the only one left there in front of the infirmary other than MacDonald and his allies and the four hostages.

"You'll never get away with this, Sergeant," Sughrue said. "You'll be hunted down and killed like the dogs you are. You must know this."

"I know that you won't do a blasted thing as long as we've got this little gal with us," MacDonald said. "And once we've let her go, it'll be simple to make a dash across the border. You might as well give it up now, Major. You'll never see us again. But if you do like you're told, you *might* see this girl of yours. You just think about that once we're gone." MacDonald turned his head, contemptuously dismissing the older man who stood in front of him, and called, "Mount up!"

Parnell poked Chance in the back with his Springfield and said, "You heard the man."

Chance cast a baleful glare back over his shoulder.

"One of these days, somebody's liable to make you eat that rifle, Corporal."

"Well, it won't be you, kid," Parnell snapped. "Move."

Ace and Chance swung up into the saddles, which were the McClellan type used by the cavalry, flatter than regular range saddles and lacking a horn since soldiers didn't have to worry about lassoing any proddy cattle. The mounts were the sturdy sort favored by the cavalry as well, built for strength and stamina rather than speed.

MacDonald lifted Evelyn and put her on the back of a horse. "I thought about making you ride with me," he told her, "but I figure it might be best for you to have your own mount. Just don't try to take off for the tall and uncut. It wouldn't end well for you."

"I . . . I'll do what you say," she replied, thoroughly cowed by what she had gone through so far and undoubtedly aware that the ordeal likely would get worse before it was over.

Ace wished he could reassure her that everything was going to be all right, but at the moment, he couldn't make that promise for any of them.

The gates had been closed after Sughrue and Evelyn came back from the cemetery, so they had to be opened before the group rode out. MacDonald waved a hand toward them and told Sughrue, "Go open those gates, Major. I reckon you can manage by yourself."

Sughrue glared at him but turned and stalked toward the gates. He struggled to lift the bar holding them closed—taking it off its brackets was normally a two-man job—but finally succeeded in shoving it loose and dragging it out of the way. Then he swung back first one gate and then the other.

MacDonald led the way with a couple of his men right behind him, then the four hostages. Evelyn and the clearly shaken Lieutenant Driscoll rode side by side, then Ace and Chance. Parnell and the rest of MacDonald's men trailed them. Any time Ace glanced back, he saw that Parnell rode with his rifle across the saddle in front of him, looking eager for an excuse to use it.

Major Sughrue stood beside the opening, puffing and red-faced from exertion. He had to lean over and rest his hands on his thighs for a moment.

"Daddy," Evelyn wailed in a miserable voice as she rode past her father. Sughrue straightened and started to take a step toward her, but MacDonald twisted in the saddle and pointed his rifle at him.

"Just stay back, Major," MacDonald warned.

"Evelyn, darling, it's going to be all right," Sughrue said. He was talking to his daughter's back now because Evelyn was already outside the fort, casting a pathetic gaze over her shoulder at him. "I'll come and find you. No one is going to hurt you, I promise."

MacDonald laughed. "You better hope that's right, Major. Do as you're told and the odds'll be a lot better." He faced forward again and called, "Come on. No draggin' your feet back there!"

The whole group moved through the gates and into the open. As they did, Major Sughrue stepped into the opening and shouted after them, "You'll never get away with this! I'll see you all dead! You'll wind up at the end of a rope, or worse!"

MacDonald's mocking laughter floated back at him.

"I can't feel too sorry for the major," Chance muttered to Ace as they rode side by side behind Evelyn and Driscoll. "If he hadn't fallen for all the lies Olsen's been feeding him, this might not have happened."

"Maybe not, but he's still got to watch his daughter riding away from here as a hostage. That's got to be pretty hard."

"Yeah, I guess," Chance admitted grudgingly. "You have any ideas what we should do next?"

"Outnumbered and outgunned like we are, I don't think we have any choice but to wait for a better hand to play," Ace said. He frowned. "And I'd still like to know where Lieutenant Olsen is this morning."

CHAPTER TWENTY-FOUR

The early morning meeting at Marshal Hank Glennon's office in Packsaddle wasn't really a council of war, because everything was going well, but Howden-Smyth insisted on these occasional get-togethers among the conspirators. A meeting of the minds, he called them.

To Frank Olsen, they were more like a waste of time, but he tolerated them because sooner or later this scheme was going to make him rich. It had already increased his stake quite a bit, but the real loot was still out there, tantalizingly close.

Portly Judge Horace Bannister waddled in and said, "Let's get on with this, gentlemen. I need to get to church. I have a Sunday School class to teach."

Olsen sat beside Marshal Hank Glennon's desk, smoking a cigar. The lawman was behind the desk nursing a cup of coffee that was probably half whiskey, judging by the smell coming from it. Olsen took the cigar out of his mouth and said, "Our English friend isn't here yet, but he ought to be showing up any time." A moment of puckish humor prompted him to add, "You teach Sunday School, Judge?"

Bannister frowned. "What's wrong with that?"

"Well, considering that you're so intimately involved with a bunch of criminals like us—"

"Stop that," Glennon said. "Everything we've done has been legal and aboveboard, isn't that right, Judge?"

Bannister hooked his thumbs in his vest. "As far as you and I are concerned, that is certainly true, Marshal. I can't speak to what happens at the fort or at Mr. Howden-Smyth's mine, of course, since such things are out of my jurisdiction and control."

Olsen looked at his two companions for a second and then laughed coldly. "Sure, you go on telling yourselves that. Those Jensen boys actually *were* deserters as far as you're concerned, I suppose."

Bannister spread his hands. "Misidentification isn't a crime. Such errors are bound to occur, and our legal system deals with them in due time."

In due time, for the Jensens, would be when they wound up in an unmarked grave in the desert, Olsen thought. He shook his head and went back to his cigars. He didn't enjoy working with a couple of toads like Bannister and Glennon, but the end result was all that really counted.

Packsaddle's main street was quiet and almost deserted at this time on a Sunday morning, so Olsen had no trouble hearing the hoofbeats of several horses coming to a stop right outside the marshal's office. A few moments later, the door opened and Eugene Howden-Smyth strolled in, followed by two of the gunmen who went everywhere with him. Arizona Territory wasn't exactly civilized yet, so the Englishman always brought his protectors along.

The lean, whip-bodied one with a face like a cadaver was Chet Van Slyke. He was Howden-Smyth's top gun and reputed to be a fast, deadly pistoleer who had killed a number of men. The shorter, beer-gutted hombre was called Navasota Jones, probably after the place he came from back in Texas. His real name probably wasn't even Jones. He carried a double-barreled shotgun under his left arm. Supposedly, he wasn't much good with a handgun, but there was nobody better at shooting folks in the back.

Nobody bothered Howden-Smyth with those two around, and the men who worked at the mine, actually hacking the precious ore out of the earth, didn't cause any trouble, either.

Howden-Smyth looked like he was in a good mood this morning. He had a cigar clenched between his teeth at a jaunty angle. Olsen had a pretty good idea what was responsible for the Englishman's jovial attitude. Or rather, *who* was responsible. From here, he and his men would accompany Olsen back to Fort Gila, where he would pick up Evelyn Sughrue, after which she would have dinner and spend the day with him.

Olsen couldn't entirely rule out the possibility that Howden-Smyth intended for Evelyn to spend the night, too. He knew Howden-Smyth had been lusting after the girl ever since the first time he laid eyes on her, and it was inevitable that he would get tired of waiting and insist on having his way with her.

Olsen hoped things hadn't reached that point yet. He didn't care what happened to Evelyn, not really, but her father would be more difficult to manage if he found out that his daughter was being subjected to all sorts of British debaucheries.

"Good morning, gentlemen," Howden-Smyth greeted the trio waiting for him. "And a beautiful morning it is, too."

Glennon grunted. "Gonna be hot as blazes later."

"Well, by then I intend to be back at my house, which is nice and cool behind those thick adobe walls. And I should have some very pleasant company with me, which makes things even better." Howden-Smyth took the remaining chair in front of the marshal's desk. Van Slyke and Jones stood behind him. "Now, shall we get down to business?"

"I'm not sure we have any business to take care of," Olsen said. "Everything's running smoothly, as far as I know."

Howden-Smyth pointed the cigar at him and said, "As far as you know. But what you don't know, Lieutenant, is that my men have spotted Apaches in the distance several times recently, watching my mine."

"Always better for Apaches to be at a distance instead of up close," Glennon said. "It's when they're up close that folks wind up dying."

Olsen said, "We're aware that the savages have been more active lately. They attacked one of our work details and nearly killed me a few days ago."

He gestured toward the bandage on his head, which was much smaller by now because the bullet graze was healing up already.

Howden-Smyth nodded and said, "I heard about that, Lieutenant. Not much goes on in this part of the territory that I *don't* hear about. I don't mind admitting that the situation makes me uneasy. The mule trains I have to use to transport the ore out of the mountains are slow and difficult to guard because so many mules are required and the line stretches out to such a great length. If that road was complete, I could load up several wagons and bring out just as much ore in half the time . . . or less. Not only that, but I could concentrate my guards around the wagon so that not even the most fanatical Apache would want to attack them."

"Never underestimate the fanaticism of a savage," Olsen said. "But you make a good point, Eugene. Unfortunately, building a road takes a lot of time, especially through such rugged terrain."

"But progress would go faster if you had more men working on it."

Olsen looked hard at him for a moment. "What do you want me to do?" he asked. "Glennon, Bannister, and I have already railroaded as many men into the guardhouse as we can get away with."

Bannister said, "I take exception to the term 'railroaded'—"

"Shut up, Horace," Howden-Smyth said. "Tell yourself whatever lies are necessary to allow you to sleep soundly at night, but don't waste my time with them."

Glennon said, "Don't look at me, either. There are only so many strangers who drift into Packsaddle. I throw as many of 'em as I can into jail, but I can't lock up the locals unless somebody actually *does* something to warrant it. Nobody cares about saddle tramps like those Jensen boys, but if you start dragging honest citizens out to the fort and put them to work, the outside authorities are going to hear about it, mark my words."

"You're probably right, Marshal," Howden-Smyth said with a sigh. "But whenever you *do* see the opportunity to throw the book at someone with reasonable justification, I know I can count on you and His Honor to do so."

"We've played along so far, haven't we?" Bannister asked in a surly tone.

"And you've profited by it," Howden-Smyth returned with an edge in his voice. He turned his head to look at Olsen. "That brings us to you, Frank."

"Vince MacDonald and his friends did us a favor by deserting when they did," Olsen said. "I don't think we can count on that happening again. And the other men at the fort have figured out by now what happens when they break some regulation." He laughed. "This situation has done wonders for discipline, I'll say that. No one wants to wind up in the guardhouse."

"Well, then, you're simply going to have to crack down harder. Find more rules for them to break, and when they do, increase their sentences." Howden-Smyth looked at Glennon and Bannister. "The same way I expect you gentlemen to be more stringent about law enforcement here in town."

Anger welled up inside Olsen, and Glennon didn't look too happy, either. The lieutenant said, "Listen, we have a deal, but that doesn't mean we're working for you. You don't give us orders."

Behind Howden-Smyth, Van Slyke leaned forward slightly, and Navasota Jones glared and shifted the shotgun a little on his arm. Howden-Smyth motioned casually to them, however, and crossed his legs as if nothing could ever disturb him.

"Quite right, my friend," he said. "I was simply pointing out the facts and stressing my opinion of what should be done about them. As you say, we are *all* in this together. It will benefit each and every one of us to make sure the maximum amount of ore is brought out of that mine and transported to the railroad as efficiently as possible." He spread his hands. "That's logical, is it not?"

"It is," Olsen admitted. "And I suppose I can talk to the major about tightening up even more on the discipline at the fort."

"And if anybody here in town gives me a reason, I'll throw the book at 'em, like you said," Bannister agreed.

"Excellent! That's all I wanted." Howden-Smyth puffed on his cigar again, then asked, "Speaking of Major Sughrue, how are he and his lovely daughter today?"

"Fine when I left," Olsen said. "They were about to walk out to the cemetery and visit Mrs. Sughrue's grave."

"It must be a dreadfully lonely life for a gentle, cultured young woman such as Evelyn. I look forward to doing something to ease her burden. In fact . . . seeing as you fellows are my friends . . . I don't mind sharing the news with you. Very, very soon now, I intend to ask the young lady to do me the honor of becoming my wife."

"Well, congratulations," Bannister said heartily, the tension of a few minutes earlier seemingly forgotten.

Howden-Smyth held up a hand again, palm out. "Not yet. I haven't asked, and the lady hasn't answered. Who knows?" He chuckled. "She might refuse."

Howden-Smyth wasn't going to allow that, Olsen thought. If Evelyn said no, the Englishman would find some way to pressure her into giving him what he wanted—if, in fact, he didn't just take it. But if Howden-Smyth wanted to maintain that façade of chivalry, it was none of Olsen's business. As long as it didn't affect the flow of gold . . .

"Since our business seems to be concluded"— Howden-Smyth got to his feet—"I suppose you and I can start on to the fort, Frank. Miss Sughrue and her father should be back from their visit to the cemetery by the time we get there."

"Yeah, plenty of time for that," Olsen agreed.

Glennon stood up as well and reached for his hat, surprising Olsen. "I'm coming with you," the lawman announced.

"What in the world for?" Howden-Smyth murmured.

"It's Sunday, ain't it? And the work detail doesn't go out on Sunday. That means those Jensen boys ought to be there."

Olsen's voice hardened as he said, "You're not going to release them."

"I never said I was going to. But if there's ever any investigation into how two civilians got locked up in an army guardhouse as deserters, I want to make sure it's known I checked on them while all the details were being sorted out."

"There's not going to be any investigation," Olsen said. "Nobody's ever going to care what happens to a couple of no-account drifters like that."

"I'm just being careful. I've got a reputation as an honest lawman to think about, you know."

"And me as an honest jurist," Bannister added.

It was all Olsen could do not to laugh in their faces. Like most men, they had to tell themselves lies in order to get through the days—and the nights. The dark nights of the soul when all of a man's past sins and shortcomings came crawling back up out of his conscience like worms leaving a rotting corpse . . .

It was a good thing he didn't have to worry about that. He jerked his head toward the door and said, "All right, then. Come on."

CHAPTER TWENTY-FIVE

Howden-Smyth had come to town in his fancy buggy, of course. Olsen had never seen the Englishman on the back of a horse, although he supposed Howden-Smyth could ride if it was necessary. As they all headed toward Fort Gila, Olsen rode on the buggy's left side, Marshal Glennon on the right, and the two gunmen, Van Slyke and Jones, brought up the rear.

The thought of Apaches lurked in the back of Olsen's mind. Since his close call a few days earlier, he had been wary of leaving the fort alone. When one of Howden-Smyth's men had shown up the day before with the message summoning him to the meeting in Packsaddle, Olsen had been tempted to refuse. It wasn't like he could take a detail with him to town. Some of the men undoubtedly had figured out that what was going on at the fort wasn't exactly on the up-and-up. Costello had known, certainly, and had made the mistake of revealing that he had figured out too much. But there was no need to rub the others' faces in it by being seen conferring with Howden-Smyth, Glennon, and Bannister.

So he had ridden to town alone, taking the fastest horse at the fort and staying as alert as possible every step of the way. He hadn't worried as much about the return trip, because he assumed that Howden-Smyth and whichever gunmen he brought with him would be riding along, too.

Having a pair of killers like Van Slyke and Jones with him eased Olsen's mind somewhat, but he still kept his eyes peeled. From time to time, the skin on the back of his neck crawled a little, as if he were being watched, but he knew that could be just his imagination.

It was past the middle of the morning by the time they came in sight of Fort Gila, and as soon as they did, a sense that something was wrong struck Olsen and made him stiffen in his saddle. He couldn't tell why he felt that way until they drew closer and he realized the gates stood wide open.

That didn't necessarily mean anything bad, but it wasn't common, either. The gates, and the wall itself, were more symbolic than anything else. They wouldn't keep out a determined attacking force.

He signaled to Howden-Smyth to stop and said, "Wait here, Eugene, while I ride ahead and take a look around."

Howden-Smyth brought the buggy to a halt, forcing Glennon, Van Slyke, and Jones to stop, as well. He frowned at Olsen and asked, "Why in the world would I want to do that, Frank?"

"Because something's not right at the fort. The gates shouldn't be open."

Glennon said, "You think the Apaches have been here?" He jerked his head from side to side, looking around nervously. He could handle being a corrupt, small-town lawman, but he was no Indian fighter.

"No, I see troopers moving around in there." Olsen could have taken out his field telescope and used it to take a better look, but he didn't believe there was any immediate danger, even though something was wrong. "Just wait here. It won't take me long."

"Forget about that," Van Slyke growled. "If there's Apaches around, you need to be behind that wall, boss. I say we all get to the fort as fast as we can."

"I agree," Howden-Smyth said. Without warning, he slapped the reins against the backs of the two buggy horses. *"Hyaaahhh!"*

The horses bolted ahead, pulling the buggy behind them. Olsen bit back a curse and joined Glennon and the two gunmen in galloping after the racing vehicle.

Someone in the fort must have seen them coming and spread the word, because a good-sized group was waiting for them just inside the gate when they rode in. Major Flint Sughrue, wild-eyed and clearly upset, hurried forward as Olsen reined in and dismounted.

"Frank, I'm glad you're here," Sughrue said. "Evelyn's been kidnapped!"

"What!" Howden-Smyth exclaimed from the buggy seat. He put a hand on the buggy's frame and vaulted to the ground. "How in blazes—"

"MacDonald got her," Sughrue went on as he gripped Olsen's upper arms. He didn't seem to have even heard Howden-Smyth's outburst. "He escaped, and some of the other men deserted, and they took Evelyn with them!"

Olsen didn't like being grabbed like that, but he resisted the impulse to shove Sughrue away from him. Instead he worked his arms loose carefully and said, "Just tell me what happened, Major."

"I told you! It was MacDonald! He took Evelyn—" The words choked off. Sughrue, pale as a sheet, lifted shaking hands to his face. "I promised Amelia I'd take good care of her. I swore it! Swore it to my poor wife on her deathbed . . ."

The major began to sob. Olsen looked around at the troopers and asked, "Where's Lieutenant Driscoll? Major Sughrue could use a sedative, and then someone else can explain to me exactly what happened here."

Corporal Cochran stepped forward and said, "MacDonald and the others took Lieutenant Driscoll with them, too, as well as those Jensen boys."

"The Jensens helped MacDonald escape?"

Cochran shook his head. "No, as a matter of fact, they tried to stop him. But MacDonald took them along, said he'd use 'em as bait to distract the Apaches if he needed to."

That sounded like something Vince MacDonald would do, all right. The sergeant was ruthless as well as brutal. At first, Olsen had seriously considered taking him in on the road-building scheme, but in the end he'd decided that MacDonald couldn't be trusted.

MacDonald had certainly proven him right about that.

"Someone help the major back to his quarters," Olsen said. "He should lie down and rest."

"We tried, Lieutenant," Cochran said. "He wouldn't go until you got back."

Howden-Smyth had listened intently to the exchange. Now he said, "Why didn't you send a rescue party after them? Those hostages should be freed as quickly as possible!"

Sughrue dropped his hands from his face and cried, "No! MacDonald said . . . said he would kill Evelyn and . . . and Driscoll if anyone came after them. But he promised he would let them go if we did like he said—"

"Nonsense," Howden-Smyth broke in. "You can't trust the word of a man such as that. The only thing he understands is force. Swift, merciless force."

Sughrue lunged at the Englishman and grabbed his shoulders, shaking him. "No! Didn't you hear me? We can't! He'll kill Evelyn—"

Olsen saw Van Slyke and Jones moving forward quickly from where they had dismounted. They were ready to counter any threat to their boss, with lethal force if necessary. Sughrue was still useful, so Olsen took hold of him from behind and pulled him away from Howden-Smyth before the gunmen could step in.

"Major!" he said. "Major, please listen to me. We'll figure out the best way to rescue Evelyn. I give you my word, we'll get her back safely."

Olsen had to wrestle Sughrue back. He looked over his shoulder at the troopers and snarled, "Somebody give me a hand with him."

"Are you officially relievin' the major of command, sir?" Cochran asked.

"He's obviously not fit to command while he's in this state," Olsen replied. "So, yes, blast it, I am!"

Cochran nodded and motioned to some of the men. They stepped forward and took hold of Sughrue. Carefully but forcefully, they led him away toward his quarters.

With strain and anger showing on his face, Howden-Smyth straightened his coat where Sughrue had grabbed him and asked, "What are you going to do about this, Frank?"

The Englishman had been mighty quick to give orders earlier, Olsen thought, but now he looked to others to take care of his problems. Olsen turned to Cochran again and said to the corporal, "Tell me everything that happened and everything MacDonald said."

Cochran did so, taking only a few minutes to fill Olsen in. When Cochran was finished, Olsen said, "So Parnell turned traitor, did he? Well, he's going to regret that. They all are."

"You're going after them, aren't you?" Howden-Smyth asked.

Olsen rubbed his chin and frowned in thought. "MacDonald threatened to kill the hostages, and he's the sort of man who'd keep his word about that."

"But surely you don't believe that he actually intends to release them! Why would he give up that advantage? The best chance to rescue them is to go after them now, before they have a chance to get farther away." Howden-Smyth's well-manicured hands clenched into fists. "I simply can't abide the thought of Evelyn being helpless in the clutches of a man such as that. There's no telling what might happen to her!"

"It's true that MacDonald doesn't have much to lose at this point," Olsen agreed. "And the bigger the lead they have, the harder it's going to be to catch up to them—"

Marshal Hank Glennon had dismounted, as well, but he hadn't said anything until now. He interrupted Olsen. "All that talk MacDonald did about heading for the border and letting Miss Sughrue go in Moss City sounds like a trick to me."

Olsen and Howden-Smyth turned to look at him. "What do you mean, Marshal?" the Englishman demanded.

"Just what I said. I think MacDonald's trying to lead any pursuit astray. He probably didn't believe that nobody would come after him, no matter what he threatened, so he figured it would be best to send 'em in the wrong direction."

Olsen thought about that and nodded. "You might be right about that. It would be a good strategic move. MacDonald never struck me as very smart, but he can be cunning when he needs to be."

"Then if they're not going to Moss City," Howden-Smyth said, "how are you going to find them?"

"Only one way. We'll have to track them." Olsen looked at Cochran. "Get a detail of twenty men together, Corporal, with good mounts and supplies and ammunition for a week. We're going after those deserters."

"You're not going alone," Howden-Smyth said. For a second Olsen thought he was going to declare that *he* was coming along, too, and Olsen didn't like that idea. But then the mine owner continued, "Chet, you and Navasota will accompany the rescue party."

"I can't have civilians along—" Olsen began.

"Chet Van Slyke is the best tracker I've ever seen, and he and Navasota will be valuable allies in any fight. I insist that you accept their help, Frank."

Olsen still didn't like it, but he supposed it wouldn't hurt to have a couple of extra guns along. After a moment, he nodded curtly in acceptance.

"When I get back to the mine, I'll send more men after you, just in case you need them," Howden-Smyth went on. "Those villains must be run to ground, Frank, and as swiftly as possible." He looked around and his gaze lit on Glennon. "Marshal, you go, too."

"Me?" Glennon said, raising his eyebrows. "I don't have any jurisdiction out here."

"What about the Jensen brothers? You were concerned about their welfare earlier, even if it *was* just for appearance's sake, and they're hostages, too."

Glennon didn't seem to like the idea at all, but he sighed and nodded. "All right. I reckon that way we'll have both sides covered, military and civilian law alike."

"Good. Just bring back Miss Sughrue safely, that's the most important thing."

He sounded like he actually meant that, Olsen thought. So something was important to Eugene Howden-Smyth besides money. The concern might not be because of any real worry about Evelyn's well-being, though. Howden-Smyth had his eye on her and already considered her his property. He wasn't the sort of man who would put up with it when somebody took something of his.

Olsen glanced at Cochran and saw that the man hadn't moved. "You have your orders, Corporal," he snapped. "Carry them out!"

"Yes, sir!"

Olsen looked toward the hills in the direction MacDonald and the others had gone. It would be best to catch up to them quickly and get back here to the fort by nightfall.

Because there were other dangers lurking in those hills, and Olsen knew it.

CHAPTER TWENTY-SIX

For probably the thousandth time since that fateful day he and his brother had ridden into Packsaddle, Ace Jensen wished he had his hat. The sun beat down with a fierce intensity on his bare head as the fiery orb rose to its zenith and then continued its journey across the western sky.

Chance looked equally miserable as he rode alongside, but no matter how bad off they were, Ace thought, this ordeal had to be worse for Evelyn Sughrue. A lot worse. Her fair skin shone pink as it began to burn. She seemed to be shrinking into herself as the horse underneath her plodded along.

The worst that MacDonald and the others could do to Ace and Chance was to kill them. Evelyn might be subjected to much more torment, so much that she would consider death a relief.

For now, however, she was safe, and MacDonald might consider it to be to his advantage that she remain so. Ace hoped the brutal noncom was smart enough to see that.

"Sergeant, how long are you going to make us ride

like this?" Lieutenant Driscoll asked in a voice that cracked with the strain he was feeling.

"I want to put some distance between us and the fort," MacDonald answered without looking around.

"But you told them not to follow us."

MacDonald laughed. "That old man might be shook up enough to do what I told him, but Olsen won't be. Whenever he gets back from wherever he went and finds out what happened, he'll be mad enough to come after us. Besides, he can't afford to lose this many workers for his precious road. But he'll kill us if he has to, make no mistake about that, because he can't afford to let anybody get away with runnin' off like this. If they did, folks might stop bein' so scared of him."

Ace knew MacDonald was right. He didn't know where Olsen had been this morning, but as soon as the lieutenant found out what had happened, he would take up the pursuit.

After a few more minutes, Chance said quietly, "Have you noticed that we're heading more to the north now, Ace? Looks like we're angling up into the ruggedest part of the mountains."

"Yeah, I saw that."

"But MacDonald said he'd let Miss Sughrue go when we got to that settlement down close to the border. That's southwest of here, not northwest."

"He lied," Ace said simply. "He was trying to throw anybody who comes after us off our trail."

Chance thought about it and nodded. "I didn't give him credit for being that clever."

"He worked out this whole thing. Reckon he's smarter than either of us took him for."

"So where are we going?"

Ace studied the slopes rising in front of them and slowly shook his head. "I don't know this part of the country well enough to say. Maybe headed up around Flagstaff? The country on the other side of there, all the way up into Utah, is supposed to be pretty empty. Lots of good places for a man to lose himself for a while. That might be what MacDonald has in mind."

The terrain through which the group rode grew more rugged. They had to follow hogback ridges to avoid brush-choked gullies. Ace didn't like that. They were too easy to spot while they were on higher ground like that. He could almost feel them being watched.

Everyone knew that bands of Apache renegades lived in the mountains. The question was whether any of them wanted to ambush a well-armed party such as this. Those bands often were small, with less than a dozen warriors to go along with a few dozen women and children.

Apaches were stubborn, though, and didn't like intruders in territory they considered their own. They might strike no matter what the odds were.

Finally, MacDonald called a halt and told everyone to dismount. Chance was off his horse fast enough to reach Evelyn's side before she could get down from the saddle. He said, "Let me help you, Miss Sughrue."

She managed a weak smile. "Thank you, Mr. Jensen."

"Please, call me Chance," he said as he reached up to assist her.

There was no situation desperate enough to keep his brother from flirting with a pretty girl, Ace thought wryly. He swung down from his saddle and leaned against the cavalry horse for a second as weariness gripped him.

Chance had his hands under Evelyn's arms as he helped her to the ground. When she was standing on her feet, Chance let go of her, but she immediately swayed and let out an alarmed, "Oh!"

Chance caught hold of her again to steady her. He turned his head and said to MacDonald, "This poor girl needs rest, and plenty of it, MacDonald. We have to stay here for a while."

It wasn't a bad place for that. They were in a canyon about a hundred yards wide, with steep, rocky walls rising on both sides. Rainwater had collected in a tank in some rocks, and half a dozen scrubby trees grew around it to provide a little shade. A few patches of hardy grass sprouted from the rocky ground here and there, as well.

Without waiting for MacDonald to respond to his suggestion, Chance started helping Evelyn over to the little pond.

"Let's get you out of the sun," he said. "You can have a drink, too. That should help you feel better."

MacDonald began, "Blast it, I didn't say that you could—" He stopped, blew out a breath, and went, "Oh, all right. We'll let the horses drink and graze a little. Won't do us any good if they get all done in. Parnell, you and a couple of men keep your eyes on those prisoners."

"Sure, Vince," Parnell said. He pointed his rifle in Ace's general direction as Ace and Lieutenant Driscoll trudged over to the natural water tank to join Chance and Evelyn.

Evelyn sank down on a rock in the shade of one of the little trees and let out a deep sigh of exhaustion. "I don't know if I can go on," she said, keeping her voice low enough that MacDonald wouldn't hear her.

Lieutenant Driscoll put both hands in the small of his back and stretched, then said, "I don't believe any of us have any choice, Evelyn. These are desperate men, and they won't hesitate to kill any of us if they think it will benefit them."

"You're right about that," Ace said. "Miss Sughrue has some value to them, though." He smiled at her. "I don't think you have to worry too much. MacDonald wants to keep you alive."

"Alive, maybe," she said, "but what might happen to me in the meantime?"

Ace couldn't answer that. Not anything that Evelyn would want to hear, anyway.

The deserters gathered around the tank and drank their fill, then let the horses drink—but not too much. They would be in trouble if their mounts foundered. The horses didn't want to leave the water, but the men led them away and picketed them where they could graze.

Ace and Chance stood to one side. Chance said quietly, "You know, I bet we could jump a couple of these fellas and grab those handguns they're wearing."

"And even if we made every shot count, we'd still be outnumbered," Ace pointed out. "Besides, you know how things go in a gunfight. Bullets fly around every which way, and some of them usually hit things they're not supposed to."

He looked meaningfully at Evelyn Sughrue.

"Yeah, you're right about that," Chance admitted. "I don't guess we can risk it. But what *are* we going to do?"

Lieutenant Driscoll had drifted closer while the Jensen brothers were talking. He overheard Chance's question and asked with a frown, "Are you talking about trying to get away from these men?"

"They don't have anything good in mind for us, Doctor," Ace said.

"That's true, but you don't know MacDonald as well as I do. He's a vicious brute. If you give him any excuse, he'll—"

MacDonald's rumble came from behind Driscoll, interrupting him. "What'll I do, Doc?" he asked. MacDonald chuckled, but the sound didn't hold any genuine humor. "You go ahead and tell me, why don't you?"

Driscoll had jerked around as soon as MacDonald spoke. He swallowed nervously and said, "I was just trying to convince these two young men that we need to cooperate with you—"

"Yeah, by talkin' about what a vicious brute I am. You know, maybe you're right about that."

With no more warning than that, MacDonald's left arm came up and around and the back of his hand smashed against Driscoll's jaw. The unexpected blow snapped Driscoll's head to the side and made him stagger back several steps. A few yards away, Evelyn let out a cry of surprise and fear.

MacDonald handed the rifle in his right hand to one of the other deserters. "I told you I'd let you go tomorrow if nobody came after us," he said as he stalked toward Driscoll, flexing his hands. "I never said nothin' about what kind of shape you'd be in, Doc. You know, you always got on my nerves, actin' so high and mighty the way you did, tellin' us what we ought to do."

"I'm a doctor," Driscoll cried shakily. The side of his face where MacDonald had struck him was bright red now. "It's my job to tell my patients how to take care of themselves."

"You ain't a real doctor," MacDonald sneered. "You're just a pill-roller and bandage-wrapper. If you'd been a real doc, you would've been practicin' in some town, instead of bein' the post surgeon at a place in the middle of nowhere like Fort Gila."

Driscoll held out a trembling hand as MacDonald crowded in at him. "Leave me alone!" he said.

MacDonald ignored the plea and hit him in the belly. Ace winced as the powerful blow sunk MacDonald's right fist in Driscoll's midsection and doubled him over. MacDonald hooked a left against Driscoll's jaw that sent the doctor rolling on the ground.

Ace and Chance both stepped forward, unable to control the reaction. They had to stop, though, when Parnell and one of the other deserters swung their rifles up and trained the weapons on them. At this range, the men couldn't miss, and MacDonald had already made it clear he didn't care that much whether the Jensen brothers lived or died.

"I ought'a stomp your guts out, Driscoll," MacDonald said as he loomed over the fallen lieutenant. "I won't, though. You know why? Because a pathetic excuse for a man like you just ain't worth that much effort."

Shaking his head contemptuously, MacDonald

turned away. Behind him, Driscoll struggled to get up. He put his hands on the rocky ground and pushed, lifting his head and glaring after MacDonald as he did so.

Ace saw something in Driscoll's eyes that he hadn't expected. The light of temporary madness blazed there. In most men, deep-seated instinct made them want to strike back when they were physically attacked. In addition, MacDonald had humiliated Driscoll. The man had to have at least some pride, or he never would have become an officer.

Put simply, MacDonald had just pushed the lieutenant too far.

Driscoll surged up off the ground, let out an incoherent cry, and lunged after MacDonald, who was several inches taller and fifty or sixty pounds heavier. Driscoll stood no chance, but he wasn't thinking about that at this moment.

Hearing Driscoll charging him, MacDonald wheeled around sharply. As he did, something flicked past him. Ace barely caught a glimpse of it, but the next instant, he saw the arrow that appeared in Driscoll's left shoulder, bringing the doctor to a staggering stop as he pawed at the shaft and howled in pain.

That howl blended with the bloodcurdling cries that suddenly filled the canyon.

CHAPTER TWENTY-SEVEN

"Apaches!" MacDonald bellowed.

Driscoll dropped to his knees and continued fumbling with the arrow lodged in his shoulder. His wail trailed off into a whimper.

Rifle shots began sounding from the rimrock on both sides of the canyon. One man pitched forward as a bullet struck him in the back of the head, killing him instantly. Another of the deserters spun off his feet as a slug ripped along his ribs.

The Jensen brothers acted instinctively. Chance sprang toward Evelyn Sughrue, grabbed her, and bore her to the round behind some of the rocks surrounding the water tank. The rocks were low enough that they didn't provide great cover, but they were better than nothing.

At the same time, Ace raced over to the trooper who'd been shot in the head and grabbed the man's fallen Springfield. An arrow whipped past him, missing by scant inches. As he lifted the rifle, he whirled and spotted the Apache warrior who had fired the arrow. The man was drawing back his bowstring to launch another flint-tipped missile.

Ace fired from the hip. There was no time to aim. But luck and skill guided his shot, and the Apache flew backward as the .45-70 round slammed into his chest. He managed to loose the arrow, but being hit threw off his aim, and the shaft sailed harmlessly over Ace's head.

A few feet away, MacDonald's rifle blasted. Ace didn't see what happened, but he heard MacDonald exclaim, "Got the red devil!" so he assumed the sergeant had hit his target.

Another Apache charged at Ace and launched with one foot off a rock into a leap that carried him toward the young man. The warrior's raised right hand clutched a knife, ready to drive the blade into Ace's chest.

Ace thrust the empty rifle up and caught the Apache in the belly with the Springfield's barrel. He fell back and heaved, and the move propelled the warrior through the air. The man cried out in alarm as his arms and legs flailed helplessly now. He smashed down on some rocks and then lay there unmoving.

Hearing a rush of footsteps nearby, Ace rolled over and scrambled up in time to use the Springfield to knock aside the barrel of a Winchester just as the Apache wielding it was about to fire point-blank at him. Ace stepped in and swung the Springfield's stock against the warrior's jaw. Bone crunched under the impact. The Apache fell to the side, and Ace leaned down to strike again with the rifle butt, crushing the man's skull.

He had been lucky so far, but the Springfield was empty and with Apaches dashing around the canyon floor bent on killing the white interlopers, Ace knew he wouldn't have time to reload even if he could get his hands on some ammunition. He dropped the rifle and dived toward the trooper who had been killed in the first volley. He unsnapped the man's holster and dragged out the .45 revolver.

As he did, an arrow thudded into the man's body. Ace thrust the Colt across the corpse's back and triggered a round at the warrior who had fired the arrow. The bullet punched into the Apache's guts and doubled him over.

Part of the way around the tank, Chance had had the same idea as his brother. He told Evelyn, "Keep your head down!" and scrambled on hands and knees toward the man who'd been wounded in the side. The man was rolling around and using his hands to try to stop the bleeding, without much luck.

Chance picked up the man's rifle and aimed at the rimrock where several Apaches had stood up now to get better shots at the group in the canyon. The Springfield roared and bucked against Chance's shoulder. Through the haze of smoke from the shot, he saw one of the warriors drop his Winchester, clutch at his belly, and pitch forward off the rim, turning over completely in midair as he plummeted toward the canyon floor.

Chance tossed the empty rifle aside and said to the wounded deserter, "Give me your pistol!"

"Wh-what?"

"Your Colt! Let me use it!"

"I . . . I can't. MacDonald would—"

Chance saw one of the Apaches who'd been hidden in the canyon running toward the rocks where Evelyn lay. He didn't waste any time arguing with the wounded man. He threw a punch that crashed into the man's jaw and stretched him out, stunning him. That allowed Chance to snatch the revolver out of the man's holster.

He thumbed back the Colt's hammer as he whirled back toward the rocks. The Apache had almost reached Evelyn, who had her head buried in her arms and probably didn't even know the renegade was there. The Apache swung his Winchester toward her, but before he could fire, Chance shot him in the head. The warrior jerked and collapsed, but his momentum carried him forward. He sprawled across Evelyn, on top of her.

The unexpected weight made her shriek in terror and writhe around frantically on the ground in an attempt to escape from it. Chance ran toward her and called, "Evelyn! Evelyn, it's all right! He's dead!"

Chance reached down with his free hand, caught hold of the back of the Apache's shirt, and hauled him off the panic-stricken young woman. Evelyn continued screaming as Chance bent toward her and started trying to reassure her.

Then he saw that she was staring wide-eyed past him, and instinct warned him. He spun around and snapped a shot at the Apache looming over him, about to plunge a knife into his back. The bullet caught the warrior under the chin and jolted his head back as it bored on into his brain. The man stumbled and went down on top of Chance, who shoved the body aside.

He knelt there beside Evelyn, the gun in his right hand, his left hand now on her shoulder to hold her down and try to calm her at the same time, as the battle continued swirling around them.

Ace spotted them there and was relieved to see that his brother was all right, at least for the moment. He raced toward them, firing as he ran, and two more Apaches fell before the Colt's hammer clicked on an empty chamber.

Vince MacDonald was close to the tank in the rocks, too, swinging his empty rifle like a club at the Apaches surrounding him. They could have shot him, but grim-faced and determined with hate, they darted in at him and tried to gut him with knife thrusts. It seemed to be cruel sport for them.

MacDonald drove them back each time, but dark stains on his gray shirt showed that he had suffered several gashes from the blades.

Ace dropped the empty revolver as he nearly tripped over a rock. He caught his balance and reached down to grasp the stone slab. With a grunt of effort, he lifted it, raised it as much as he could, and ran toward the Apaches who were attacking MacDonald. They didn't see him coming, so he was able to throw the heavy rock into their midst without warning. It crashed into one man's head and knocked him sprawling into two more.

That gave MacDonald an opening to take the fight to the enemy instead of staying on the defensive. He bulled forward, whirling the empty Springfield, and two more warriors went down as the stock smashed their skulls.

But one of the remaining Apaches lunged in and buried his knife in MacDonald's side. The sergeant roared in pain and twisted to drive the rifle's stock into the man's face, turning it into a red, misshapen ruin. MacDonald staggered, plucked the knife out of his flesh, and thrust it into the throat of another warrior. Then his strength deserted him and he fell to his knees.

One of the Apaches was about to ram his knife into MacDonald's back when Ace tackled him. They sprawled on the ground. The warrior jabbed the blade at Ace, who grabbed the man's wrist to stop the thrust. He twisted hard and threw his weight against the Apache. The knife, turned now so that it pointed the other way, went cleanly into the man's chest. The warrior bucked up once from the ground, then sagged back as his face turned slack and lifeless.

A big hand closed hard around Ace's upper right arm. He jerked his head around, ready to fight some more, then saw it was MacDonald who had hold of him. Wounded or not, the burly noncom still had plenty of strength. He hauled Ace to his feet and shoved him toward the rocks where Chance and Evelyn were.

The wounded Lieutenant Driscoll had crawled over there, too, and four more of the deserters were close by, including Corporal Parnell. Some of the men still held rifles or revolvers, but evidently the weapons were out of ammunition, because no one was firing anymore.

Ace and MacDonald joined the little group. The Apaches had backed off a ways, but they still ringed the rocks. Another rush would overrun the whites, now that they didn't have any firepower.

"Thanks for your help, Jensen," MacDonald rasped

to Ace. "Wouldn't have blamed you if you'd let those savages have me."

"We're in this together," Ace replied.

"Yeah, I reckon. Not that it's gonna do any good. There are too many of the red devils—"

He fell silent as the circle of Apaches suddenly parted and a man strode through the opening. He was slightly taller and slimmer than the rest of the warriors, who tended toward short, stocky builds. He had a blue headband around his hair and a blue sash at his waist, tied around the long white shirt he wore.

A gunbelt was buckled around his waist as well, with the attached holster containing what appeared to be a long-barreled Remington .44. The warrior carried a Winchester at a slant across his chest. His bearing, as well as the way the other Apaches stepped back to let him through, told Ace that this man was the chief.

The man lowered the rifle and made a leisurely, sweeping gesture with his left hand, indicating to the other warriors that they should step back. He faced the group of whites huddled next to the water and said in good English, "I am called Ndolkah. It means mountain lion in your tongue. You have killed several of my warriors, but I will spare your lives if you will lay down your arms and promise to fight no more."

"You mean you'll let us go?" MacDonald asked harshly.

The ghost of a smile flitted across the chief's lips. "This I did not promise," he said. "But if you surrender, some of you may live . . . for a while. If you fight, all of you will die, here and now."

"We surrender!" Driscoll cried. "Just . . . just don't kill us!"

"Shut up," MacDonald growled. "That heathen ain't gonna let any of us live except maybe the girl . . . and she won't want to!"

The wheels of Ace's brain turned over swiftly. He didn't think they had much of a chance, either—but they had no chance the way things were.

And one slim hope still existed to which they might cling. Despite the warnings MacDonald had issued back at Fort Gila, Ace thought it likely that Lieutenant Olsen and a search party would have set out after the deserters as soon as Olsen got back to the fort. So help *could* be on the way—if they could survive long enough for it to find them.

"Lieutenant Driscoll is right," Ace said. "We have to surrender or be wiped out."

Chance stared at him in disbelief. "Ace, have you gone loco? Jensens don't give up—"

"This time we do," Ace said. "We don't have any choice."

Ndolkah smiled again. "You are wise beyond your years, young white man. Perhaps you will live the longest." He gestured to his warriors again, this time curtly. "Take them!"

The Apaches closed in again. MacDonald and a couple of the other men put up a fight, but it didn't last long before they were overpowered and borne to the ground. Then all the prisoners' hands were tied and their captors prodded them into a defeated walk on up the canyon.

CHAPTER TWENTY-EIGHT

The Apache village was a couple of miles higher in the mountains, in a narrower canyon that had an actual spring in it, so they didn't have to rely on rain caught in tanks for their water. The clean, cool stream that trickled out of the rock wall was a tiny one, but it was enough to form a small pool, and in a harsh, unforgiving land such as this one, that was almost a luxury.

Perhaps thirty mud hogans were scattered around the canyon, so Ndolkah's band was neither one of the smallest nor a very large one. He had lost almost a dozen warriors in the ambush, with Ace, Chance, and MacDonald doing most of the damage, so the attack had been a costly one. Wailing from the women who had lost their husbands filled the air.

"If they let those women have us . . ." Chance muttered as the prisoners trudged into the village.

"I know," Ace said. He and Chance had never clashed with Apaches until the ambush on the work detail, but they had heard enough stories to be aware that it was the women who took torturing prisoners to new, awful heights, not the men.

"Frank will find us," Driscoll babbled. "He's got to."

"Shut up," MacDonald told him. "That big buck who's their leader savvies our talk. No point in lettin' him know that a patrol might be on our trail." He laughed. "If anybody at that fort's smart enough to figure out I was tryin' to put 'em on a false scent with all that talkin' I did."

"Somebody will figure it out," Ace said. He hoped that was true, because it was their only chance.

Some of the women rushed toward them and spat at them. Children pelted them with rocks. Evelyn whimpered in fear and pain. Chance wanted to put his arms around her and comfort her, but with his hands tied behind his back, he couldn't. Instead he walked as close to her as he could and said, "It's going to be all right. You'll see."

The tear-streaked face she turned toward him showed that she didn't believe that for a second.

The warriors poked them with Winchester barrels and herded them over to an area where part of the canyon wall bulged out and created an overhang. The area underneath it was ten feet deep, maybe twice that long, and the sloping roof no more than five feet high. All the prisoners had to bend to clear it as they were forced into the cave-like den, even Evelyn.

MacDonald banged his head on the rock and cursed. His shirt had a large bloodstain on the side where he'd been stabbed. Nothing had been done about the wound. The Apaches probably didn't think it mattered, since in their eyes MacDonald wasn't long for this world anyway, and the big sergeant seemed to share that feeling.

When they were all sitting down against the canyon wall under the overhang, though, Ace said, "Lieutenant Driscoll, you ought to take a look at that wound in MacDonald's side."

"MacDonald's wound?" Driscoll said in a voice that bordered on hysterical. "What about this arrow in my shoulder?"

It was true that the arrow was still lodged in the lieutenant's shoulder. That wound hadn't bled as much as the gash in MacDonald's side, though.

Driscoll went on, "I'll see if I can lean over so somebody can get hold of the shaft and pull it out."

"Don't be a fool," MacDonald snapped. "You know better than that. You've removed arrows from men who were hit. Pull it out and you'll do a lot more damage."

That was true. The only practical method to remove an arrow like that was to break off the end of the shaft and then push the head the rest of the way through. That created an exit wound to deal with, but that was still less dangerous than the other way.

Driscoll sobbed. "You're right," he choked out. "But it doesn't matter. We're all going to die."

"Don't give up yet," Ace said quietly. "As long as we're alive, there's a chance we'll get out of here."

A gloomy silence fell over the group. Three of the Apache warriors stood just outside the makeshift prison, holding Winchesters at the ready. Now and then some of the women approached the prisoners and spat at them again. The guards allowed that but ran off any children who came up intending to throw more rocks.

It was difficult to tell how much time had passed,

but Ace tried to keep track of it by watching the play of sunlight in the canyon and the way its slant increased. He estimated that it was late afternoon when Ndolkah strode toward them and came to a stop in front of the overhang.

The chief studied them for a long moment. Whatever he had in mind, Ace figured it would be a good idea to postpone it for as long as possible, so he asked, "How is it that you speak English so well?"

Ndolkah looked annoyed by the question, but he said, "I learned at the reservation school, when I was a child. It was the first reservation on which the white men tried to force my people. They had not yet learned that we are not animals to be penned up."

MacDonald said, "Maybe if you'd learn to live like human beings instead of animals, you wouldn't get treated that way."

Ndolkah moved his hand to the knife sheathed at his waist, attached to the gunbelt he wore. "You have no right to tell us how to live, white man. When you try, *we* tell *you* . . . how to die."

He turned his head, looked along the line of prisoners, and pointed to the two troopers at the other end. He gave a guttural command in his native tongue, and warriors sprang forward to bend down and grab hold of those two.

The men had started to look terrified as soon as Ndolkah's gaze landed on them and lingered. Now they screamed and yelled and tried to writhe around as strong hands lifted them from the ground. One of them kicked at the Apaches and received a powerful blow that left him half-stunned and unable to fight.

Both men were forced to their feet and dragged away from the others.

MacDonald roared curses and said, "Leave those boys alone! They ain't never done nothin' to you or your people!"

"They do not belong here," Ndolkah responded calmly. "Some of my men died today, brave men, and their deaths must be avenged. The women and children cry out for justice."

"It ain't justice! You just like killin'! You're monsters, all of you!"

Ndolkah ignored him and walked away.

"They're going to kill them," Driscoll said hollowly. "They're going to torture them and kill them."

Evelyn sobbed. Her head drooped forward and she didn't lift her eyes, which Ace figured was a good thing. Whatever was about to happen, she didn't need to watch it.

"Shoemaker and Barnes," MacDonald said. "Them's their names. All of you ought to know that, and remember 'em in the time you've got left."

Chance said quietly to Ace, "With what they've done, I shouldn't feel sorry for those men. Given the opportunity, I would have drilled them myself when we were trying to stop them from deserting."

"That doesn't matter," Ace said. "They don't deserve what's about to happen to them. None of us do."

The Apaches were like a completely alien species that lived by different rules. There was no room for compassion in their makeup, only cruelty. That was the way it seemed to Ace, anyway, as the two troopers, Shoemaker and Barnes, were staked out and the women went to work on them with knives.

Scream after scream ripped through the hot, late afternoon air as razor-sharp blades cut and sliced and peeled away skin and flesh. The men's voices grew hoarse and raw as shrieks of agony took their toll on vocal cords. At first Shoemaker and Barnes bucked up off the ground and tried to fight against the bonds, but their strength deserted them as their blood flowed and seeped and oozed from the scores of cuts. Finally, all they could do was lie there, whimpering and quivering, as the Apache women continued to inflict torment beyond imagining.

Evelyn slumped against Chance's shoulder. Her eyes were squeezed tightly shut, but Chance knew she could still hear the cries. He began talking, not really paying attention to what he was saying, just spewing an endless stream of words in an effort to drown out the terrible sounds that filled the Apache village and echoed back from the canyon walls. He couldn't cover them up completely, but he could at least blunt their effect.

MacDonald began cursing, a low, monotonous drone of obscenity, and oddly enough, that helped, too. Ace listened and almost took comfort in it.

While that was going on, some of the warriors erected a pole framework with a thick crossbeam at the top. When they had it lashed together securely, the women who weren't involved in torturing Shoemaker and Barnes began building a fire underneath the crossbeam, using broken branches from the scrubby trees around the spring. They fed it carefully until the flames burned steadily without being overly large. There wasn't an abundance of fuel in these parts—but what the Apaches had in mind made using some of it worthwhile, where they were concerned. By now the sun was down and shadows were beginning to gather in the canyon, which made the fire seem even brighter.

The women moved back away from the prisoners as the men approached. Ndolkah stood to one side, arms folded across his chest, watching, as his warriors freed Shoemaker and Barnes from the pickets that had held them spread-eagled. They tied the men's ankles together, then lashed their hands behind their backs. They carried the troopers over to the fire, threw ropes over the pole framework, looped those ropes around Shoemaker and Barnes's ankles, and then hoisted the men so they hung head-down over the flames.

The two troopers looked more like bundles of bloody rags than they did anything human. So much blood covered the men's faces and bodies that they appeared black in the firelight. Enough still oozed from their wounds to form fat drops that fell into the fire. From where Ace sat, he could hear each grotesque sizzle as those drops landed in the flames.

Instinctively, even in their half-dead state, Shoemaker and Barnes tried to escape the terrible heat rising from the fire. Trussed up as they were, all they could do was wriggle frantically, like worms impaled on a fishing hook. They couldn't twist enough to get away.

Their suffering gave them enough strength, though, that their desperate struggle provided great sport for the watching Apaches. The women hooted and screamed in joy. The children capered around and giggled. The men looked on solemnly, nodding in satisfaction as the prisoners' writhing grew more and more frantic, then progressively weaker and weaker.

Finally, Shoemaker and Barnes stopped fighting and just hung there like sides of meat. They had either passed out or were already dead. Either way, it was merciful, because after a while their brains swelled from the heat and burst their skulls like shattered melons. Judging by their reaction, the Apaches thought that was the most entertaining thing they had ever seen.

MacDonald was sitting next to Ace. He leaned his head closer and whispered, "Listen to me, Jensen. Before they get around to you . . . if you get a chance . . . you kill that girl. You hear me? You swear it to me!"

Ace glanced at Evelyn, shivering against Chance's side, and had to swallow hard before he was able to say, "I hear you. And I promise . . . I will."

CHAPTER TWENTY-NINE

The death of Privates Shoemaker and Barnes evidently satisfied the Apaches' savage lust for the time being, because they didn't approach the prisoners for the rest of the night. Eventually, exhaustion claimed all the captives. The human mind could only cope with so much horror before it retreated into whatever oblivion it could find.

But when they awoke in the morning, that horror was still right in front of them. The Apaches had left Shoemaker and Barnes hanging from the framework as the fire burned down, so by now the bodies were nothing but charred husks. And the smell that still lingered in the canyon . . . !

"How long is this going to last?" Driscoll muttered. He was pale and drawn, and every time he moved even the tiniest bit, he grimaced in pain from the arrow. Blood had dried and crusted around the wound, but now and then some fresh crimson would seep out of it.

"Well, there are seven of us left," MacDonald said, "but that counts the girl and they won't kill her.

They'll make her a slave, and the bucks'll take turns with her."

"Shut your mouth, MacDonald," Chance flared. "There's no need for filthy talk like that."

"I'm just tellin' it the way it is, kid. If you don't like it, take it up with those savages." MacDonald paused, then went on, "Anyway, as I was sayin', with six of us to kill, they'll probably do two every night. So that means the *lucky* ones who go last probably have three more days to look forward to."

Quietly, Ace said, "There's still a chance we'll be rescued. We need to hang on as long as we can."

"Keep tellin' yourself that," MacDonald said with a cold grin.

Ace was doing more than that. Now that the shock of their captivity had worn off slightly, his brain had begun to work again. If there was a way out of this deadly dilemma other than just sitting there helplessly and hoping, he was determined to find it.

Only two warriors were standing guard over the prisoners today. That was a slight improvement. If he and Chance could get loose, they could overpower those guards, free the others, take the Winchesters, and maybe make it to the far end of the canyon, which was steep but not too sheer to be climbed. Even better, there were enough rocks and trees on the slope to provide some cover. The Jensen brothers would be able to put up a fight and hold the Apaches off while the others escaped.

They would still be on foot, in the middle of a harsh landscape filled with enemies, but that was better than being helpless captives destined for torture and death.

The first step was figuring out a way for him and Chance to get loose . . .

Ace looked to his left at his brother. Evelyn was on Chance's left, leaning against him and resting her head on his shoulder. Under other circumstances, Chance would have been pleased as punch about having her so close to him, but not now. Evelyn's eyes were closed, but she was breathing in such a jerky rhythm that Ace didn't think she was asleep, just trying to shut out her surroundings. Chance just stared ahead dully, as if he'd been stunned.

Ace's gaze fell on the brooch pinned to Evelyn's blouse. Even after everything that had happened, it was still there. The pin holding it in place had to be pretty sturdy.

Ace's heart began to slug a little harder in his chest.

"Chance," he whispered to his brother. "Chance!"

A little life came back into Chance's eyes. He turned his head toward Ace. "What?"

"Look at Evelyn's bosom."

Chance frowned. "Blast it, this isn't the time or place—"

"I'm talking about the brooch pinned to her blouse."

"What?" Chance said again. "I don't understand . . ."

Even as he spoke, though, he had turned his head to look where Ace had said, and his voice trailed off as he stared at the piece of jewelry.

"That brooch has a pin on it," he said softly.

"Yeah."

"It's not like it'll cut through those rawhide strips around our wrists, though."

"No," Ace said, "but you might be able to use it to pick at them enough to loosen them. Then you could untie them."

"And if my hands are free, I can untie the rest of us."

"Seems like it's worth a try."

"It's going to take a long time, though," Chance warned.

"What do we have, other than time?"

"Yeah, but only a limited amount of it."

"MacDonald doesn't think they'll torture any more of us until night falls again," Ace said. "We probably won't want to make our move until it's dark, anyway. Easier to give them the slip then."

Chance grunted. "It won't be easy any time, but I guess we should take whatever gives us the best odds. I ought to get started, though. They're not watching us very close. They don't think there's anything we can do."

"Let's prove them wrong."

The brothers had carried on the conversation in urgent whispers. Now Chance turned his head the other way and said, "Evelyn. Evelyn, listen to me."

"What?" she murmured without opening her eyes.

"I'm going to lean forward, and when I do, you slide down behind me."

That answer was unexpected enough to make her open her eyes and look up at him in confusion.

"What? I don't—"

"Just lean over far enough that my hands can reach your chest."

Her eyes widened. "Chance, I . . . I thought you were a gentleman—"

Through gritted teeth, he said, "I'm going to get

that brooch and try to use the pin on it to work the bonds on my wrists loose."

"Oh! I . . . I think I see what you mean. But do you really believe it will work?"

"We have to do *something*. We're not going to just sit here and wait for the Apaches to kill us."

Evelyn swallowed hard and then nodded. "All right. I think I can do it. When?"

"There's no time like the present." Chance hunched his shoulders a little and leaned forward, grunting with the effort it took to do so in this position. Like a tree toppling slowly at first and then falling faster and faster, Evelyn leaned to her right behind him.

"What in blazes are you doin' over there?" MacDonald asked.

Ace was watching the two Apache guards, who appeared to be paying no attention to what the prisoners were doing. "Just be quiet," he told MacDonald. "Chance and I are trying something."

"If it gives us a fightin' chance—" MacDonald began.

"Wait!" Ace said. He had spotted Ndolkah coming toward them. The chief's determined stride made it clear that he intended to visit the prisoners. "Chance, Ndolkah's coming!"

Chance had been fumbling with his bound hands at the front of Evelyn's blouse. He got his fingers on the brooch, but not before they unintentionally explored the soft mounds of flesh underneath the fabric. He hadn't been the sort to blush since he was a kid, but his face felt warm now.

He saw the Apache chieftain approaching, too, and whispered, "Evelyn, sit up!"

He felt her struggling behind him. "I . . . I don't know if I can!"

He understood. Since she couldn't use her hands, she had no way to gain any leverage and lift herself back to a sitting position.

He got his hands against her shoulder and tried to push. That was something for her to brace against, anyway, and he felt her rise a little. She struggled to come up more. He twisted, managed to hook his left shoulder against her right one, and pushed her up farther. The contact between them slipped loose and Evelyn started to topple over again, but Chance pressed his heels against the rocky ground in front of him and shoved back hard, flattening himself against the wall behind him. Evelyn wound up falling with her head in his lap.

"Oh!" she exclaimed.

"Just lay there," Chance grated. "I know it's . . . undignified. But you can, uh, pretend you fell asleep that way."

"Oh," she said again, this time sounding utterly mortified. Chance just sat there next to Ace with his face impassive as they watched Ndolkah walk up.

The chief hunkered on his heels in front of the prisoners. "The women will bring you food and water," he said.

"What if we don't want your heathen swill?" MacDonald asked.

Ndolkah shrugged. "You will not starve or die of thirst in the time you have left, so it does not matter whether you eat or drink. But you might as well satisfy your bellies while you can."

"That's not a bad idea," Ace said. He didn't see any point in antagonizing their captors. Doing so would just make the Apaches pay more attention to them, and that was the last thing they wanted right now. "Thank you."

Ndolkah looked at Evelyn and smiled. "The woman sleeps?"

"That's right," Chance said. "She's exhausted."

"She will learn. A slave's life is not an easy one. She will learn . . . or she will die. As simple as that."

Ace changed the subject by saying, "You're not like the other warriors in this band, are you?"

Ndolkah frowned and tapped his chest with a fist. "I am Apache!" He shrugged. "But it is true that my mother was a Mexican, a captive. Mostly of Spanish blood, she claimed to be, or so my father told me. I never knew her. She was weak and died giving birth to me."

"I'm sorry," Ace said.

"Do not be. If she had lived, she might have passed that weakness on to me. By dying, she freed me to be a true Apache!"

Driscoll spoke up. "Chief, I . . . I really need something done about this arrow in my shoulder. I think the wound is infected. I . . . I feel like I have a fever . . ."

"Very well," Ndolkah said, nodding. "I will do something for you, white man, so you will not suffer. When evening comes, we will see how well you die."

"No!" Driscoll wailed. "That's not what I—"

Ndolkah wasn't listening. He straightened to his

full height, gazed contemptuously at the captives for a moment, and then turned to walk away. Driscoll just slumped against the wall and sobbed quietly and miserably.

"Well, that makes it pretty plain," Ace said. "By nightfall, we need to be ready to make our move."

CHAPTER THIRTY

Chet Van Slyke leaned over in the saddle and spat next to the corpse of a trooper with a good-sized chunk of his head blown away. The man's body had been mutilated, probably after he was dead—*hopefully* after he was dead, if anybody had any sympathy for the poor varmint—and flies had covered the bloody flesh. They had risen in a black swarm when Van Slyke rode up.

"Told you we were on the right trail," the gaunt gunman said to the riders reining in nearby.

Lieutenant Frank Olsen nodded. He felt no real loyalty to the men under his command, but the sight of the hacked-up bodies lying around on the canyon floor made his gorge rise. The place looked and smelled like a charnel house.

Olsen looked over at Corporal Cochran and said, "If you can find a place where the ground's not too hard, give these men a decent burial. If you can't . . . well, pile some rocks on them, anyway."

Cochran swallowed hard and said, "Yes, sir." He turned in the saddle and called out the names of six troopers to form a burial detail.

"Post lookouts, too," Olsen snapped. "I don't think it's likely the Apaches will come back here any time soon, but you can't ever tell with those savages."

While the troopers got busy with their grim chores, Chet Van Slyke and Navasota Jones dismounted and led their horses over to the tank in the rocks so they could drink. The sight of such violent death clearly didn't bother the two gunmen at all.

Olsen wasn't particularly shaken by it, either. He was just relieved that they hadn't found Evelyn Sughrue's body along with the others. Evelyn was the only one of the captives he really cared about rescuing, although it would be nice if some of the men could be brought back safely, too—and put back to work on building that blasted road.

Olsen brought his own mount over to the water. As the animal lowered its muzzle to drink, Olsen said to Van Slyke, "Do you think you can pick up the trail from here?"

"I brought us this far, didn't I? Yesterday evenin', you figured I had lost the trail, but I led us right here."

Both of those things were true. Olsen had been convinced that Van Slyke was leading them astray when they kept going more and more toward the northwest, away from the border. That was just the opposite direction from where Vince MacDonald had indicated the deserters were going.

However, the theory that MacDonald's words had been meant to decoy any possible pursuit away from them still was possible. If they had misjudged the situation, though, then MacDonald and his cronies—and Evelyn—would be getting farther and farther away from them with each mile that fell behind the rescue party.

The situation was uncertain enough that every nerve in Olsen's body had been stretched almost to the breaking point by the time they made camp the night before. He had hoped to catch up and rescue Evelyn before darkness fell, but frustratingly, things hadn't worked out that way.

Van Slyke had remained confident, though, and now that confidence had proven justified with the discovery of this battleground, along with the bodies of the troopers who had been left behind.

"How far ahead of us do you think they are?" Olsen asked.

"Those fellas have been dead since sometime late yesterday afternoon, I'd say," Van Slyke replied. "So the Apaches have a five- or six-hour lead on us with their prisoners. That's assumin' they holed up somewhere and didn't travel all night. For all I know, they might've even made it back to their village."

"You're certain the Apaches won this fight?"

Van Slyke grunted. "Aren't you? You don't see any redskin carcasses layin' around, do you? They had time to gather up their dead and wounded and take 'em with them when they left. If MacDonald and his bunch had won, wouldn't they have buried those dead troopers and left the 'Paches where they fell?"

"MacDonald might not have taken the time to bury those men," Olsen said. "It would depend on how big a hurry he was in. And the savages could have come back later to retrieve the ones who were killed."

"Whatever you say, Lieutenant." Van Slyke hauled

on his horse's reins and lifted the animal's snout from the tank. "We ought to be able to tell for sure, though, once we pick up the trail again." He jerked his head at Jones. "Come on, Navasota. We'll scout around while the soldier boys are plantin' their friends."

The burial didn't take long. The troopers were only able to scratch shallow graves out of the ground. More than likely, scavengers would get the bodies anyway, but the dead men were beyond caring and Olsen hadn't cared to start with. He'd made the gesture, and that was enough to satisfy the men in the rescue party. He didn't want them turning on him.

By then, Van Slyke and Jones had located tracks leading on up the canyon. Van Slyke pointed them out to Olsen in one of the rare stretches where a thin layer of sandy soil overlay the rock.

"You got a dozen or more Injun ponies and eight or nine whites afoot," Van Slyke said. "You can make out the boot prints. And that smaller track there, that must've come from one of the girl's shoes."

"So she's still alive."

Van Slyke's narrow shoulders rose and fell. "Could've expected that much when we didn't find her body with the others. Not even Apaches would go to the trouble of totin' along the body of a dead girl, and they ain't hardly human."

"So there's still hope," Olsen said.

Jones scratched a lucifer to life and held the flame to the tip of the quirley he had just rolled. Grinning around the smoke, he said, "Well, there's hope . . . and then there's hope. Can't never tell. Right now, that little gal may be hopin' that it won't be too much longer 'fore she dies."

Once Ndolkah was gone, Evelyn rolled toward Chance's knees, then strained and struggled until she was sitting up again. Chance said, "I'm sorry about all of this—"

"Don't be," she told him as she pushed with her feet and scooted back against the wall. "I admit, I was . . . embarrassed . . . but a little embarrassment doesn't mean a thing compared to our lives. Shall we try again?"

"Wait a little bit," Chance said. "Those guards are paying too much attention to us right now. They'll get bored again after a while."

On Ace's other side, MacDonald whispered, "You better tell me what you boys are up to, Jensen. I don't want to be taken by surprise."

"I planned on telling you," Ace whispered back. Keeping his voice low enough that only MacDonald could hear, he explained the plan, then said, "As soon as Chance and I are free, we'll untie your hands, too, and you can let the others loose. You'll need to be really careful about it, though, so the guards won't notice what we're doing."

MacDonald grimaced. "We'd stand a better chance of gettin' away if it was just the two of you, the girl, and me. We can move a lot faster than if the whole bunch makes a break."

"You'd leave Parnell and the rest of your friends here?" Ace asked. The thought of abandoning the others to the Apaches made him aghast.

"I don't have friends," MacDonald snapped. "There are folks who can help me get what I want, and folks who can't." He paused for a long moment, then blew out a breath. "But after seein' what those devils did to Shoemaker and Barnes . . . no, I don't reckon I could leave any white man to that, not even a snivelin' wretch like Driscoll. But I ain't gonna tell *him* what's goin' on until I have to. He might sell us out to the savages in the hope of gettin' some sort of break from them."

"The only break they might give him is a quick bullet in the head."

"After seein' what we saw last night . . . he might think that's worth it."

Ace couldn't argue with that. He fell silent and sat back to wait for Chance and Evelyn to try again on the first part of the plan.

When Chance thought the Apache sentries were no longer watching them closely and it was safe to try again, he told Evelyn, "I'm going to lean forward, but instead of lying down behind me, just hunch over a bit and I'll try to raise my hands as high as I can. You can tell me when I'm getting close to the brooch."

"All right," she said. "Just be careful."

He moved forward and turned a little so she was partially behind him. Then he strained to raise his arms and reach toward her with his bound hands. Evelyn leaned toward him and his fingertips brushed the front of her blouse.

"About a foot higher than that," she whispered. "Can you raise your arms that much?"

"I don't know," Chance said, "but I'm sure going to try."

He leaned forward a little more to give himself a better angle and then attempted to reach higher. His muscles creaked, and bones ached as they were forced to move farther in their sockets than nature had intended. If he dislocated his shoulders, Chance thought, then all this effort and risk would have been for nothing.

His mind flashed back to a traveling show he and Ace had seen one time over in Kansas. One of the performers had been a girl who could twist herself in all sorts of unnatural ways, bending her limbs until it looked like her head was on backwards and the upper and lower halves of her body were going in different directions. The India Rubber Girl, she was called, and she had lived up to the name. Chance would have given a lot to have just a small part of her abilities right now.

He was thinking about that when Evelyn breathed, "You've almost got it . . . Just a little more . . ."

Chance gritted his teeth and stretched his arms and felt the brooch with the fingers of his right hand. He closed them around the hard, round shape and hung on for dear life.

"You've got it!" Evelyn whispered.

"I'll see . . . if I can . . . work it loose . . ."

"Just rip it off of there," she told him. "I don't care about the blouse."

"Let me get . . . a better grip on it . . ."

When Chance was ready, he pulled and Evelyn leaned back away from him at the same time. He heard cloth tearing, and the brooch came free. The sudden release of tension made him sag forward.

One of the Apache guards glanced over his shoulder, probably having seen the movement from the corner of his eye. Chance thought fast and leaned forward even more, lowering his arms behind him so the warrior couldn't see him clutching the brooch and a small piece of fabric attached to it in his right hand. He acted like he was gagging and about to throw up, but after a moment he pretended that the spasm had passed and straightened to a regular sitting position. The Apache just shook his head, sneered at the white weakling, and looked away again.

"Got it?" Ace whispered.

"Got it," Chance said.

Now it was a matter of seeing what he could do with it.

CHAPTER THIRTY-ONE

"Ouch," Chance said quietly.

"Poke yourself again?" Ace asked.

"Yeah, but a little pain is worth it. I'm getting there. This rawhide's the loosest it's been so far."

Chance had been working at his bonds for an hour. He'd had to stop for a while when a couple of the Apache women brought gourds of water and bowls of some sort of mush to the prisoners. They spat in the food and used their hands to shove it into the captives' mouths, then allowed them to drink from the gourds, being so rough about it that more water got spilled than went down their throats. It was a miserable experience but eventually was over with.

Now Chance paused to rest for a few moments. His wrists were bleeding in several places where he had jabbed the brooch's pin into his flesh instead of hooking the rawhide strips. He mentioned that to Ace, then added, "It's a good thing, though. Rawhide stretches more when it's wet, even with blood."

"You lose enough blood to make much of a difference and you're going to be in pretty bad shape."

Chance chuckled. "No, I've got plenty of blood. Blood to spare."

Ace hoped that was the case.

Chance got back to work. MacDonald whispered to Ace, "How's he doin'?"

"Getting there," Ace replied.

The day crawled on. The Apaches cut down the bodies of Shoemaker and Barnes and dragged them off somewhere. The air freshened slightly after that. The heat grew worse as the sun climbed higher, and the prisoners dozed. With their time quite likely running out, it seemed as if they would want to spend every second awake, clinging to every last bit of life they had left, but that wasn't the way it worked. Heat, fear, and exhaustion all took their toll. It was hard to stay awake.

Evelyn leaned against Chance's shoulder and slept soundly, despite the small, continual movements he made as he tried to work the bonds loose. After a while, those movements stopped, and Chance's head sagged forward.

Ace was in a semi-stupor himself, but after a while he came awake with a jerk of his head. He didn't know how long Chance had been sitting there like that, either asleep or passed out.

"Chance!" he hissed. "Chance, wake up!"

Chance blinked, lifted his head, shook it vehemently. "Wha . . . what happened?"

"You went to sleep," Ace told him. "We both did."

"Ace—" Alarm filled Chance's voice. "The brooch is gone."

"Don't panic," Ace said. "It probably just slipped out of your fingers when you dozed off. Can you feel around behind you and see if you can find it?"

"Yeah . . . Lemme try . . ." Chance's shoulders twisted back and forth as he searched for the brooch. After a minute or so that seemed longer than it really was, he heaved a sigh of relief and said, "I've got it."

"What's goin' on over there?" MacDonald asked.

"Nothing," Ace said. He didn't see any point in explaining how close their plan had come to being ruined. They still had hope, and that was all that mattered.

Chance continued working. Evelyn woke up and spoke to him in low, encouraging tones. Ace watched the play of sunlight in the canyon and tried to estimate the time. On down the line of prisoners, Driscoll whimpered and complained until Vince MacDonald said savagely, "If you keep that up much longer, I'm gonna roll down there and head-butt you to death! The Apaches won't have a chance to kill you!"

That made Driscoll shut up for a while. His complaints choked off in a sniveling sob.

"I can't stand a coward," MacDonald said. "Give me the rottenest man in the world over one who doesn't have any guts."

Ace wasn't going to debate philosophy with the big noncom. Instead he whispered encouragement to Chance, too.

It was past midday when Chance suddenly took a sharp, indrawn breath. Ace looked over at him. He could tell that his brother was making an effort to keep his face impassive rather than excited and triumphant, just in case any of the Apaches happened to glance in this direction at just the wrong second.

"You got it?" Ace breathed.

"I got it," Chance said. "My hands are loose."

Ace twisted a little and thrust his bound wrists toward his brother. "See if you can reach over and untie mine."

Without drawing attention to themselves, they worked on freeing Ace. The rawhide strips were difficult for Chance to untie, even with his hands loose. But even though it took a while, it was still a lot easier task than Chance had accomplished by freeing his own wrists.

The next step was untying their ankles. Ace watched the guards closely, and when the warriors weren't looking and none of the other Apaches were close by, he whispered to Chance, "Now!"

They had been flexing their fingers and rolling their shoulders to restore the feeling in their arms and hands. Even so, their efforts were clumsy as they reached in front of them and started tugging at the rawhide strips lashed around their ankles.

MacDonald saw what they were doing and exclaimed, "Hey! Get me loose, blast it!"

The other prisoners realized what was going on, too, and started babbling questions and pleas. Ace saw one of the guards start to turn his head to look around. He hissed a warning to Chance, and both of them had to jerk their arms behind their backs as quickly as possible so it would look like they were still tied up.

"Shut up!" MacDonald told the others in low, urgent tones. "Everybody just shut up!"

The other prisoners fell silent. The guard studied them for a few seconds, then said something to his companion in their guttural native tongue. The other warrior glanced back, shrugged, and replied. Ace couldn't understand any of the words, but he thought the man didn't sound concerned at all. The captives still appeared to be helpless and mired in despair.

After a moment, the first guard laughed, made some sort of comment, and both warriors resumed their negligent attitudes. They didn't consider these white men to be much of a threat.

MacDonald leaned over to the man on the other side of him, who happened to be Brunner, the trooper with the broken foot who had been the key to their escape. He whispered orders for the men to be quiet and pretend that nothing was going on and told Brunner to pass that along to the others.

Then MacDonald whispered to Ace, "I still don't trust Driscoll, but there's nothing we can do about that now. We'll just have to hope he doesn't give us away. You'd better make it fast, though, and get me loose! If nothin' else, I want to kill some more Apaches before I die."

Ace understood that feeling. If there was no way out, it was better to go down fighting.

As soon as it seemed safe again, he and Chance went back to untying their ankles. They pulled the knots free but left the rawhide strips looped around their ankles so it would look like they were still tied.

When that was done, Ace reached behind MacDonald's back and started working on the sergeant's bonds. Farther down the line, Driscoll whined again.

"I don't know about this—" the surgeon began.

"Blast it, Driscoll, keep your mouth shut!" MacDonald warned him. "If you don't, the first thing I'm gonna do when I'm loose is come down there and rip your tongue out! I don't even care if we get away, as long as I get to close your trap for you!"

Those threats made Driscoll subside. He grimaced again from the pain of the arrow wound but didn't say anything else.

While Ace was working on MacDonald's bonds, Chance freed Evelyn. As the rawhide fell away from MacDonald's wrists, he growled, "Are you sure the three of us shouldn't just grab the girl and get outta here?"

"We'll stand a better chance of fighting our way clear if we all stick together," Ace said.

"Yeah, yeah," MacDonald muttered. "I suppose." He went to work untying his ankles, glancing up at the guards every few seconds to make sure they still weren't paying attention.

More than once, Ace had to hiss a quick warning when one of the Apaches wandered in the direction of the overhang where the prisoners were being kept. They all sat as still as possible and hung their heads as if in the throes of despair. Only when the Apaches had gone on did they resume their stealthy efforts to escape.

By late afternoon, everyone was free. MacDonald kept insisting it was time they make their move, but Ace counseled, "Wait a little longer. Let the shadows start to gather."

MacDonald didn't like it, but he controlled the impulse to act. Ace worried that the sergeant might not be able to restrain himself much longer and wished that twilight would go ahead and get here.

Finally, when he saw the women beginning to gather firewood again, he knew they couldn't wait.

Soon, warriors would come for two more prisoners and drag them off to be tortured before they were strung up over the flames to have their brains cooked.

During the afternoon, whispered instructions had been passed along the line. Ace and Chance would jump the two guards and get their rifles. MacDonald would herd Evelyn and the other three prisoners toward the far end of the canyon and get them up the slope there as quickly as possible. But now, at the last minute, MacDonald changed the plan.

"Listen, Jensen . . . Ace," he said. "You take charge of the girl and the rest of this bunch. I'll help your brother with the guards."

"Wait a minute, MacDonald," Ace said. "You're wounded. I know you haven't said much about it, but you lost quite a bit of blood—"

"You reckon I don't know that, kid?" MacDonald snorted. "Even with half as much blood as I'd normally have, I'm more'n a match for any of those dirt-eatin' savages. I want a gun in my hands just as soon as I can get one, understand? Anyway," he added grudgingly, "your brother did most of the work gettin' us free. He deserves a better chance of gettin' out of here."

Chance would have argued about that, but just then Evelyn squeezed his arm and when he looked around at her, he could tell that she wanted him to go along with MacDonald's suggestion.

Ace saw that, too, and reluctantly said, "All right, MacDonald, we'll do it your way." He was so accustomed to fighting alongside Chance that any other option just hadn't occurred to him, but he knew from experience that MacDonald was quite an effective battler, too.

He looked along the line of prisoners and asked, "Is everybody ready?"

Grim nods of agreement came from all of them, even Lieutenant Driscoll with the arrow stuck in his shoulder.

Ace and MacDonald drew their legs up. Each braced a hand on the ground to give themselves some balance. They looked at each other in the gathering dusk and exchanged curt nods.

Then, with no more sound than the rustle of clothing and the whisper of boot leather, they sprang into action.

CHAPTER THIRTY-TWO

The guards heard them coming and started to turn around. Ace leaped at the man closest to him and caught hold of the Winchester's barrel as the warrior swung it toward him. He lashed out with his other fist and crashed it into the man's jaw.

MacDonald reached his man in time to get an arm around the guard's neck from behind before he could bring his rifle into play. MacDonald grabbed that arm with his other hand to lock it into place and the muscles in his back and shoulders bunched as he heaved and twisted with all his massive strength. The Apache's neck snapped with a brittle crack like a branch breaking. He slumped bonelessly in MacDonald's grip.

Ace tore the rifle out of the other guard's grasp and drove the butt into the man's throat, crushing his windpipe. The man gagged and struggled for breath as he stumbled backward, but he wasn't out of the fight yet. He clawed at the bone handle of the knife sheathed at his waist.

So far, the battle had been relatively quiet. Neither guard had managed to raise a cry of alarm, and with one dead and the other unable to breathe, that wasn't going to happen now. But the commotion was going to attract attention within a matter of seconds. There was no avoiding it.

From the corner of his eye Ace saw Chance, Evelyn, and the rest of the captives sprinting toward the far end of the canyon, and he knew there was no more need for stealth. When the choking guard pulled the knife and lunged at him, Ace turned the rifle and shot the man.

The bullet fired at close range struck the Apache in the chest and flung him backward. Ace turned toward the village, where several more warriors were already running to see what was going on. He opened fire, spraying lead among them as fast as he could work the Winchester's lever. A couple of the Apaches tumbled to the ground as Ace's shots found their mark. A few feet away, the rifle MacDonald had taken away from the other guard barked a deadly rhythm, too.

Ace stopped after four rounds and bent to rip away the bandolier of ammunition from the first man he had shot. "Let's go!" he called to MacDonald.

The sergeant loosed one more shot that knocked a warrior sprawling, then he grabbed the bandolier from the man whose neck he had broken. He and Ace both turned and ran for the far end of the canyon.

MacDonald's gait was more ragged and unsteady, and he puffed heavily. Ace figured the untreated wound in the big man's side had taken more of a toll than MacDonald was willing to admit. But MacDonald's longer legs allowed him to keep up even though he was staggering.

Ace reached out with his left hand to grab hold of MacDonald's arm and steady him. MacDonald snarled and jerked away.

"I don't need your help!" he yelled. "Just keep moving!"

Shots began to ring out behind them. A few arrows flew through the air around them. Ace felt the wind-rip of a bullet near his right ear.

Ahead of them, Chance and Evelyn had reached the slope and started up it, with Chance holding her arm to help her. One of the other captives—a trooper whose name he didn't even know, Ace realized—wasn't far behind them. That left Driscoll, who stumbled along holding the arrow shaft so it wouldn't move around as much as he ran, and Brunner, who was hobbled because of his injured foot and couldn't move very fast.

Brunner stumbled, cried out, fell to his knees, and struggled back up again. He turned toward Ace and MacDonald and put out his hands toward them.

"Vince! Vince, you gotta help me—"

He stopped short, his eyes widening as his head jerked back. A black hole had appeared suddenly in the center of his forehead. Ace realized that one of the shots fired at him and MacDonald had missed them and gone on to strike Brunner. Brunner reached out to them again, but that may have been purely a reflex action since he already had a bullet in his brain. His knees buckled and he pitched forward on his face as Ace and MacDonald hurried past him.

"Poor devil," MacDonald muttered. It was more of

an expression of sympathy than Ace expected to hear from MacDonald.

They reached the base of the slope. MacDonald stopped, waved Ace on, and said, "I'll slow 'em down!"

"We fight together!" Ace told him. He started to turn back toward the pursuing Apaches as another bullet sang past them.

"Blast it, boy!" MacDonald roared. "Get outta here, or I'll shoot you myself!"

The fierce expression on the man's face made Ace believe that he meant it. He said, "I'll go partway to the top, then stop and cover you while you catch up. If we do it like that, we might both get away."

"Just go!" MacDonald turned, brought the Winchester to his shoulder, and opened fire again. Ace saw now that he had a fresh bloodstain on his side, probably as a result of that knife wound opening up again. He didn't think either of them had been hit by Apache rifle fire.

Ace scrambled up the slope, bounding in big steps when he could, putting a hand down for balance or grabbing hold of a rocky outcropping or a bush when he had to. When he reached a stone slab jutting out from the slope, he threw himself belly down on top of it and shouted, "MacDonald! Come on!"

From that prone position, Ace had a good angle to fire back down into the area between the Apache village and the end of the canyon. The warriors weren't chasing them anymore, he saw. Instead, they had taken cover behind trees and rocks and were peppering the slope with bullets. Several slugs pounded into the front of the stone slab where he lay, but stretched out like he was, he didn't present much of a target.

He stayed cool and picked his shots, and two more warriors showed too much of themselves and went down under his lethal fire.

He wished he could get a clear shot at Ndolkah, but so far he hadn't spotted the chief.

MacDonald clambered up the slope, really struggling now. Ace couldn't go to help him, though. He had to keep firing at the Apaches, to distract them and make them keep their heads down, if nothing else.

Rocks rattled behind him. He jerked his head around, thinking for a second that he was under attack from that direction, but then Chance dropped down onto the slab beside him.

"I got everybody else to the top," Chance reported. "They're holed up in some rocks. It's good cover, but the bad news is, I don't know how much farther they can go. It's kind of a box, and the walls are too sheer to climb. You and I might be able to make it, but Evelyn and Driscoll can't." Chance paused. "Where's Brunner?"

"He didn't make it," Ace said. "A stray bullet from the Apaches got him."

"Too bad," Chance said, but he didn't really sound that sympathetic. Brunner had played a vital part in MacDonald's escape plan, and that was what had landed all of them in this dangerous mess.

About twenty yards below them, MacDonald suddenly collapsed. Ace hadn't seen him get hit, so he thought the sergeant's strength might have just deserted him.

Chance saw what happened, too, and said, "We can't just leave him there. For one thing, he's got the other rifle!"

Before Ace could say anything, Chance leaped up and started down the slope toward MacDonald, covering the distance in huge bounds. The Apaches threw a few shots at him, the bullets kicking up dirt and rocks when they struck, but none of them came very close to Chance, who was moving too fast for them to draw a bead on him.

He slid down next to MacDonald, grabbed the rifle with one hand and the sergeant's arm with the other. Ace had thumbed more rounds from the bandolier into his Winchester and opened fire again, so he couldn't hear what Chance was saying to MacDonald, but his brother was being emphatic about it. MacDonald shook his head stubbornly at first but then started climbing again. Chance knelt and fired down into the canyon.

When MacDonald made it to the stone slab, he slumped down beside Ace and gasped for breath. The side of his shirt was soaked with blood now.

Ace paused in his shooting and told him, "As soon as you can, head on up. Chance said the others are holed up in some rocks at the top."

He didn't mention the other thing Chance had said, that there might not be a way out up there. Talking about it wouldn't change anything.

Between puffing for air, MacDonald said, "You oughta . . . get outta here . . . while you can. Leave me . . . with that rifle and bandolier . . . Get your brother . . ."

Ace stared at him. "You're offering to sacrifice yourself for us?"

"I just want to . . . kill more of those . . . savages! Now . . . go!"

Ace shook his head and called, "Come on, Chance! I'll cover you!"

Chance retreated up the slope, throwing a few more shots down into the canyon as he did so. Between the sound of the shots fired by his brother and himself, Ace heard MacDonald cursing. But then the big noncom heaved himself up and started toward the top of the slope again.

Chance reached the slab and threw himself down beside Ace again. Ace said, "MacDonald just offered to hold them off while we got away."

"Really? If that doesn't beat all! You think maybe he's got a shred of decency left in him after all?"

"Don't get carried away," Ace said. The rifle cracked and bucked against his shoulder again. He saw one of the warriors fall back, clutching a bullet-torn arm. "We need to get out of here. Want to go together?"

"Wouldn't have it any other way," Chance replied with his usual reckless grin. They reloaded the Winchesters, then started shooting as fast as they could work the levers as they stood up and backed toward the top of the slope.

CHAPTER THIRTY-THREE

One of the soldiers galloped up to the front of the little column and told Olsen, "Looks like riders coming up fast behind us, Lieutenant."

Olsen reined in and signaled for the rest of the men to halt. He was riding with Marshal Hank Glennon while Chet Van Slyke and Navasota Jones were up ahead, scouting the trail. The gunmen would turn back when they realized the others had stopped, more than likely.

Olsen hipped around in the cavalry saddle and peered toward the rear. He saw the haze of dust rising there and knew the report was correct. Riders were approaching at a good clip. A fairly large number of them, in fact. At least a dozen, Olsen estimated.

"You think those blasted Apaches got behind us?" Glennon asked nervously.

"Anything is possible where Indians are concerned," Olsen said. "But there's another possibility, as well. Eugene said he would send more of his men from the mine to join the rescue party."

Glennon rubbed his chin and nodded. "Yeah, he did,

didn't he? Let's hope that's who it is. But hadn't we maybe better get ready for a fight, just in case it ain't?"

"That would be wise," Olsen agreed. "Cochran!"

The corporal moved his horse forward. "Sir?"

"I'm giving you a field promotion. You're a sergeant now."

Cochran stared at him. "Can you do that, sir?"

Olsen reined in the anger that welled up inside him at having one of his decisions questioned. "I can do whatever I deem necessary for the success of this mission."

For all practical purposes, he was in complete command of the garrison at Fort Gila, and his grip on power would be even stronger once he brought Major Sughrue's daughter back safely. That would also solidify his position with Howden-Smyth, since the Englishman wanted the girl for himself. He would string them all along, including Glennon and Judge Bannister, until he was ready to cut them out and seize everything for himself.

"Yes, sir," now-Sergeant Cochran said. "What are your orders?"

"Prepare for a possible engagement with hostiles. Have the men dismount and form a skirmish line."

"Yes, sir!"

Cochran snapped a salute, wheeled his horse, and hurried to carry out the orders.

The swift rataplan of hoofbeats made Olsen look the other way again. Van Slyke and Jones were on their way back, as he'd expected. The two gunmen reined in, and Van Slyke nodded toward the rear.

"Is that some more of our boys comin' up?" he asked.

"Probably, but just in case it's not, I'm preparing for trouble."

Cochran spread the men out and detailed a couple of troopers to hold the horses well behind the skirmish line. The rest of the soldiers knelt on one knee and readied their Springfields. Olsen, Van Slyke, and Jones remained mounted. The two gun-wolves drew Winchesters from saddle sheaths and jacked cartridges into the firing chambers.

Olsen took the telescope from his saddlebags, extended it, and lifted it to his right eye. Squinting through the lens, he focused the glass on the dark shapes at the base of that dust cloud. As they grew larger and came into better view, he sighed in relief. He lowered the glass and called, "They're white men, not Apaches!"

"Must be more of the boss's crew," Van Slyke said. "Come on, Navasota, let's find out for sure."

They rode around the skirmish line and went to meet the newcomers. A few minutes later they were back with a dozen more hard-featured men in range clothes. One of them actually *was* an Indian, not white, a hawk-faced man wearing a round-crowned black hat with an eagle feather stuck in its turquoise band. He was a Navajo, Olsen recalled, a tracker and gunhand known simply as Ash. Olsen figured that was short for some heathen gibberish of a name.

"Have the men mount up again, Sergeant," Olsen told Cochran. "We'll be pushing on momentarily."

"Yes, sir," the new sergeant responded.

Van Slyke and Jones rode up with the newcomers. "The boss sent these boys, just like he promised," Van Slyke said. A grin stretched his face and made it look even more like a skull. "Reckon we've got enough guns now to take on the whole Apache nation if we need to."

"I think you're exaggerating," Olsen said, "since the United States Army hasn't yet been able to run all the savages to ground."

"That's because those fools back in Washington have some loco idea about pacifyin' 'em," Van Slyke said. "What they really need is killin', and we're mighty good at that."

Olsen wasn't going to debate military and political strategy with this hired gun, especially since he agreed with him. The only solution for the Indian problem that would work in the long run would be to wipe out all the savages. The world would be a better place if that were to be accomplished.

Instead he changed the subject by asking, "Are the tracks we've been following still leading in the same direction?"

"Yeah, up into the mountains. There are some high canyons there that have water and grass for horses—"

Van Slyke stopped short and lifted his head, cocking it slightly to the side in a listening attitude. Olsen knew why, too, because he heard the same thing himself.

Gunshots in the distance, a whole slew of them. Maybe not enough for a war, but definitely plenty for a battle.

"That's them!" he said. "It has to be. MacDonald and the Jensen boys and the rest of them got their hands on some guns somehow, and they're trying to break free from the Apaches."

Cochran rode up hurriedly and asked, "What are your orders, Lieutenant?"

"We'll follow those shots." Olsen wheeled his horse and waved his arm. "Column . . . *ho!*"

A bullet tugged on the sleeve of Ace's shirt as he and Chance retreated up the slope, but that was as close as any of the Apache slugs came to the Jensen brothers. When they reached the top, they dived into the cluster of boulders and pine trees that filled a slight depression about fifty yards in diameter. Around the other sides of that little bowl rose steep, rocky walls bare of vegetation.

Ace tipped his head back and saw more trees up on the rimrock seventy or eighty feet above them. As Chance had said, those walls looked like they could be climbed by strong, agile young men—but not by Evelyn or wounded men like MacDonald and Driscoll.

"We can make a good fight of it here," he said. "They can't come up that slope without being exposed to our fire."

"Yeah, we've got the high ground, all right," Chance agreed. Ace knew the enthusiastic tone in his brother's voice was just to make it sound like their situation wasn't as hopeless as it really was.

MacDonald wasn't fooled for a second. "We've got two rifles and a limited amount of ammunition. No food or water. Doesn't look to me like we've got a chance in Hades." He glared at Ace. "You should've left me down there with both rifles and all the bullets. I could've held 'em off for a while."

"What good would that do?" Driscoll asked. "We'd still be trapped here!"

"You and me and Crawford, maybe," he said, referring to one of the wounded troopers. "But these youngsters *might* be able to climb out of this hole."

"No," Evelyn said as she looked at the rock walls. "I . . . I couldn't." She shook her head vehemently. "I just couldn't."

"It might be the only way you'll get out of here alive," Chance told her. "If you want to give it a try, I'll help you."

"I'm terrified of heights," Evelyn insisted. Her voice trembled. "I always have been. It was difficult enough just climbing up here." She clutched Chance's arm. "Please don't make me!"

Ace and Chance looked at each other. Trying to make that climb was probably suicide, anyway. And Jensens always preferred fighting to running . . .

"All right," Chance said. "We'll stay here and see what happens." He smiled. "I've always believed that somewhere, a miracle comes true every day."

And that was exactly what they would need.

MacDonald sat down on one of the rocks and grimaced. Evelyn said, "Would . . . would you like for me to take a look at your wound, Sergeant?"

Before MacDonald could answer, Driscoll protested, "Nobody's done anything about this blasted arrow in my shoulder for more than a day now!"

"That arrow needs more attention than we can give it, Lieutenant," Ace said. "You'll just have to hang on until we get out of this."

Driscoll sat down, too, and passed a shaky hand

over his face. "I already have a fever. It's going to kill me. I know it is."

Evelyn ignored him and went over to sit beside MacDonald. He shook his head, though, and said, "Forget it. There's nothing you can do for me, and I'd just as soon not have anybody pokin' around at that wound."

"But I can at least look at it—"

"I said leave it alone!"

"Hey!" Chance objected. "Watch your mouth, MacDonald. The lady's just trying to help you."

MacDonald scowled. "Why in blazes would any of you try to help me? I'm the reason we're here. Well, along with that snake Olsen and your crazy father, miss."

"He's not crazy," Evelyn said. "Just . . . just overcome with grief . . ."

"And we're all in this together, MacDonald," Ace said. "No need to worry about settling grudges when it looks like the Apaches may do it for us."

"If I could, I'd leave all of you here and get away," MacDonald growled. "The savages could have the whole blamed lot of you."

He didn't really sound like he meant it, though. Desperate circumstances made for unexpected allies.

And these circumstances were about to get more desperate, because the other trooper—Crawford, MacDonald had called him—was kneeling behind one of the rocks watching the lower slope and the canyon, and he called out in alarm, "Here they come!"

CHAPTER THIRTY-FOUR

Ace and Chance had been thumbing fresh rounds into the Winchesters while they talked. About half the loops on the bandolier Ace held were still filled. They could put up a good fight—for a while.

But it would be dark soon, and when night fell, they wouldn't be able to see the Apaches sneaking up on them. That was when the main attack would come, Ace thought as he hurried over to where Crawford was kneeling behind the rocks. This thrust was probably just to feel them out.

Chance dropped to a knee beside his brother. "Where are they?" he asked as he brought the rifle to his shoulder.

"There in that clump of brush," Crawford replied, pointing. "I just saw something movin' around in there."

Ace frowned. "So you're not even sure what you saw was Apaches?"

Before Crawford could answer, muzzle flame spurted from the gloom down the slope, in the brush the trooper had indicated. A slug whined off a rock somewhere nearby, and the next instant more shots rang out.

"Get your heads down!" Ace called to the others. He and Chance hunkered low behind the rocks. Crawford threw himself belly down on the ground. Slugs whipped through the air and ricocheted wickedly.

The shooting went on for several long seconds, then died away and left an echoing silence behind. Chance started to raise up and return the fire, but Ace said, "Let them burn powder. We'll need ours later."

"Yeah, you're right," Chance said grudgingly. "But I don't like it."

"Neither do I."

After a few minutes, the Apaches thundered another volley up the slope. Again, the fugitives stayed low and hoped that no stray bullets or ricochets would penetrate the little bowl. It was a harrowing experience. In a lull between shots, Ace heard Driscoll whimpering again, along with MacDonald cursing the wounded, terrified surgeon.

A rock rattled somewhere nearby, and Ace glanced up to see a figure looming out of the shadows. The Apache warrior let out a bloodcurdling cry as he launched himself at Ace and Chance. Ace tipped the Winchester up and fired one-handed.

The bullet flung the Apache backward, where he collided with another warrior who had crept up the slope unseen while the barrage of shots had everyone keeping their head down. Chance came up on his knees and shot that man, who was so close that the tongue of flame that licked out from the

Winchester's muzzle almost touched his chest. He flew backward down the slope as well.

So they weren't going to wait for full dark after all, Ace thought as he levered the rifle. Movement caught his eye and he swung the barrel to the right to fire at another shape hurtling toward them. That warrior staggered but didn't fall. In fact, he threw himself over the rock behind which Ace crouched and crashed into him, bashing him over backward.

The impact knocked the breath out of Ace and left him stunned, but only for a split second. As the Apache raised his arm over his head, Ace recovered his senses enough to see the knife gripped in the man's hand. He jerked his head to the side as the warrior struck. The blade swept past his ear and threw sparks as it hit the rocky ground. The Winchester was trapped between Ace and his attacker, so he couldn't bring the rifle to bear.

Then the crushing weight went away abruptly. An even larger shadow loomed above Ace. It took him a second to realize that was Vince MacDonald. The renegade sergeant had grabbed hold of the Apache and lifted him off of Ace. With a grunt of effort, MacDonald hoisted the kicking, flailing man above his head and threw him down the slope, where he slammed into two more warriors and knocked them off their feet.

Ace pushed himself back up. Chance was still firing, sweeping his rifle back and forth as he worked the lever and triggered. Ace joined in and sprayed the slope with lead.

It wasn't enough to break the back of the charge. Warriors swarmed over the rocks into the bowl. Ace heard Ndolkah's shouts urging them on. He emptied the Winchester and saw several more men fall before the deadly hail of bullets, but for every warrior that fell, two more took his place.

MacDonald waded into them with his bare hands, roaring his defiance. He grabbed men, flung them away, caught others by the head and broke their necks with a savage twist of his powerful arms. His hammer-like fists lashed out, broke jaws, and sent warriors flying.

Ace and Chance used their empty rifles as clubs, slashing back and forth around them. The Apaches could have stood off and riddled them with bullets, but their hate led them to want to kill the Jensen brothers up close, so they could see Ace and Chance suffer. Clearly, though, they hadn't counted on the brothers being such deadly fighters.

Behind Ace, Chance, and MacDonald, deeper in the bowl, Crawford had scuttled backward to join Evelyn and Driscoll. He grabbed Evelyn, thrust her behind him, and said, "I'll protect you, ma'am!"

He had nothing with which to protect her, though. One of the warriors got past the bottleneck in the rocks and charged at them, howling in rage. The man slashed at Crawford with a knife. Crawford jerked back, grabbed the warrior's wrist, and struggled with him, trying to gain possession of the blade.

While that fight was going on, another Apache headed for Driscoll, who had backed against a tree and stood there sobbing with fear. The warrior leered, obviously anticipating an easy kill.

As he reached Driscoll, though, the lieutenant summoned up what courage he had left and did something unexpected. He grabbed the shaft of the arrow in his shoulder and ripped it free, spraying blood from the wound that had just been torn open even larger. Driscoll turned the arrow and thrust it out in front of him with all the strength he had left.

The flint head caught the Apache in the throat and drove deep, the penetration aided by the warrior's own momentum. The man stopped short, made a grotesque gagging sound, and then reeled backward as he pawed feebly at the arrow lodged fatally in his throat.

Driscoll fell to his knees, blood pouring from his wounded shoulder now. He raised a hand toward it, but before he could do any more, another warrior appeared in front of him and slammed a knife into his chest. The blade went in all the way up to the hilt. Driscoll opened his mouth in a soundless cry. The Apache ripped the knife free and stabbed Driscoll again and yet again. On his knees, Driscoll leaned back against the tree behind him. He died that way, still upright, with his head falling forward and hanging limply over his ruined chest.

Ace, Chance, and MacDonald were still battling fiercely, surrounded by warriors determined to kill them. Blood dripped from several cuts the brothers had received in the fighting, but they hadn't been wounded seriously—yet. It was only a matter of time before they were overwhelmed, though.

Ace heard Evelyn scream. He twisted in that direction, saw one of the Apaches striking down Crawford, who appeared to have been trying to protect the girl. A knife ripped across the trooper's throat, spilling a dark flood over his chest. The warrior reached for

Evelyn next. He probably wouldn't kill her, but in his blood lust, there was no telling what he might do.

Ace swung the Winchester and shattered the stock on the skull of an Apache, which also broke under the impact. Clutching the broken rifle, Ace ran toward Evelyn. He hit the warrior from behind, swinging the rifle and crushing the man's skull with the breech. He would keep whaling away with it until nothing was left but the barrel if he had to, he thought as he grabbed Evelyn's arm. She was sinking toward the ground in horror.

"Are you hurt?" he asked, raising his voice to be heard over the tumult in the bowl.

"No, I . . . I don't think so—"

She screamed again as she looked over his shoulder. Ace whirled and knocked aside the knife being thrust at him. The tip raked a fiery line across his ribs. He slashed the broken rifle across the warrior's face and sent him to the ground.

Chance broke free of the struggle and raced to the side of Ace and Evelyn. He said, "Get back against the big rock. Ace and I will hold them off!"

They were all doomed, Ace knew, but he and his brother would fight to the bitter end. As Jensens, they couldn't do anything else. They stood shoulder to shoulder in front of Evelyn as she backed against one of the boulders.

"Look!" Ace suddenly exclaimed. "It's Ndolkah!"

The Apache chief had entered the fray. He was wrestling with MacDonald, who was so covered with blood that his clothing appeared black rather than gray. MacDonald was taller and heavier than Ndolkah, but he was badly injured and rapidly losing his strength. He had his left hand locked around Ndolkah's right wrist, trying to hold off the knife in the chief's hand. MacDonald tried to get his right hand on Ndolkah's throat, but the Apache fended it off.

Then Ndolkah hooked a foot behind MacDonald's left ankle and jerked that leg out from under him. MacDonald lost his grip on Ndolkah's wrist and fell. Ndolkah's lips drew back from his teeth in a grimace that was half savage grin, half hate-filled snarl. He raised the blade to strike . . .

Then stumbled forward as a gun boomed once, twice, three times behind him. Ace saw the muzzle flashes in the gloom. The slugs crashed into Ndolkah's back and hammered him forward into oblivion. Men poured over the top of the slope. Ace saw their wide-brimmed hats and knew they weren't Apaches. Colt flame bloomed in the gathering darkness, and with each swift shot, another warrior fell.

The reinforcements weren't totally unexpected. Ace had hoped that a rescue party from Fort Gila would catch up to them, and it appeared that was what had happened. He heard more shots from down in the canyon and realized fighting was going on down there, too. He would have thought that most of the warriors were up here, trying to catch the escaping prisoners, but maybe . . .

A thought struck him and made a chill go down his back. There were women and children down there in the Apache village, and despite everything that had happened, even the torture of Shoemaker and Barnes, he didn't want them massacred.

Right now, though, he turned to Evelyn, who had

slumped to the ground next to the boulder, and said, "Looks like it's going to be all right—"

"Ace." Chance's voice was sharp with warning.

Ace looked back around and saw a man in cavalry uniform striding toward them with a revolver thrust out in front of him. Lieutenant Frank Olsen smiled coldly at them and said, "You Jensen boys have led us on a merry chase, but it's over now."

CHAPTER THIRTY-FIVE

The Apache women had built cooking fires as evening approached, and those flames still leaped and crackled merrily. The scenes they illuminated were anything but merry, though. The massacre Ace had worried about had indeed taken place.

The bloody, huddled corpses of women and children littered the ground all over the village, along with the bodies of the few warriors who had been down here when Olsen and the other men arrived, shooting and yelling, blasting some of the Apaches while riding down others and trampling them into something unrecognizable. Evelyn couldn't bear to look at the carnage and kept her eyes downcast and almost closed as she stumbled along between Ace and Chance.

MacDonald was behind them, staggering from weakness. All four survivors had their hands tied again, but their feet were loose so they could walk. Ace was a little surprised Olsen hadn't gone ahead and shot him and his brother, along with MacDonald, and just taken Evelyn back to the fort.

He supposed Olsen believed he could get some more work out of them on that road of his.

The combined force of cavalry troopers and Eugene Howden-Smyth's hired guns had lost three men during the fighting, all of them soldiers. Taking the Apaches by surprise as they had, they had wiped out Ndolkah and all his band. As they returned to their horses, Olsen said, "I want to make camp for the night somewhere else. The air here smells too much like freshly spilled blood."

"Reckon there's a good reason for that," a gaunt gunman said with a wolfish grin. "What do you want us to do with all them redskin bodies, Lieutenant?"

"Why do anything with them?" Olsen snapped. "The scavengers will take care of that."

"My thinkin' exactly," the gunman agreed. He called to the other hired killers. "Mount up, boys."

"You'll ride with me," Olsen said to Evelyn. "I assure you, I have no lecherous motives. Eugene has his eye on you, and I wouldn't interfere with that. But I intend to keep you safe until we get back and I put you in his hands."

Ace said, "Sergeant MacDonald needs a horse. As bad a shape as he's in, he can't walk very far."

"Speak for yourself," MacDonald growled. "I'm fine."

He was far from fine, obviously, but he was too stubborn to admit that.

"You'll all be mounted, so as not to slow us down," Olsen said. "A couple of my troopers can double up until we make camp. You Jensens can share one of the horses, and MacDonald can have the other. After we've buried the men we lost, well away from here,

you can have their horses. Sergeant Cochran, see
to that."

"Yes, sir," Cochran said.

MacDonald grinned at the man and said, "You're
a sergeant now, Cochran? Well, don't let it go to your
head. The only rank that really matters around here
is Olsen's, and he figures he might as well be king of
the Arizona Territory!"

"King of Arizona," Olsen repeated with a smile.
"You know, I rather like the sound of that, Vince. Perhaps I'll work on that, one of these days. But until
then, I want to get away from this slaughterhouse."

Ace couldn't argue with that sentiment, no matter
how despicable the man who had uttered it.

Within minutes, the whole group was mounted
and heading back down out of the canyon. Night
had fallen, but the light from millions of stars that had
winked into existence in the black heavens was
enough for them to see where they were going.

They rode for about half an hour before Olsen
called a halt and declared that they would make
camp. They were on a broad, grassy bench, and Ace
recalled from the earlier trip as captives of the
Apaches that at the far side of that level ground was a
steep drop-off with a trail that zigzagged back and
forth down it. Trying to navigate that path by starlight
probably wasn't a good idea. The drop-off wasn't that
high, but a misstep could still cause a fatal fall.

"Build a good big fire," Olsen ordered. "We don't
have to worry about those savages anymore."

He was probably right about that. Ndolkah's band
wasn't the only one lurking in the mountains and

foothills, but in all likelihood, there weren't any others close by.

The four prisoners sat on the ground with two troopers nearby to guard them. One of the hired guns, a stocky man with a shotgun tucked under his arm, sauntered over to join them.

"No offense to you blue-bellies," he said with a cocky grin that showed he didn't care if he offended them or not, "but I'm gonna keep an eye on these prisoners, too. They've made a habit of gettin' away from you soldier boys, and I know my boss don't want that happenin' again."

"Please," Evelyn said, "Sergeant MacDonald needs medical attention—"

"That's none of my business," the gunman interrupted her. "Anyway, we ain't got a doc along, and from what I understand, the post surgeon from Fort Gila is one of the fellas who got killed up there in that fight with the Apaches. So you're outta luck, MacDonald."

"It wasn't me who asked for help," MacDonald growled. "The whole bunch of you can go to blazes. I wouldn't let any of you skunks touch me."

The gunman laughed. "Ain't none of us wantin' to!" He leered at Evelyn. "This little gal, on the other hand—"

"Hush that kind of talk, mister," one of the troopers snapped. "This is our commanding officer's daughter, and she's a lady."

"You don't give me orders." The shotgunner's voice hardened. "You best remember that."

An uneasy silence fell over the group. After a while,

one of the troopers brought over plates of beans and bacon and cups of coffee. The prisoners' hands were freed so they could eat and drink, but several of Howden-Smyth's men stood by with drawn guns the whole time, so any attempt to get away was impossible. After supper, they were tied up again, except for Evelyn. It was Lieutenant Olsen's order that she remain unbound, one of the soldiers explained.

Olsen himself walked over a short time after that. He took off his hat, smiled at Evelyn, and said, "Miss Sughrue, there's no need for you to spend any more time with these men. MacDonald kidnapped you, after all, and intended to use you as a hostage, so I'm sure you don't want anything more to do with him. I apologize for having you restrained. It was more for simplicity's sake than anything else, until we got well away from those Apaches."

"I thought all the Apaches were dead," Evelyn said. A shudder ran through her. "From what I saw in the village, I can't imagine that any of them survived."

"They didn't," Olsen said, his voice harder now. "We made certain of that. An unpleasant thing, but necessary. Now more than ever, though, any other savages in the vicinity ought to understand that they need to leave the army, and Mr. Howden-Smyth's mine, alone in the future." He smiled again, put his hat on, and held out a hand to her. "Please, come with me. I've had the men set up a shelter for you. It's not an actual tent, it's made out of blankets and some rope and poles, but it'll afford you a bit of privacy, at least."

Evelyn hesitated. "I want medical attention for my friends."

"What friends?" Olsen asked, frowning. "These deserters?"

"Ace and Chance aren't deserters! They're not even in the army."

"A matter still being worked out among the proper authorities. But in any event, they still face serious charges in Packsaddle, and since Marshal Glennon has accompanied our party, they're his responsibilty." Olsen looked at the Jensen brothers and shook his head. "Anyway, they don't appear to be seriously injured. A few bumps and bruises and scrapes, that's all."

"Sergeant MacDonald *is* seriously injured. He's lost a great deal of blood—"

"Blast it, stop tryin' to look out for me, woman," MacDonald said. "The lieutenant's right. You were never anything but a hostage to me, a way to keep your crazy pa from comin' after us."

Ace could tell that the harsh words hurt Evelyn, but she said stubbornly, "You're still a human being and deserve decent treatment."

"I'll have someone take a look at MacDonald's injuries, if that will make you feel better," Olsen said. He beckoned to Evelyn again. "Now, please, if you'll come away from here . . ."

She looked at Ace and Chance. Ace nodded, and Chance said, "Yeah, go with him, Evelyn. It's all right. We'll be fine."

"If you're sure . . ."

"We're sure."

She sighed, took Olsen's hand, and let him help her to her feet. She cast a glance over her shoulder as the lieutenant led her away, and Ace could tell that she hoped she wasn't making a big mistake.

"She'll be better off with him," Chance said quietly, so that the men guarding them wouldn't overhear.

"She's important to him," Ace said. "He'll see to it that nothing happens to her."

MacDonald said coldly, "Yeah, she's important to him, all right. Olsen's gonna trade her to that Britisher when he gets back to the fort. Wouldn't surprise me a bit if he made Howden-Smyth agree to cut him in for a bigger share of the mine's profits before he hands over the girl."

"Evelyn doesn't understand just how crooked Olsen is," Chance said. "She still thinks that because he's an officer, he must be honorable."

MacDonald scoffed. "That polecat wouldn't know honor if it came up and bit him."

Ace said, "Do you really think he's going to force Evelyn to marry Howden-Smyth?"

"That's what the Englishman wants. And he's got the gold mine, so he's got the leverage to get what he wants." MacDonald made a face. "Actually, I reckon the gal will be lucky if there's a preacher involved. Howden-Smyth could just take her and keep her locked up in that big house of his, up at the mine, and do whatever he wants with her."

"We can't allow that," Chance said.

MacDonald laughed. "How are you plannin' to stop it, kid?"

"We have to get away," Ace said. "If we could just

get to Major Sughrue and make him see what's actually going on . . ."

His voice trailed off as MacDonald leaned forward and started breathing harder. "Sergeant?" Ace said. "What—"

MacDonald toppled over on his side, apparently unconscious—or worse.

CHAPTER THIRTY-SIX

With his hands tied behind his back, it wasn't easy, but Ace scrambled over to MacDonald and leaned down toward him.

"Sergeant! Sergeant, are you all right?" That was a stupid question under the circumstances, Ace knew, but it was what people said at times like this.

The answer took him completely by surprise. MacDonald opened his eyes just a slit and whispered, "Act like I'm dead, you idiot."

"Sergeant—"

"Raise a ruckus, and then when everybody's looking at me, you and your brother back off and make a break for it." MacDonald had his face turned away from the guards, and his lips were barely moving anyway. "I got my hands just about loose—those troopers never could tie a blasted knot to save their lives—and I'll keep 'em occupied while you and Chance get outta here."

"But you—"

"I'm done for, kid, and I know it. I'm startin' to feel empty inside, like I been hollowed out. Let me go out makin' things worse for that snake Olsen. And you two . . . do what you can for . . . the girl . . ."

Ace could tell now that MacDonald really was on the verge of dying. And what the sergeant said made sense. He was hurt too badly, had lost too much blood to last. There was a very good chance he wouldn't make it until morning. So if he wanted to give the Jensen brothers one last chance to save themselves and Evelyn . . .

"Thank you, Sergeant," Ace said.

"Shut up . . . and make it . . . look good . . ."

"What's going on over there?" one of the guards demanded.

Ace looked up and said loudly, "It's Sergeant MacDonald. I think he's dying!"

He didn't know if any of the soldiers would care about that. Howden-Smyth's hired guns surely wouldn't. But he called loudly enough that Evelyn ought to hear, and since Olsen had already promised her that someone would see about MacDonald's wounds, that ought to get some action.

It did. A few moments later, Olsen himself strode toward the prisoners, trailed by several troopers. Ace scooted back over next to Chance as the lieutenant approached.

"Is MacDonald—" Chance began.

"He's going to provide a distraction for us," Ace said. "Get ready to make a run for it down that trail."

Chance didn't have time to ask anything else. Olsen stalked angrily up to MacDonald and demanded, "Well, is he dead?"

MacDonald moaned and seemed to be trying to

say something. Frowning, Olsen leaned closer.

"So you're *not* dead. That's a shame. What are you trying to say?"

Instead of answering, MacDonald must have summoned every bit of strength he had left. He suddenly rolled toward Olsen. His big hands shot up and caught hold of the lieutenant's leg. MacDonald heaved, and the startled Olsen flew up into the air, yelling and waving his arms.

In a continuation of that movement, MacDonald surged to his feet and lunged at the closest trooper. He got his hands on the man's rifle and rammed the butt into the soldier's stomach.

Olsen landed on his back with the wind knocked out of him, too stunned and breathless to shout any orders.

At the same time, Ace and Chance leaped to their feet and sprinted toward the steep trail leading down to the lower elevations. One of the hired gunmen yelled, "Hey! Stop those two!" and shots blasted.

Once they were out of the circle of firelight, though, Ace and Chance weren't very good targets, especially moving as fast as they were. Bullets whipped and whined around them, too close for comfort, but none of them found the Jensen brothers.

The landscape fell away in a sweeping black gulf as Ace and Chance reached the top of the trail. They paused and glanced back toward the camp. A big knot of struggling men marked MacDonald's location. MacDonald flailed around with a rifle he had grabbed from one of the men, but as they fell back, space opened up around him and Olsen and several of the hired guns blasted away at him.

The multitude of orange muzzle flashes split the night. Bullets pounded into MacDonald's burly form, driving into his chest and making him jitter backward in a macabre dance. As much blood as he had lost in the past couple of days, it almost seemed impossible that he had more to lose, but dark crimson welled from the wounds.

That was the last Ace and Chance saw of him, because pursuers were running after them, and Colt flame still spurted in their direction, too. Time for them to light a shuck out of here.

Ace bounded down the trail, taking as much of it as he could with each leap. Chance was right behind him. With their hands tied, keeping their balance was difficult, and Ace was all too aware that it would be easy to slip and fall and tumble out of control down the slope.

More shots sounded from the top of the trail. Firing downhill in the dark made accuracy impossible, but if their pursuers sent enough lead in their direction, some of the flying slugs might find their mark. A lucky bullet could kill just like a well-aimed one.

"Ace!" Chance called. "Jump down from level to level!"

"What? Are you loco?"

"We'll get down a lot quicker either way!"

He had a point there, Ace thought grimly. He skidded to a halt and looked over the edge of the trail. The next zigzag was down there somewhere in the darkness. Not too far down—maybe a dozen feet. He could stand a drop like that.

A bullet zinged overhead. Ace muttered and jumped.

He landed hard, sooner than he expected, on a slope where it was impossible to remain upright. He went down and rolled, and as he did, he heard Chance's *"Ooof!"* as he landed a few feet away. Both of them came up on their feet.

"We lived through it!" Chance said. "Let's do it again!"

"Why not?" Ace said. Once again, they leaped out and dropped through the darkness.

The landing wasn't quite as much a surprise this time, but Ace fell again anyway. He slid and came to a stop with his legs hanging out into empty space. Guns were still going off above them, but as far as he could tell, none of the bullets were coming anywhere close now. And he could see trees not too far below them, so he knew that they were almost to the bottom.

He pulled his legs in and struggled to his feet. "Come on," he said to Chance, who had landed nearby. "If we can get into those trees, we can lose them."

"That's what I was thinking. And then we'll get these blasted ropes off!"

Ace hoped so. He had spent altogether too much time tied up recently. He didn't like the feeling at all.

As they charged on down the trail, the shooting stopped, probably because the gunmen couldn't see them anymore. Shouts drifted down from above.

Men were giving chase now, probably thinking that they didn't have anything to worry about since Ace and Chance were unarmed and had their hands tied behind their backs.

If they got a chance, the Jensen brothers would show those hombres just how wrong they were.

They reached level ground and dashed into the pines but had to slow down so they wouldn't run full-tilt into the tree trunks. The shadows were so thick it was utterly black in here. Ace grunted as he bounced off a rough-barked trunk.

"It'll take them a few minutes to find us," he said as he came to a stop. "We'd better try to get those ropes off while we can."

"Good idea," Chance said, unseen in the darkness but close by. They fumbled around until they found each other, then turned so that their backs were to each other.

"I'll see if I can get you untied—" Ace began.

"No, let me try first with you," Chance interrupted. "I've spent so much time handling cards that my fingers are a mite more deft than yours, I'm thinking. No offense."

"None taken," Ace assured him. He held out his bound hands from his back. "Go ahead."

A moment later, he felt Chance's fingers working at the ropes. Chance was right. All the hours he had spent shuffling and dealing the pasteboards had given his fingers enough strength and dexterity that he was able to work the knots loose in a matter of minutes. As the ropes fell away from Ace's wrists, he pulled his arms back in front of him and began rolling his shoulders and flexing his fingers.

Somewhere not too far off in the darkness, a man called, "They've got to be in here somewhere."

"Shut up," another man responded. "You want them to know where *we* are?"

A chuckle came from the first man. "What does it matter? It's not like they have guns."

"Yet," Ace whispered to Chance. "Turn around and let me get to work on those knots."

The sounds of the men searching through the trees grew louder as Ace fumbled with the rope. His pulse hammered in his head. He forced himself to breathe slowly and regularly and concentrate on what he was doing. The knots began to loosen, and once they did, he needed only moments more to finish freeing Chance's hands.

"Those two are coming in this direction," he breathed.

"Yeah, and there are probably more out here searching for us, too," Chance replied. "So we need to take care of them without any racket, if we can."

Each of them put his back to a tree trunk, about ten feet apart. The rustling footsteps weren't far off now. The moon had started to rise, and a little of the silvery illumination penetrated the pine branches. Ace's eyes had adjusted to the point that he could make out vague shapes.

Because of that, he was able to see when the two men walked between the trees where he and Chance waited. One of the searchers whispered, "I don't know why Olsen cares so much about findin' those two. They're afoot, and they'll never make it back to the fort. Even if they do, he can just have 'em shot as deserters."

"I reckon they've given him so much trouble already, he's bound and determined to get rid of them. Anyway, Chet's the one who told us to go along with Olsen's orders, and I don't want to argue with a gunhand like him—"

They couldn't afford to wait any longer. The two gunmen were in perfect position. Ace and Chance leaped through the shadows at them.

CHAPTER THIRTY-SEVEN

Even though the distance was short, the men heard Ace and Chance coming and tried to turn around to meet the attack. Ace lowered his shoulder and rammed into his man from the side, knocking him off his feet. Ace's momentum carried him to the ground, too.

He threw his left arm out blindly. His forearm struck the barrel of the gunman's rifle and knocked it to the side. Ace grabbed the barrel with that hand and hung on while he estimated where the gunman's face was and threw a punch with his right. He knew he might break his hand if he judged wrong and hit the ground instead.

His fist crashed into flesh and bone and he felt the hot spurt of blood across his knuckles from a pulped nose. The man bucked wildly underneath him. Ace tried to hang on, but he was thrown off to one side.

He took the rifle with him when he went, though, wrenching it out of the gunman's grip.

The man leaped to his feet and clawed at the gun on his hip. Ace rolled over and came up on his knees in time to see that and strike first. Since he had hold of the rifle's barrel, he lashed out with the stock, driving it into the gunman's groin.

The man forgot about pulling his revolver and doubled over as he moaned in pain. Ace lunged up and whipped the rifle around. The stock caught the man in the jaw this time and laid him out cold.

A few yards away, Chance had tackled his man around the waist and knocked him off his feet. They rolled across the ground, which was littered with pine needles, and struggled over the gunman's rifle. Chance had both hands on it, but his opponent clung to it stubbornly. As the man panted with exertion, Chance smelled raw whiskey on his breath. The Jensen brothers escaping had ruined a perfectly good night of drinking and carousing after slaughtering all those Apaches.

They both clambered onto their feet as they continued to wrestle over the rifle. They staggered back and forth. Chance didn't know how Ace was doing, but no shots had rung out so far. Chance wanted to keep it that way.

The men hadn't yelled for help, either. He supposed the attack by supposedly helpless men had surprised them enough that they weren't thinking straight yet. But they would recover their wits soon enough, Chance knew.

In fact, he heard the man he was battling take a sharply indrawn breath and knew the hombre was about to yell. Chance lunged forward, driving hard with his feet. That forced the gunman backward, and Chance kept bulling ahead until he forced the man into one of the tree trunks. He heard a solid *thunk!* as the back of the gunman's head hit the rough-barked trunk. The man said, "Uh!" and his knees buckled. His hands slipped off the rifle.

Chance lifted the stock into the man's jaw. The man slithered loose-limbed down the trunk. He was out.

Chance turned, saw another shadowy figure on its feet, and hazarded a whisper. "Ace?"

"Yeah. Is your man down?"

"He sure is. Yours?"

"Out cold, and I've got his rifle."

"Let's get their Colts," Chance said.

That sounded like an excellent idea to Ace. He bent, found the buckle on the gunbelt of the man he had knocked out, and unfastened it. A moment later, as he strapped the belt around his own hips, he felt the familiar and reassuring weight of a six-gun against his thigh.

"That's more like it," he said.

"What now?" Chance asked.

That question made Ace frown. "Olsen has close to thirty men, and he's going to be keeping Evelyn mighty close to him. Even if we took them by surprise, there's no way we can outgun a force like that and get her away from them."

"I don't reckon there's any point in wondering about MacDonald."

Ace shook his head in the darkness. "I saw probably half a dozen shots hit him. There's no way he survived. But at least he went out fighting, like he wanted to."

"I guess he wasn't *all* bad . . ."

"Mostly he was," Ace said. "But you're right, not all."

They stood there in silence for a second, until Chance said, "If we can't rescue Evelyn, that just leaves getting back to the fort and trying to talk sense into Major Sughrue, like you said earlier."

"It's our only shot," Ace agreed.

"Can we make it on foot? And get there before Olsen does?"

Honestly, Ace didn't see how they could, especially the second part of Chance's question. But they had no other option except to try.

"If we don't get to the fort in time, we'll circle around it and head for Packsaddle. We need to find a telegraph and get word to Washington."

"Might as well get started, then."

They trotted off into the darkness, trusting to instinct to guide them in the right direction.

They traveled most of the night, pausing only occasionally to rest. Leaving Evelyn behind, knowing that she was in Frank Olsen's hands, was disturbing, but they also knew that getting themselves killed trying to shoot it out with Olsen's men wouldn't do Evelyn any good.

When the sky lightened enough with the approach of dawn for them to look around at their surroundings, Chance asked, "I don't suppose you have any idea where we are?"

"Not exactly, but I know we're headed in the right direction." Ace pointed to the south, where foothills rolled into the distance. "I know the road Olsen is building is in that direction, so Howden-Smyth's mine must be that way." He swung his arm back to the west. "Which means the fort is southeast of us, and I can tell from where the sun's fixing to come up in a little while that we're aimed toward it."

Chance turned and squinted back in the direction they had come from. "I haven't seen or heard anybody on our trail, but that doesn't mean they're not back there. What are the odds of Olsen sending somebody to try to track us?"

"Pretty good, I'd say," Ace replied. "Or pretty bad, depending on how you look at it. But I wouldn't be surprised if he did, I can tell you that."

They moved on, because there was really nothing else they could do at this point, and a short time later came to a small creek where they were able to drink. Their bellies were getting empty by now, but there was nothing they could do about that. Ace spotted a couple of rabbits and could have easily knocked them over with the Winchester he had taken away from the gunman, but he didn't want to risk a shot giving away their position.

They paused to rest again at mid-morning, not far from a gully that angled across the landscape. They were nearly out of the foothills now. Ace looked out over the rolling, trackless, semi-arid plains and didn't see anything moving.

"I wonder if there are any ranches around here where we could get some horses," Chance said.

"Not likely. This isn't really ranching country, as far as I—"

Ace didn't finish his statement, because at that instant, the crack of a rifle shot and the whistle of a bullet past his ear sounded simultaneously. He whirled around and saw three riders burst out of a stand of trees fifty yards away. They rode hell-bent for leather toward the Jensen brothers, firing as they came. Powder smoke billowed from their guns.

Ace flung the Winchester to his shoulder and slammed out two shots toward the attackers. Beside him, Chance did likewise. As the echoes filled the air, Chance shouted, "Head for that gully over there! It's the only cover around here!"

He was right about that. Ace didn't see any trees or rocks nearby. He turned, raced to the gully, and slid down its bank. Chance leaped into it beside him.

The gully was only about five feet deep, so Ace and Chance had to crouch as they flattened themselves against the bank and thrust their rifles over the edge. "We don't have a lot of bullets," Ace said. "Pick your shots."

"They're splitting up!" Chance said. "They're going to try to flank us!"

Ace saw that. It was good strategy, too. One of the men galloped straight at them while the other two veered left and right.

The man in the center wore a black, round-crowned hat with a turquoise band and a feather sticking up. Ace recalled seeing him with the gunmen Eugene Howden-Smyth had sent to join forces with Olsen. He was an Indian—his coppery, hawklike face made that obvious—but not an Apache and except for his hat he dressed more like a white gun-wolf. Ace would have been willing to bet this man was the one who had tracked him and Chance.

Ace drew a bead on him and squeezed the trigger, but the Indian's instincts must have warned him. Either that or it was blind luck, but he jerked his horse aside and Ace knew his shot had missed. He jacked another round in the chamber but then fell back as the Indian fired and a bullet hit the ground right in front of the gully and kicked dirt and rocks into Ace's face.

Ace heard hoofbeats pounding to his right and rolled in that direction. The man who had flanked them in that direction had gotten his horse down into the gully and was thundering toward the Jensen brothers. Ace fired, hating to kill the man's horse, but from this angle, he didn't have a shot at the rider.

The horse collapsed as the bullet slammed into its chest. Its forelegs folded up and the gunman suddenly found himself catapulted over the animal's head. He landed hard, rolled over a couple of times, and tried to come up on his feet as he clawed at the revolver on his hip, which had somehow stayed in the holster during that wild fall.

Ace shot him in the head, a single shot that drilled through the man's brain and exploded out the back of his skull. The upper half of his body went backward while momentum kept his legs trying to run forward. This resulted in an awkward collapse as the man wound up twisted in death on the gully floor.

There was a bend about twenty yards away in the other direction, so the man approaching on that side had some cover. Slugs slammed into the bank near Chance, and when he threw himself backward and turned that way, he spotted the rifle barrel sticking around the bulge in the gully's bank. The hired gun had dismounted and was using that for cover.

Chance rolled again as a bullet plowed into the ground next to him. He wound up on his belly and fired twice, chewing chunks of dirt away from the bank as he forced the gunman to duck back. Then, leaving the rifle on the ground, he sprang up and sprinted toward the bend. When he saw a flicker of movement, he dived forward. Something tugged at his shirt as another shot blasted. He went down, somersaulted, and came up with the Colt in his hand.

The gun roared and bucked against his palm. He had a clear shot at the man now. The slugs pounded into his chest and drove him back against the bank, pinning him there for a second as if he'd been nailed in place. The rifle he had been firing at Chance slipped from nerveless fingers, and the man pitched to the ground right after it.

That left just the Indian tracker. As if sensing that he was suddenly on his own, he snapped a couple of final shots toward the gully and then reined in, wheeling his horse so he could gallop back the other direction. Ace stood up and tried to draw a bead on the man. The Indian bent forward over his mount's back, making himself a smaller target. Ace fired, but the galloping horse never broke stride and the rider didn't budge.

Chance hurried over and asked, "Did he get away?"

Ace lowered the rifle and frowned as the Indian disappeared back into the trees. "Yeah, looks like it. Which means he'll hightail it back to Olsen and tell him where we were when he found us."

"We'd better not be here if anybody comes back to look for us, then. But that varmint probably figured out that we're heading for Fort Gila. Maybe we'd better consider some other plan, Ace, or we're liable to find Olsen waiting for us."

Ace nodded and was about to agree with that, but the sudden rataplan of hoofbeats that filled the air made both Jensen brothers wheel around and lift their guns. They froze as half a dozen cavalrymen reined to a halt on the other side of the gully and trained Springfield rifles at them.

CHAPTER THIRTY-EIGHT

For a second, Ace thought that some of the troopers who'd been with Olsen had gotten behind them somehow. With the way those soldiers had the drop on them, he and Chance wouldn't be able to shoot their way out of this fix. And if they were captured again, Olsen wouldn't make the same mistake twice. He would go ahead and have them killed, especially if he could do it without letting Evelyn know what had happened.

But just then, an officer rode up beside the troopers and called, "Hold your fire!" To Ace and Chance, he ordered, "You men lower your weapons."

The man wore the insignia of a lieutenant. He was young and lean-faced and Ace had never seen him before. But he wasn't Frank Olsen, and that might make all the difference.

Ace lowered the Winchester but didn't drop it. Chance did likewise. The mounted troopers didn't relax when the Jensen brothers did that, however. They maintained their air of deadly readiness.

From horseback, the officer asked, "Who are you, and what's going on here?"

"I reckon we could ask the same thing of you, mister," Ace said.

The lieutenant's mouth tightened. "I'd say that under the circumstances, I get my answers first. We heard a lot of gunfire." His gaze swung both ways along the gully, taking in the sight of two dead gun-wolves and a dead horse. "Are you responsible for killing these men?"

"It seemed like the thing to do at the time," Chance drawled. "They were doing their best to kill us."

This officer definitely hadn't been with Olsen, and Ace didn't recall seeing him at Fort Gila when the Jensen brothers were there. That might mean he wasn't part of Olsen's crooked scheme. Ace decided they would just have to run the risk of being honest.

"My name is Ace Jensen. This is my brother Chance. Yes, we killed these men, but like my brother said, it was self-defense. They gave us no choice. They're hired guns working for a man named Eugene Howden-Smyth."

"The mine owner?" the lieutenant asked with a frown.

"You know him?"

"I know *of* him. He was mentioned in a report I read. And that report is the reason for me being here." The lieutenant studied Ace and Chance intently. "You say these men worked for Howden-Smyth?"

"That's right."

"Why would they want to kill you? Did you attempt to steal gold from Howden-Smyth's mine?"

Chance snorted in disgust. "We're not gold thieves or outlaws of any sort. It was our bad luck to be forced into working on that blasted road being built between the mine and Fort Gila."

That made the lieutenant's interest perk up even more. "So you know about that road?"

"Mister, we nearly busted our backs breaking rocks on it!"

The officer seemed to make up his mind about something. He said to the troopers, "Lower your weapons, men, but remain alert. Private Otterson, Private Thomas, burial detail. I want these men buried properly. Private Simmons, you stand guard while they're doing that. Private Burton, ride back and fetch the rest of the men."

The troopers saluted and set about carrying out the orders. The lieutenant turned back to Ace and Chance and went on, "Climb up out of there. We need to talk."

"I reckon we do," Ace agreed. Something told him they could trust this young officer. He hoped his instincts weren't letting him down.

A few minutes later, they stood with the now dismounted lieutenant, chewing on some jerky he had offered them from his saddlebags. While they were doing that, the man introduced himself.

"I'm Lieutenant Patrick Slattery. I work for the War Department in Washington. I was sent out here to Arizona Territory, along with a small detail of men, to investigate a rather puzzling situation."

"An army post furnishing the men to build a road to a gold mine owned by an Englishman?" Ace guessed.

Lieutenant Slattery's eyebrows rose in surprise. "That's exactly why I'm here."

"How did you find out about it?"

"The War Department received a report from Major Flint Sughrue, the commanding officer at Fort Gila. It was very matter of fact, detailing the progress on the road he'd been ordered to build, but the thing of it is—"

"Nobody in Washington or anywhere else ever ordered him to build that road," Chance interrupted. He glanced over at Ace. "I guess one of those reports the major sent in slipped past Olsen without him knowing about it."

Ace nodded. "That's the only explanation that makes sense."

"Olsen," Slattery repeated. "You mean Lieutenant Frank Olsen, who's also posted to Fort Gila?"

"That's right," Ace said. "For all practical purposes, he's the commanding officer there now. He's got Major Sughrue buffaloed and going along with whatever he says."

"But that's insane! Why would the major go along with that? And why would Lieutenant Costello allow it? He's supposed to be Major Sughrue's second in command."

"Costello is dead," Ace said flatly. "Before that, he was a prisoner, being forced to work on that road to the mine like quite a few of the other soldiers."

Slattery's expression was grim as he said, "I need to hear more about this . . . this debacle."

For the next few minutes, Ace and Chance filled him in on everything they had heard about and experienced in the past week or so. Lieutenant Slattery's face reflected his disbelief at first. Ace could tell he thought they were crazy, or else lying for some other reason.

But gradually, as they laid out all the details, Ace saw that Slattery was starting to believe them. Reluctantly, granted, but still, he could tell that their story had the ring of truth to it.

Finally, he said, "We were aware that Major Sughrue's wife had passed away, but no one had any idea that her death affected him so strongly."

"Because Olsen didn't let anybody find out," Ace said. "There are probably quite a few men at the fort who don't actually realize how bad the situation is. As far as they know, the major really was ordered to get that road built."

Shaking his head, Slattery said, "Why would Olsen do such a thing? I don't know the man personally, but I looked into his record. I checked the records of all the officers at the fort before I came out here. Olsen appears to have been a decent officer. Nothing really exemplary in the record, but nothing bad, either. How could he . . . why did he . . ."

"We're not sure if he came up with the idea or if Howden-Smyth approached him with it," Ace said, "but I reckon it all comes down to gold. That stuff can make a man do things nobody ever thought he would. It can make him do things *he* never thought he would."

Chance said, "And a fella never really knows what he's capable of until the opportunity is right there in front of him, gleaming and beckoning him on."

Slattery sighed and nodded. "I suppose you're right. I hope you know, however, that I'm still going to have to corroborate your story. I'm not going to accept Lieutenant Olsen's guilt on your word alone."

"You start talking to the men at the fort and you'll find out plenty," Ace said.

"Talk to Evelyn Sughrue, too," Chance added. "She knows all about it now, and she's seen what Olsen is capable of, first hand."

"Like wiping out those Apaches." Slattery shrugged. "Engaging a band of hostiles isn't going to be looked on with disfavor in Washington. Although the number of casualties among the women and children *is* rather disturbing. But I believe everything else you've told me is sufficient justification for taking Lieutenant Olsen into custody while I continue my investigation."

"You mean you're going to arrest him?" Ace asked.

"That's right." Slattery saw the frown on Ace's face and went on, "You don't think that's a good idea?"

"How many men do you have with you, Lieutenant?"

"Nine troopers. The detail including myself is ten men."

"Olsen has at least twice that many who are in on the scheme, I'd say. It's likely they'd back him if it comes to a showdown. Plus there are all the other men who *don't* know the truth but might follow him anyway because they're used to him giving the orders."

"Olsen's mighty slick," Chance put in. "He might convince the whole garrison that *you're* the one in the wrong, Lieutenant. He could say you're some sort of renegade, or a deserter, or something else to turn the men against you. And it's likely that Major Sughrue would believe him and back him up, which would just make things worse."

Slattery looked at the Jensen brothers and said, "Then what *do* you suggest would be an appropriate course of action? And mind you, I'm not in the habit of asking civilians for advice!"

Ace rubbed his chin and said, "Seems to me there's only one thing that might work. Somebody's got to get through to Major Sughrue and let him know what's really going on. It won't be easy to convince him, but if he can grasp that Olsen and Howden-Smyth are the real dangers to his daughter, I'm sure he'll turn on Olsen and the honest troops will follow him. Then when you ride in, you'll be able to arrest Olsen."

"When you say that someone has to talk to Major Sughrue . . . are you talking about yourself and your brother?"

"Well, two men can get into the fort easier than a whole detail, seems like."

"But you're civilians," Slattery argued. "The major is much more likely to believe me. If I show him my credentials from the War Department, his sense of duty will almost compel him to accept the truth. You two will be needed to explain the details to him, though."

"So you're saying all three of us will have to sneak into the fort," Chance said.

"That seems to be the best plan of action."

"We can give it a try," Ace said. "You can leave the rest of your detail somewhere near the fort and arrange a signal for them to come on in."

"Indeed." Slattery looked back and forth between them. "I'd very much like to end this affair without firing a shot, gentlemen."

"So would we, Lieutenant," Ace said.

But at the same time, he thought that was just about the unlikeliest thing he had ever heard.

CHAPTER THIRTY-NINE

When Ash rode back with the news that the Jensen brothers had gotten away, Olsen was tempted to pull his gun and shoot the Navajo right then and there. The furious impulse was strong in him.

But he controlled it. Ash worked for Howden-Smyth, not him, and the Englishman probably wouldn't like it if Olsen executed one of his men. Besides, that might turn Chet Van Slyke, Navasota Jones, and the rest of the hired gunmen against him, and they outnumbered the cavalry troops. A situation like that could turn ugly in a hurry.

So instead of giving in to the murderous urge, he said, "Take a couple more men and run them to ground. Take more than that, if you need to. But *don't* let them get away this time."

Van Slyke sat his horse close enough to hear the exchange. He spoke up, pointing out the same thing that had just crossed Olsen's mind. "We don't work for you, Lieutenant. I didn't have a problem with Ash goin' after those Jensen boys, because I don't like 'em, either, but now I've lost two men. Why are the Jensens important enough to risk more?"

Olsen looked around. Evelyn sat on her horse about twenty yards away, with a trooper on either side of her, guarding her. Protecting her from harm, as far as she knew, but actually they were there to keep her from getting away again. Even so, Olsen didn't want her overhearing what he had to say.

"They know the truth," he told Van Slyke quietly. "They're too much of a danger to just let them roam around loose. They might find someone who would believe their story."

"As long as you've got Sughrue backing you up, it don't matter what those boys say." Van Slyke looked over toward Evelyn. "And you've just rescued the major's daughter not only from the deserters who kidnapped her, but also from a bunch of filthy red-skins, as well. He's gonna be so grateful to you that he'll never go against you."

"I'd like to think so," Olsen said, "but I want to eliminate any possibility of it."

Ash said, "If it makes any difference, I want to go after them again. I don't like failing. Never have."

Van Slyke shrugged and said, "All right, if that's the way you feel about it, go ahead. Just don't get yourself killed."

"I don't intend to," the Navajo replied. He turned his horse and rode over to the group of hired guns, pointing out three of them to take with him. They rode off, heading in the same direction the Jensen brothers had been traveling in earlier. Ash was a good tracker. He wouldn't have any trouble picking up the trail where the fight had taken place.

As the group moved out again after that brief halt, Van Slyke nudged his horse alongside Olsen's and said, "You know, that girl spent a lot of time with those Jensens. No tellin' what sort of things they filled her head with. She might not be exactly safe to have around, either."

Olsen stared over at him. "What in blazes are you suggesting, Van Slyke? No harm's going to come to Evelyn—"

The gunman held up a hand to stop him. "I'm not sayin' anything should happen to her. If we didn't have all these soldier boys around, *maybe* somethin' like that would be the smartest thing to do. But as it stands, we might all be better off if she didn't get a chance to do a lot of talkin' to her pa. If she was up at the mine, say, in the boss's house, she wouldn't be much of a threat anymore."

Olsen considered that and slowly nodded. "It would be even better if she was married to Howden-Smyth. A wife being kept close to home by her husband wouldn't raise any suspicions. And I know that Eugene had something very much like that in mind . . ."

"I could send a man ahead on a fast horse and have him tell the boss to bring the rest of the boys and be at the fort when we get there. We could reunite the gal with the major and then have a weddin' right away, before she had a chance to talk much to him."

"Evelyn would have to go along with that. I'm not sure she would."

"She would if she knew her pa's life depended on it," Van Slyke said.

Olsen drew in a deep breath. "You mean threaten to kill the major if she doesn't marry Howden-Smyth? That crosses a line!"

"You got to decide, Lieutenant. Are you an officer and a gentleman?" The mocking tone in the gunman's voice made Olsen's face darken in anger. "Or are you a man who's gonna have himself a nice little fortune in gold when this is all over?"

For a long moment, Olsen glared at the man riding beside him. Then the truth of the matter soaked in on him, and he knew there was only one answer to Van Slyke's question.

"Send the rider to your boss," he said. "And tell him not to waste any time!"

As Ace and Chance were riding toward Fort Gila with Lieutenant Slattery and the rest of the lieutenant's detail, Slattery asked, "Where is this gold mine and the road to it that I've heard so much about?"

Ace pointed to the southwest and said, "The mine is in that direction. I haven't been there, so I don't know exactly where it is. And the road doesn't run all the way to it yet. Most of the way there's only a trail fit mostly for horses or mules. Howden-Smyth's buggy is the only vehicle that can travel over it. That's why Howden-Smyth was so set on having a road built, so he could transport the gold out easier in big ore wagons."

"If the man owns a gold mine, why not just *hire* men to build the road?"

Chance said, "Some men can never have too much money, Lieutenant, and if there's a way to save some and put it in their pocket instead of spending it, they're going to take it. I suppose Howden-Smyth is that sort of man."

"As is Lieutenant Olsen, if what you've told me about him is correct." Slattery shook his head. "I hate to think about an officer in the United States Army doing such a thing. But I suppose corruption can be found anywhere."

Ace said, "I'm curious what you were doing up in the foothills, Lieutenant. Why didn't you just go straight to Fort Gila?"

"Because I was sent to investigate the situation and that's what I was trying to do," Slattery answered crisply. He sounded a bit more abashed as he added, "I wanted to take a look at the road first. I just hadn't, ah, found it yet . . ."

In the awkward silence that followed, Ace said, "Well, it was lucky for us you and your men came along, Lieutenant. I'm sorry a couple of the troopers had to double up so we'd have horses."

"Have you been in Arizona Territory before, Lieutenant?" Chance asked.

"No, this is actually my first time west of the Mississippi. I'm from Ohio, and all of my previous postings have been at forts in the east."

"And now you work in Washington," Ace said.

"That's correct."

"It's a lot different out here."

Slattery looked around and said, "I can see that. The landscape is rather . . . empty . . . isn't it?"

Ace smiled. "An old mountain man friend of ours named Preacher says the West is getting so blasted crowded that a man can't hardly breathe anymore. So I guess it's just a matter of what you're used to."

As they traveled on, Ace kept an eye out for other riders. If they ran into Olsen's bunch, it might mean a running battle, and the Jensen brothers and their companions would be badly outnumbered. Stealth and speed were important now, but out here on these open, sandy plains, there weren't many places to hide if they needed to. And they could only push their mounts so hard, too, which meant they had to stop now and then to rest the horses.

It was late afternoon before their path intercepted the road and Ace knew they weren't far from the fort. They all reined in, and Ace pointed to a cluster of boulders and rock spires that stuck up from the ground about two hundred yards to the north.

"We can wait there until nightfall, Lieutenant, and then the three of us can try to get into the fort and talk to Major Sughrue. Your men can wait in the rocks until you signal them. I'd suggest that three shots, then two more, would be a good signal for them to ride on in."

"Very well," Slattery said. "But if we're unsuccessful and they haven't heard from us by daybreak, I think they should return to Packsaddle and send a wire to the War Department asking for reinforcements."

"That would probably be too late to do us any good," Chance said, "but it's a good idea anyway.

Somebody needs to put a stop to what's going on around here."

They rode into the cover of the rocks and dismounted. Lieutenant Slattery shared his canteen with Ace and Chance. It had been a long day, but both brothers sensed that the end of this dangerous ordeal was getting closer. They were more than ready to have it over with.

While they were waiting, Ace spotted some dust rising not too far away, along the road leading into the foothills. He asked, "Do you have some field glasses I can borrow for a minute, Lieutenant?"

"Of course," Slattery said. He opened one of his saddlebags and reached inside. As he brought out the glasses, he went on, "What's wrong?"

"We're not the only ones headed for the fort."

"Olsen's bunch?" Chance asked.

"The angle's wrong, I think," Ace said as he took the glasses from Slattery. "More like somebody's coming from that mine of Howden-Smyth's."

He lifted the field glasses to his eyes and peered through them, adjusting them slightly until he was able to locate the dark figures at the base of the rising dust. As they came closer, he could make out more details and realized he was looking at Eugene Howden-Smyth's buggy, followed by a dozen riders, no doubt more of the mine owner's hired guns.

"That's Howden-Smyth and some of his gunwolves," he told Chance and Lieutenant Slattery as he lowered the glasses. "Looks like they're heading for the fort, and if they're up to anything good, I sure can't figure out what it might be."

"Blast it," Chance said. "We need to be in there right now, talking to Major Sughrue."

Ace shook his head. "If we try to waltz in in broad daylight, it won't get us anything except thrown back in the guardhouse, if we're lucky." He sighed. "No, we're still going to have to wait until nightfall . . . and hope that things don't go completely to hell before then."

CHAPTER FORTY

Once they were in sight of the fort, Olsen dropped back so that he was riding alongside Evelyn Sughrue. He motioned for the troopers guarding her to move away. Marshal Hank Glennon rode nearby as well, so Olsen said, "Marshal, why don't you take the lead for now?"

Glennon started to object. As a civilian, he had no right to lead a cavalry detail. But when he saw the look Olsen gave him, he caught on, nodded, and nudged his horse ahead. Olsen and Evelyn rode side by side with no one else around them now, giving them some privacy.

Evelyn frowned over at him and said, "This is rather strange, Lieutenant. I get the feeling that something is wrong."

"No, not really," Olsen said. "It's just that the two of us need to get some things straight between us."

"I can't imagine what that might be," Evelyn replied coolly.

"Well, it has to do with your father. I think very highly of the major."

"I'm glad to hear that, because I certainly do, too, of course."

"And I'd hate to see anything bad happen to him."

Evelyn shot a sharp glance at him. "Why would anything bad happen to him?"

"This is a rugged land, after all," Olsen said with a shrug. "It's filled with hostile Indians. One of the Apaches might sneak into the fort some night and stab your father in his sleep, and no one would ever know about it until it was too late."

Evelyn stared at him. "What a perfectly horrible thing to say!" she exclaimed.

"Or there might be an accident. A gun going off while it's being cleaned, say. But even terrible tragedies like that might not be as bad for the major as it would be if he was relieved of his command, discharged from the army, and disgraced. I think he would prefer a knife or a bullet to that, don't you?"

Evelyn looked angry now, not just surprised. "What's your purpose in saying all this to me, Lieutenant?"

"I just want to be sure that we're in agreement when it comes to protecting the major."

"Of course," Evelyn snapped.

"So you'll do anything in your power to see that no harm comes to him?"

"I think that you had better speak plainly, Lieutenant Olsen, or else I'm riding ahead and this conversation will be over."

"All right," Olsen said. "I know Major Sughrue would like to see you married and well taken care of. Setting his mind at ease where you're concerned is the best way to protect him. When we get to the fort,

Eugene Howden-Smyth will be there, and I think the two of you should get married immediately, or at least as soon as we can get Judge Bannister out here from Packsaddle."

"Married?" Evelyn repeated, evidently astonished by the very idea. "To Mr. Howden-Smyth?"

"Eugene," Olsen said with a smile. "You should get used to calling him Eugene, since he's going to be your husband."

"But he hasn't asked me, and I certainly haven't agreed!"

"Yes, but I know he wants to marry you. He's mentioned that to me on several occasions. That big house he built for himself up at the mine is lonely without a woman in it, I suppose. You won't ever want for anything, Evelyn, I can promise you that."

"This . . . this is all happening too fast . . ."

"And if you're married and living at the mine, your father won't have to worry about you anymore. You won't have to worry about him. I'm sure he'll be absolutely fine."

"It . . . it almost sounds like you're threatening him, Lieutenant. That if I don't agree to marry Howden-Smyth, then something *will* happen to my father . . ."

"Arizona Territory is a dangerous place," Olsen said. "Nobody can predict what's going to happen."

For a long moment she stared at him, clearly struggling to understand and accept what she was hearing. Finally, she said, "Ace and Chance Jensen were right. You *are* a villain."

He restrained the urge to slap her. Now that things were out in the open, he said in a flat, hard voice, "Do as you're told and nothing will happen to your father. But you've got to cooperate. That means you'd better smile and act like you're fine with the idea of marrying the Englishman. If you do, everything will be all right."

"I . . . I don't have any choice, do I?"

"Not really."

Another long moment passed until Evelyn said, in a voice little more than a whisper, "All right. I'll do as you say, Lieutenant. But only if you promise that no harm will come to my father."

"You have my word that *I* won't do anything to harm him." He chuckled. "I'm afraid I can't speak for the Apaches or any other natural threats, but that was always the case, wasn't it?"

Evelyn stared straight ahead as she said, "I don't know exactly what you're up to, Lieutenant, but I'm severely disappointed in you."

"Well," Olsen said, thinking about the gold, "I suppose I'll just have to live with that."

When they rode into the fort, the sun was low in the western sky, not far from touching the peaks of the Prophet Mountains. Reddish gold light filled the air. Heat still lay heavy on the landscape, but a bit of a breeze had sprung up, offering hints of the coolness that would settle down with the shadows of evening. Normally, this was one of Evelyn Sughrue's favorite times of day.

But not today. She didn't like anything about today.

Her mind whirled madly. She had never felt any great fondness for Frank Olsen. There had always been something about him that made her slightly uneasy. Not his ambition, exactly, because she had known ambitious officers before, but perhaps a sense that he would go to greater lengths to get what he wanted than some men would.

She never would have dreamed, though, that he would threaten to kill her father if she didn't go along with his demands. And he wasn't even making demands of her for himself, but rather for Eugene Howden-Smyth . . .

She had liked the Englishman, more than Olsen, anyway, and she'd known that he was attracted to her. She wondered now if he knew that Olsen was going to force her to marry him. Olsen seemed to have come up with that idea on his own, but she had no way of knowing what the two men might have discussed in the past.

All that mattered was that she protect her father, she told herself. She drew in a deep breath through flaring nostrils as she rode into Fort Gila with Olsen at her side.

It looked like the entire garrison had turned out to greet them, along with Howden-Smyth and some of his men, who waited over by the headquarters building while the troops were lined up on the parade ground. Evelyn's father strode toward her, a smile on his rugged face. He was there to help her dismount when she reined in.

When her feet were on the ground, he put his hands on her shoulders and looked intently at her. "You're all right?" he asked in a voice drawn taut with emotion and strain.

"Yes," she forced herself to say. She glanced at Olsen to be sure that he heard her saying what she was supposed to. "I'm fine, Father."

He looked at her for a second longer, then abruptly drew her into his arms and embraced her. "Thank heavens," he said fervently. "I . . . I'm not sure I could live with myself if anything ever happened to you, my dear." He stepped back and rested his hands on her shoulders again. "I should resign my commission so we can go back east. I thought I couldn't do such a thing because . . . because your mother is laid to rest here, but I see now that it might be best. It's the safest thing—"

Evelyn's eyes darted to Olsen again. He gave a tiny shake of his head, so faint that anyone not looking for it might not see it. But Evelyn did, and she knew what it meant. He had no intention of allowing Major Flint Sughrue to resign, because that meant Fort Gila would get a new commanding officer—and that would ruin all of Frank Olsen's carefully laid plans.

"You can't do that, Father," she said, interrupting him. "I want to stay here."

"You do? Even after everything that's happened?"

"Y-yes. I do. I've . . . grown to like it here."

Sughrue frowned, but he didn't appear to disbelieve her. Before the conversation could continue, Olsen stepped up, snapped a salute, and said, "Mission accomplished, Major. I'm happy to say that Miss Sughrue has been returned safely, and Sergeant MacDonald and the other deserters have been dealt with."

Sughrue turned toward him, returned the salute, and said, "I don't see any prisoners, Lieutenant."

"They, ah, would not allow themselves to be taken into custody, sir. Regretfully. And some had already been lost to the Apaches."

"I'll expect a full report on my desk in the morning, Lieutenant," Sughrue said sternly.

Olsen inclined his head slightly. "And you'll have it, sir."

That report wouldn't tell the whole story, Evelyn thought—but it would tell the story Frank Olsen wanted it to.

Eugene Howden-Smyth couldn't contain himself any longer. He started walking toward them and broke into a trot along the way. As he came up to Evelyn, he swept his hat off and said, "Evelyn, my dear! You're not harmed?"

She shook her head and managed to smile again. "I'm fine."

"That's superb news! Like the news we have for your father, eh?"

His words made her heart sink. She had hoped—vaguely, and without any real reason to—that he didn't know what Olsen was up to and wouldn't force her to go along with this.

Clearly, though, Olsen had gotten word to him somehow, not only to be here to meet them but also to be prepared to marry her. This was their way of imprisoning her, she realized. It would be a luxurious prison, in the form of Eugene Howden-Smyth's house at the mine, but still, she would be locked up there, unable to see her father or communicate with him unless Howden-Smyth was right there with her, controlling what she said and manipulating her strings as if she were a puppet.

"What's this about news?" Sughre asked with a frown.

Howden-Smyth put his arm around Evelyn's shoulders. She wanted to flinch away from him but didn't dare.

With a broad grin on his face, Howden-Smyth said, "You had no way of knowing this, Major, but your lovely daughter has done me the great honor of agreeing to become my wife."

Sughrue stared at him and after a couple of seconds repeated, "Wife?" He looked at Evelyn. "You and this man are getting married?"

"Y-yes, Father." Howden-Smyth's arm tightened warningly. Evelyn smiled. "We love each other."

The major's frown deepened. "Well, I certainly want you to be happy. Goodness knows, you've had little enough joy in your life since we came out here. First, just living in this wilderness and then . . . and then losing your mother . . ."

Sughrue drew in a deep breath, squared his shoulders, and visibly steeled himself against the emotions running rampant inside him.

"If this is what you want, Evelyn, then I give you my blessing," he said. He glared at Howden-Smyth for a second. "Although it's customary for the prospective bridegroom to *ask* the bride's father for that blessing before things go this far."

"You're absolutely correct, sir," Howden-Smyth said easily, "and I apologize for not doing things according to proper form. The circumstances were a bit irregular, though."

Sughrue grunted. "Most things on the frontier are." He paused. "Very well. With that settled . . . when will the ceremony take place?"

"We were hoping as soon as possible, and to that end, I've dispatched men to Packsaddle to fetch Judge Bannister." Howden-Smyth answered. "Perhaps . . . this evening?"

"That soon?" Sughrue looked at Evelyn.

This was for his life, she reminded herself as she said, "Please, Father."

"All right." He smiled. "Anything my little girl wants."

She managed not to scream in anger and frustration, but it wasn't easy.

CHAPTER FORTY-ONE

Ace, Chance, and Lieutenant Slattery took turns observing through the field glasses as the afternoon waned. They had seen Eugene Howden-Smyth and his men arrive at the fort, and then later they saw the detail led by Lieutenant Frank Olsen ride in. Evelyn was near the front of the group, riding with Olsen. Her red hair shone brightly in the sun.

Ace took the glasses and swung them toward Howden-Smyth's hired guns bringing up the rear. He searched for the Indian who had tracked them down earlier and then gotten away after the brief gunfight. There was no sign of the man, and Ace found that troubling. The Indian could still be out there somewhere, searching for them.

"At least Evelyn looks like she's all right," Chance commented as Ace lowered the field glasses.

"She's too valuable to Olsen for her *not* to be all right. The question is, how soon is he going to turn her over to Howden-Smyth?"

"It's too late in the day for them to start back to the mine," Chance said. "They won't leave until in the morning. So we've got tonight to turn everything around, but that's all."

Slattery said, "You two strategize like military men, despite your youth. Are you sure you've never been in the army or had military training?"

"Nope, we haven't," Ace replied.

He didn't explain that living on their own had given him and Chance some wisdom and maturity beyond their years—at least most of the time. Also, they had spent quite a bit of time around Smoke, Luke, and Matt Jensen, as well as the mountain man called Preacher, and those hombres were some of the deadliest natural fighting men the West had ever seen. Some of their knowledge was bound to have rubbed off on the brothers.

"Have you given any thought to how we're going to get into the fort?" Slattery asked.

"The wall's not really high enough to keep anybody out," Ace said. "It's just there to give the troops some protection if they have to fight off an attack. But guards patrol all the way around the inside of it at night. I heard some of the men talking about having that duty. So we'll have to go over the wall at the back of the fort and time it so we can slip between the sentries."

"Which won't be easy since they're not very far apart," Chance added. "And we'll need to do it before the moon rises, or else they'll spot us for sure."

"From there we'll need to make it to Major Sughrue's quarters and hope that he's there," Ace continued. "If we can talk to him alone, or even if Evelyn is there, I'm sure we can convince him of the truth."

Chance said, "Then he can send a detail to take Olsen by surprise and arrest him before he knows what's going on."

Slattery nodded slowly and then said, "That sounds like a reasonable plan, but what about this man Howden-Smyth? If he's part of Olsen's criminal enterprise, as you claim he is, then he's liable to try to free Olsen. And he has a number of dangerous professional gunmen with him."

"That he does," Ace agreed. "That's why we'll need the rest of your detail to get there as quickly as possible and reinforce the troops who'll be loyal to Major Sughrue. Those hired guns aren't fools. They won't take on a force of cavalrymen that large."

"Two things concern me," Slattery said. "The first is being absolutely certain that I can trust the two of you and that you're not playing me for a fool."

Ace said, "All we can do is give you our word that we're not, Lieutenant. And you have to admit, the story as we've told it to you *does* explain that mysterious report from Major Sughrue that reached the War Department."

"It does," Slattery admitted. "My other worry is the major himself. We're basing the success of our entire plan on being able to reason with a man who's evidently half-mad with grief. Lieutenant Olsen has had months to work on him and weave his web of deceit. Will we be able to convince him in a matter of minutes that everything he believes is wrong?"

Ace shook his head and said, "I can't answer that, Lieutenant. And you're right, there's a lot riding on it. But I don't know anything else to try."

Slattery lifted the field glasses to his eyes, peered

through them, and muttered, "I wish we had a better view of what's going on in there. I can't help but think that there are going to be some surprises waiting for us."

"There usually are," Chance said.

Night fell suddenly, as it did in these desert climes, darkness crashing down like a dropped curtain. Ace and Chance still wore the clothes they'd had on when they were brought to the fort from Packsaddle, but in the intervening days those garments had gotten sweat-drenched and filthy so many times, they were now just a mottled shade of grayish brown. That meant they would blend into the shadows well, as would Lieutenant Slattery's dark blue uniform. Slattery left behind his hat with its crossed sabers insignia that might catch a reflection of starlight, as well as his scabbarded saber. The three men took off their gunbelts, shoved revolvers in waistbands, and draped shirttails over them, also to guard against a glint of silver from the stars. Extra cartridges went in their pockets.

"Stay low when we start out," Ace said, "and then when we get closer to the fort, we'll need to get down and crawl."

"Watch out for rattlers," Chance added dryly. "Crawl over one of those varmints, and you're liable to let out a yell that'd wake folks up in Packsaddle."

The brothers heard the lieutenant swallow hard. "I appreciate the advice, despite the fact that you're civilians. I have to admit that even though I've been in the army for several years, I've never, ah, taken part in any action against the enemy."

Ace said, "It's a shame the first time has to be against fellow soldiers."

"If Olsen has engaged in the activities you've told me about, he doesn't deserve to be called a soldier any longer." Slattery nodded firmly. "Shall we go?"

Ace squinted up at the stars coming out in the ebony sky and nodded. "Yeah, I reckon it's late enough. Come on."

Slattery had a few last words for the nine troopers under his command, then he and Ace and Chance slipped out of the cluster of rocks and headed toward the fort.

They moved quickly but as silently as possible, the only sound to mark their passage being the faint crunch of sandy soil under their boots. They circled toward the rear of Fort Gila, and when they were about two hundred yards from the wall, Ace motioned for them to get down on the ground.

From there they went ahead on their bellies, using the small patches of shadow cast by clumps of brush as cover for their movements wherever possible. Time seemed to drag as they crawled toward the adobe wall.

Ace listened closely for the telltale whir that would tell him he was approaching a rattlesnake, but he didn't hear anything of the sort. Luck was with them, and none of the scaly monsters were in their path tonight.

He wished they'd had a chance to study the frequency of the guard patrols, but maybe once they reached the wall, they could lie there for a few minutes and listen to the footsteps on the other side enough to get an idea of when would be the best time to make their move. He could communicate that to Chance and Slattery when they got there.

Another few yards . . . Ace pulled with his elbows and pushed with his boot toes, and then the wall loomed right above him. He put out a hand and touched Chance and Slattery on their shoulders, stopping them. Leaning close to Chance's ear, he breathed, "Listen for the guards. We need to know how often they come around."

Chance nodded and passed that along to Slattery. The three of them lay there, motionless and silent, as more long minutes dragged by.

Ace heard the sentries' footsteps passing by and counted the seconds between each set. About a minute went by from one passing to the next. He wished there was a bigger gap than that. Only one man could go over the wall at a time. More movement than that would represent too great a risk of being spotted.

He heard something else while he was lying there. Somewhere in the fort, men's voices were raised in talk and laughter, almost like there was a party going on. What could they be celebrating at Fort Gila tonight? The safe return of Evelyn Sughrue? Or something else?

They would find out when they got in there, Ace told himself.

Again he whispered in Chance's ear. "I'll go first. If they happen to spot me, I'll put up enough of a fight and cause enough commotion that you and the lieutenant ought to be able to slip inside without being noticed. Go on and get to the major, like we planned."

"Blast it, Ace, don't get yourself killed!" Chance whispered back.

"I don't intend to. After I've gone, count sixty and then send Slattery. That ought to have him going over between two sentries. You can come a minute after he does. I'm going to head for the nearest building and wait there in its shadow until the two of you join me, assuming I don't get caught. All of that clear?"

"Yeah," Chance said, "but I don't like all this skulking around. Jensens kick down the door and start shooting."

"Not when they're as outnumbered as we are. Remember when Smoke killed those nineteen gunslingers in one battle up in Idaho, or wherever it was? He had to be smart about it, not just bull his way in."

"Yeah, I know. I'm just ready to see Olsen get what's coming to him."

"Me, too," Ace agreed. "And with any luck, it'll be soon." He pushed up on hands and knees, listened to the regular footsteps of a trooper crunch past on the other side of the wall, and counted to thirty. Then he breathed, "Here I go," stood up, pulled himself onto the wall, and rolled over it to drop feetfirst into the fort.

CHAPTER FORTY-TWO

He landed with almost no noise, dropped into a crouch, and looked to his left. Movement at the corner of the compound caught his eye. The sentry coming toward him had just made the turn. The back of the blacksmith shop was ten normal steps away. Ace made it in five.

No shout came from the soldier on guard duty. Ace pressed himself against the wall in the thick shadow at the building's corner and listened. The trooper's pace never altered.

It was a good thing he wasn't an Apache, Ace thought. Otherwise hostiles would be inside the fort now.

The soldier passed on by. Ace counted inside his head, and so he knew when it was time for Lieutenant Slattery to make his appearance. The lieutenant rolled over the wall—a little more clumsily and not as quietly as Ace had managed—and darted over to the blacksmith shop in response to Ace's hissed summons. Slattery was panting as he pressed himself against the wall.

"Quiet as you can, Lieutenant," Ace whispered.

"Of . . . of course. This is rather nerve-wracking."

It was nothing so far, Ace thought, but he didn't see any point in saying that.

Chance joined them a minute later. Since they had worked out their plans ahead of time, nothing more needed to be said. Ace led the way as they crept around the building. Staying in the shadows beside it, he edged up to the front corner and studied what he could see of the fort. From this position, most of the buildings on both long sides of the compound were visible.

The headquarters building was lit up brightly, and yellow light glowed in all the windows of the house Major Sughrue shared with Evelyn. Lamps burned in the barracks as well. Howden-Smyth's men were gathered in front of the sutler's store, some of them passing in and out as they no doubt sampled the whiskey for sale inside.

Ace looked again at the headquarters building. Four men stood on the porch: Lieutenant Frank Olsen, Eugene Howden-Smyth, Marshal Hank Glennon, and Judge Horace Bannister from Packsaddle. The four main conspirators in the scheme that had cost the lives of a number of men and placed an innocent young woman in jeopardy. Ace wished there was a way to strike at them while they were all there together, but right now any such attempt would just backfire.

He pointed them out, though, to Lieutenant Slattery and explained who each man was.

"They'll be dealt with in due course," Slattery

whispered, "but right now we need to find Major Sughrue."

"Follow me," Ace told him.

He catfooted his way through the darkness and started along the rear of the line of buildings leading to the commanding officer's quarters. Chance and Slattery trailed him. They all paused now and then to let one of the sentries pass by without noticing them.

"The discipline here is very lax," Slattery commented during one of those moments. "Those men aren't being the least bit vigilant!"

"I'm sure actual military discipline has slipped since Olsen's been running things," Ace said. "He was only interested in putting men in the guardhouse so he could make them work on that road, not in keeping up with all the other duties."

"And the major's been too busy wallowing in his grief to notice," Chance added. "I hate to say that, but it's the truth."

The sentry had passed on by. The three men resumed their stealthy mission.

When they reached their destination, Ace slipped along one of the side walls toward a lighted window. The shutters were open to let in the cooling night air, and as he paused beside it, flattening against the adobe wall, he heard muttering from inside.

At first he thought he was eavesdropping on an actual conversation, but then he realized he heard only one voice—and that belonged to Major Flint Sughrue. It quickly became obvious who the major was talking to.

"—so proud of her, darling," Sughrue was saying. "I'm sure she'll be the most beautiful bride this part of the territory has ever seen. No, the most beautiful bride in all of Arizona!" He paused, then said, "I just wish I could be certain that she's doing the right thing . . . What's that? Yes, yes, Eugene is a wealthy man and will be even more so in the future, but wealth isn't everything. He's not . . . well, he's not a military man, and I thought Evelyn might find some excellent young officer, one of these days . . . But as long as she's happy, I suppose that's all that matters. The thing is, dear, I'm not convinced that she is . . ."

Ace edged his head into the window enough to look through a gap in the curtains over the opening. He saw Major Sughrue pacing back and forth in the house's parlor, hands clasped behind his back and a worried frown on his face. He wore dress uniform, complete with saber, for his daughter's wedding.

Despite everything that had happened, Ace felt sorry for the man. He hadn't asked for the sorrow that had unhinged his mind, and he'd had no reason to suspect that one of his junior officers would turn out to be so ruthless and corrupt. As Slattery had pointed out, there was nothing in Frank Olsen's military record to indicate that he was going to turn bad.

That was what had happened, though, and now that evil had to be dealt with.

"I'll go in first," he whispered to Chance and Slattery as Sughrue continued to pace inside the room.

"We'll be right behind you," Chance said.

Ace waited until Sughrue turned his back and stalked toward the other side of the room. Then, with quick, lithe agility, Ace pulled himself up on the windowsill, swung his legs through the opening, and dropped his feet to the plank floor.

Sughrue heard him and turned around. The major's eyes opened wide in surprise. Ace was already moving toward him, slipping the gun from his waistband as he did so. He didn't want to hurt Sughrue, but he couldn't allow the man to make an outcry, either.

Sughrue opened his mouth to yell while at the same time reaching for the scabbarded saber on his hip. Ace lunged at him, clamped his left hand over Sughrue's mouth, and rammed the major against the wall. He stuck the Colt's barrel under Sughrue's jaw and said, "Don't do it, Major! Let go of that sword."

Sughrue glared hate at him, but he let go of the saber's grip and the blade slid back down the three or four inches he had withdrawn it. Sughrue's angry gaze darted over Ace's shoulder. He knew Chance and Slattery were climbing through the window. Maybe the sight of Slattery's uniform would calm Sughrue down.

"Listen to me, Major," Ace said with urgent intensity. "We're on your side. You may not believe that, but it's true. We just want to help you . . . and Evelyn."

At the sound of his daughter's name, Sughrue let out some angry grunts behind Ace's muffling hand. The words weren't coherent, but the major's state of mind was obvious.

Chance came up on Ace's right, Slattery on his left. The young officer snapped to attention and lifted his hand in a salute. That was a good move, Ace thought. Familiar military routine might get through to Sughrue better than anything else.

"I'm Lieutenant Patrick Slattery, sir, here on a

special mission for the War Department. I'd like to show you my orders and give you my report. Permission to do so?"

Ace saw the anger fading in Sughrue's eyes, to be replaced by confusion. He said, "I'm going to take my hand away from your mouth now, sir, if you'll promise not to yell. Can you do that?"

The anger came back for a second, but then Sughrue nodded curtly. Ace lowered his hand and took the gun away from Sughrue's jaw.

Slattery was still standing rigidly at attention, holding the salute. Sughrue straightened and brushed off his jacket, then returned the salute and asked, "What's the meaning of this, Lieutenant?"

Slattery relaxed slightly. "As I said, sir, I'm here on orders directly from the War Department." He reached inside his jacket, took out a folded piece of paper, and handed it to the major. "I was sent in response to a report you submitted about the construction of a road from Fort Gila to a mine located in the Prophet Mountains."

"Yes, yes," Sughrue said impatiently. He unfolded the paper Slattery had given him and looked at it for a few seconds, then seemed to be satisfied with its genuineness. "Work on the road is progressing at a satisfactory pace, and that's what I reported." He looked at Ace and Chance. "What are you doing with these two deserters? I should summon the sergeant of the guard—"

"Ace and Chance Jensen are not deserters, Major, and that road you've been building . . . the War Department never ordered that such a road be constructed."

Sughrue stared at him. "What! That's ridiculous! Of course those were my orders."

"Did you actually *see* those orders, Major?" Slattery asked.

Sughrue's frown deepened. "Certainly, I . . . Well, now that I think about it . . . I know my aide filed them. They'll be over in my office. Lieutenant Olsen told me about them . . ."

"Olsen's a crook," Chance said. "He and Howden-Smyth are in it together. They're just using you to get that road built so they can make more money off that mine."

Ace might have eased into it more, but Chance was probably right: best to get things out in the open, because they had no idea how much time they had.

"That's a very serious accusation, especially from a deserter," Sughrue responded.

"We're not—" Chance broke off in frustration.

"Major, I give you my word as an officer that these men are *not* deserters." Slattery nodded faintly to Ace and Chance, which Ace took as an indication that he had finally accepted their story as the truth, now that he had seen Major Sughrue's state of mind for himself. "They're simply innocent civilians who got caught up in Lieutenant Olsen's scheme and almost lost their lives as a result of it."

"And that's not the worst of it, sir, by any means," Ace said. "Olsen is *forcing* your daughter to marry Howden-Smyth so they can make her a prisoner up at the mine and keep her from telling you the truth."

"Evelyn," Sughrue breathed. "You say she's being *forced* to marry that Englishman?"

"That's right, sir. She knows what's really been

going on. They threatened *your* life to make her go along with them. If you talk to her, I'm sure she'll tell you. But you have to have Olsen arrested first."

For a second, Ace had seen rational thought in Sughrue's eyes and knew they were getting through to the man. But now the major exclaimed, "Arrested! But . . . but I rely on Frank. Without his help, I couldn't have kept going here at the fort after . . . after my wife . . . No! This is a pack of lies! I've been following orders—"

Sughrue stopped short. He turned his head and peered past Ace, Chance, and Slattery as if looking at something else. For a moment, they seemed to have disappeared from the room as far as Sughrue was concerned. He was totally focused on something beyond the three of them.

Finally, he said, "I . . . I understand, dear. If you believe this story is the truth, then . . . it must be. I know I never . . . never really trusted that Englishman . . ."

He brought his hands up, clapped them over his rugged face, and shook with soundless sobs.

Ace had a pretty good idea who Sughrue had been talking to. If that was what it took to get him to see the truth clearly, then Ace had no problem with that. Besides, despite his youth, he knew not to condemn such things out of hand as delusions. He remembered the line from Shakespeare: *There are more things in heaven and earth, Horatio, than are dreamt of in your philosophy* . . .

"It's all right, Major," Lieutenant Slattery said gently. "You've been through a great deal, and all that matters now is setting things right. To make a start on doing that, you need to call some men in here and order them to take Lieutenant Olsen into custody. But discreetly, so that he doesn't know what's happening—"

Sughrue's hands dropped away from his face, which was mottled red with rage now. His brain had cleared enough for him to realize how much Olsen had duped and used him, and he didn't like it. Not one bit.

Sughrue wheeled around and started toward the door. Ace called, "Major! Major, stop! Where's Evelyn?"

Stopping short, Sughrue looked back over his shoulder and snapped, "In my office, waiting for me. The ceremony was to begin as soon as I got there."

"Call the sergeant of the guard and some of his men in here," Slattery suggested. "You can give them their orders—"

Again, madness swept over Sughrue's features, wiping away the last vestiges of control. He yanked his saber out of its scabbard and shouted, "I'll kill that traitor!" He rushed for the door.

Ace and Chance leaped after him, but too late. Sughrue slammed the door open and stepped outside. He raised the saber high and bellowed, "Olsen!"

Heads snapped around all over the fort as the major charged across the parade ground, yelling incoherently and brandishing the saber.

That was when the gates swung open, hoofbeats pounded, and four riders raced into Fort Gila, led by the Indian tracker. "Those Jensen boys!" he shouted over the commotion. "They're here!"

CHAPTER FORTY-THREE

No matter how well you planned—and they really hadn't had a chance to do that in this case—things went wrong, Ace told himself as he sprinted after Major Sughrue. On the porch of the headquarters building, the four men had turned to stare at the major in surprise. Olsen saw Ace and Chance spill out of the house behind Sughrue, and his face twisted in anger as he shouted, "Stop them!"

Howden-Smyth's gunmen took that to mean permanently. Revolvers flew out of holsters and swept up in hardened hands.

Ace dived after Sughrue, tackled him around the waist, and drove him to the ground as shots roared and bullets ripped through the air where they had been a split second earlier.

"Sergeant of the guard! Sergeant of the guard!" Slattery called as he hurried out onto the parade ground, too. "Arrest Lieutenant Olsen!"

He thrust his pistol into the air, triggered three times, waited a beat, and fired twice more. The men they had left in the rocks ought to hear that signal and ride hard for the fort.

The troops posted at Fort Gila didn't know Slattery, but he wore an officer's uniform and orders were orders, at least for some of them. They started across the parade ground toward the headquarters building, and some of the hired guns turned their shots in that direction. The cavalrymen fired back, since they were under attack. Most of the men had no real idea of what was going on, but in the blink of an eye, the parade ground was chaos, as clouds of powder smoke rolled over the hard-packed earth and bullets whipped back and forth in the air.

The melee grew even worse when Olsen shouted at some of the soldiers near the headquarters building and they opened fire on their fellow troopers. Few of them knew for sure who was a friend and who was an enemy.

Ace knew, though. As he tried to keep Sughrue from standing up in the storm of lead, he heard hoofbeats coming closer and a slug kicked up dirt beside him. Twisting, he saw the Indian tracker galloping in his direction, seemingly oblivious to all the wild shots screaming around him. The Indian seemed to have some sort of mystical protection against those bullets, too, since none of them found him or his horse.

Ace rolled to the side to give himself a better angle and lifted the Colt. It roared and bucked in his hand, and he saw the Indian jerk back as the bullet punched into his chest. The tracker fired again with the rifle he held. Ace felt the slug's hot breath on his cheek as he fired a second time.

This shot hit the Indian above his right eye and snapped his head back. He dropped his rifle and tumbled backward out of the saddle, but one of his feet hung in the stirrup and the horse, crazed by the noise and the smell of smoke and blood, continued running, dragging the limp body alongside it.

Ace turned his head and saw that Sughrue was up again. The major still had hold of his saber and waved it over his head as he charged toward the head-quarters building. On the porch of that building, Eugene Howden-Smyth struggled with Evelyn, who must have run outside when the shooting started. She wore a simple white dress, not a wedding gown but one that would have served that purpose. As Ace watched, Howden-Smyth dragged her back inside while she screamed, "Father! Father!"

Chance passed Ace at a run. He was headed for the headquarters building, too. Ace saw Marshal Hank Glennon drawing a bead on his brother. Shooting a lawman, even a crooked one, went against the grain for Ace, but Glennon gave him no choice. Ace came up on one knee and fired twice. Glennon dropped his gun and clutched at his chest with both hands. Crimson welled between his fingers as he crumpled to the porch.

A few feet away, Judge Horace Bannister was on both knees, bent forward with his arms over his head as if to protect it from flying lead. He looked a little like he was praying, and maybe he was—praying for his own corrupt hide.

Chance passed Major Sughrue. Olsen snapped a shot at him, but before Olsen could fire again, Ace triggered a shot at him that missed but chewed splinters from a porch post less than a foot from Olsen's head. That made Olsen duck, and while he was doing that, Chance leaped to the porch and charged into the building after Howden-Smyth and Evelyn.

By that time, Major Sughrue had reached the steps and started up them. Ace had one more round left in his gun, but he couldn't fire because Sughrue was between him and Olsen.

Ace saw the muzzle flashes as Olsen triggered again and again. He saw the major's body jerk as the slugs hammered into him. But Sughrue never slowed down. With the saber thrust out in front of him, he rammed forward against Olsen and drove him back against the wall of the building behind him. Ace watched as both men stood there for several long seconds. Then Sughrue slowly slid down to the porch while Olsen stayed against the wall, pinned there by the steel that had gone all the way through his body and stuck in the adobe. Olsen made a few feeble twitches, and then his head drooped forward and he didn't move again.

Ace didn't have time to look in that direction any longer, because at that moment another bullet sizzled past his face. Jerking his head to the right, he saw two of Howden-Smyth's gun-wolves closing in on him. He recognized them as the pair that had been with Olsen's detail when they attacked the Apache village. He didn't recall their names, but one was tall and gaunt, the other stocky and wielding a shotgun. The cadaverous one was firing at Ace, but remembering that he had only one bullet left in the Colt and no time to reload, Ace targeted the shotgunner instead.

The bullet slammed into the man's midsection and doubled him over before he could fire the scatter-gun. Instead it slipped from his fingers and fell to the ground.

Ace dropped the revolver and leaped up, then threw himself forward. As he landed, rolling, he snatched up the shotgun and had time to hope that the barrels hadn't gotten fouled with dirt when the man dropped it. That was all he had time for, though, because the gaunt gunman was practically on top of him. A bullet from the man's gun burned along Ace's ribs.

He tripped both triggers and as flame gouted from the twin muzzles, the double load of buckshot tore into the gunman at an angle, lifted him off his feet, and flung him backward. He landed as limp as a rag doll. The whole front of his torso was shredded.

Ace tossed the empty shotgun aside, scooped up the revolver the gunman had dropped, and ran toward the headquarters building. From the corner of his eye, he saw the other members of Lieutenant Slattery's detail galloping into the fort. Slattery was there to wave his arm and shout orders to them as the battle continued with Howden-Smyth's hired guns and the troopers who were part of Olsen's scheme.

Inside the headquarters building, Chance heard Evelyn's cries and followed them to the major's office. As he charged past the aide's desk and on into the office, he spotted Howden-Smyth and Evelyn on the other side of the room. The mine owner had one arm wrapped around her waist while she struggled and flailed at him. He had a gun in his other hand and was cursing bitterly at her.

He saw Chance come into the room and turned the gun toward him. Flame geysered from the barrel. Chance veered away from the wind-rip of the bullet next to his ear, but he couldn't risk a shot with Evelyn in the way.

"Give it up, mister!" Chance yelled. "The War Department knows about your scheme. It's over!"

Howden-Smyth cursed him instead and swung the gun up for another shot. Evelyn stopped fighting wildly but grabbed his arm and jerked it toward her. Her teeth locked in the fleshy ball of his hand. Howden-Smyth howled in pain and hammered his other fist against her head, knocking her loose.

But that knocked her out of the way, as well, and as Evelyn slumped to the floor, Chance had a clear shot. He and Howden-Smyth triggered so close together that the two reports sounded like one. The Englishman's bullet smacked into the wall beside Chance while the slug from the young man's gun left a smoldering hole in the breast pocket of Howden-Smyth's expensive coat. Howden-Smyth stumbled forward, eyes widening in shock, pain, and disbelief.

"You . . . you've shot me!" he gasped. "It . . . can't be! I was . . . going to be . . . rich . . ."

He pitched forward on his face and didn't move again.

Chance swung around fast as rapid footsteps sounded behind him. He held off on the trigger as he recognized his brother. "Ace!" he cried. "Are you all right?"

"Fine," Ace said, although his side hurt like blazes where that bullet had grazed him. "Howden-Smyth?"

"Dead. Olsen?"

"Dead," Ace said. Unless the lieutenant had figured out a way to survive being run through with a cavalry saber, and Ace didn't think that was very likely. "Where's Evelyn?"

Chance stuck his gun back in his waistband and hurried over to the girl. Ace was right beside him. They helped her up, and as Ace looked over the white dress, he didn't see any bloodstains on it.

"You're all right?" he asked her.

"I . . . I think so." She summoned up a weak smile. "Somehow, I'm not surprised to see you boys."

"We do seem to turn up wherever there's trouble," Chance said.

Evelyn's eyes widened as she remembered something. "My father!" she exclaimed. She started to hurry past Chance. "I have to find—"

Ace shook his head, and Chance reached out to take hold of Evelyn and keep her from rushing out.

"Let me go!" she cried. "I have to go to him!"

"Miss Sughrue," Ace said, "I'm sorry . . ."

"No!" She looked at him in horror, and tears began to roll down her cheeks. *"No!"*

Chance drew her into his arms and she buried her face against his chest as sobs shook her entire body.

Ace heard someone else coming into the building and turned, raising the revolver he had picked up outside. He lowered it when he saw that the newcomer was Lieutenant Patrick Slattery. The lieutenant had a cut on his cheek that oozed blood, and another red stain on his left arm where a bullet appeared to have nicked him, but otherwise he seemed unharmed.

"Miss Sughrue?" he asked.

"She's all right," Chance said as he held Evelyn and

patted her lightly on the back in a mostly futile effort to comfort her.

"What about her father?" Ace asked.

Grim-faced, Slattery replied, "Still alive, but fading fast."

Ace nodded to Chance. "Better take her out there."

Chance shepherded Evelyn out of the office. As Ace and Slattery followed, Ace said quietly, "For somebody who hadn't seen any action, you seem to have acquited yourself pretty well, Lieutenant."

Slattery smiled a little. "There was hardly time to do anything else."

"I don't hear any more shots. The fighting is over?"

"It is," Slattery replied with a nod. "Some of those hired gunmen working for Howden-Smyth survived, but they reached their horses and got away. The soldiers who fought on Olsen's side surrendered when they saw that he was dead. I believe most of them regret their actions, but they'll be spending time behind bars for them, anyway." Slattery paused. "Do you think those gunmen will return?"

"Not likely," Ace said. "Especially once they hear that Howden-Smyth is dead. That breed doesn't fight unless there's a good payoff involved. Now there's no more money for them to make here."

They stepped out onto the porch and saw that Evelyn was sitting on the planks with her father's head and shoulders in her lap. The front of Sughrue's uniform jacket was sodden with blood. He looked up into her crying face, blinked, and struggled to make his mouth form words.

"Ev-Evelyn . . . I . . . I'm sorry . . . To think of . . . what I almost did . . ."

"Don't worry about that, Father," she said, her voice choked with emotion. "You hang on, we'll help you—"

"N-no! Don't . . . want any help . . . Just want to . . . go on . . . be with my darling . . . Amelia . . . again . . . Evelyn . . . dear . . . know that . . . we'll always . . . be looking down . . . and loving . . ."

His last breath went out of him in a sigh. Evelyn clutched him and sobbed harder, but he was gone.

Ace looked around, spotted Bannister standing at the other end of the porch looking sick and shaken, and went over to the portly jurist. Bannister saw him coming and a panicky look appeared on the judge's face, as he was afraid Ace might shoot him.

Instead, Ace said, "Listen to me, Bannister. You're as big a crook as Olsen, Howden-Smyth, and Glennon were—"

"No, I . . . I was just trying to cooperate with the army—" Bannister began protesting.

"Shut up," Ace said. "I don't know if Howden-Smyth had any relatives, but if he didn't, that gold mine ought to go to Evelyn. He intended to marry her, after all. I know that doesn't give her any real legal standing—"

"But I can arrange it," Bannister said hastily. "The young lady will never want for anything again, I promise you. I'll see to it."

Ace nodded. "Things will probably go easier for you if you do. You might even wind up not spending any time behind bars."

"Just leave it to me, Mr. Jensen."

"And as for that murder charge against me and my brother—"

"Gone! Wiped out! Have no doubts about that, sir."

"Good, because if we ever find out that we're fugitives from the law because of that, we'll be hunting you up . . . and we won't have anything to lose."

Bannister swallowed hard.

"One more thing. Where are our horses and all the gear we left behind in Packsaddle?"

"The horses are in the livery stable, and your things are, ah, still in Marshal Glennon's office, I believe."

"Good."

Ace turned away from the judge and joined Chance and Slattery, who were watching from a discreet distance as Evelyn held the body of her dead father. He put a hand on Slattery's shoulder and said quietly, "You'll look after Miss Sughrue?"

Slattery frowned in surprise. "Of course. But I thought the two of you—"

"We're going to take a couple of horses from the bunch that belonged to Howden-Smyth's men so we can ride to Packsaddle, reclaim our own mounts, and get our gear from the marshal's office. Isn't that right, Chance?"

Chance looked at Evelyn, sighed regretfully, and nodded. "Yeah, that's probably the best thing to do. Evelyn needs somebody who doesn't have the sort of restless nature I do." He grinned at the young lieutenant. "Maybe somebody with a nice, stable career in the army."

Blinking rapidly, Slattery said, "Wait. What? I was hoping I could persuade the two of you to stay here and help me clean up this mess. Perhaps you might even be interested in enlisting—"

He was talking to himself. The Jensen brothers were already striding away through the thinning haze of powder smoke.

CHAPTER ONE

Beneath a black sky torn apart by a raging thunder-storm, the sidelamps of the Patterson stage were lit as Red Ryan and Patrick "Buttons" Muldoon approached the town of Cottondale, some sixty miles east of El Paso, Texas.

Buttons drew rein on the tired team and shouted over a roar of thunder, "Hell, Red, the place is in darkness. How come?"

"I don't know how come," the shotgun guard said. Red wore his slicker against the hammering rain. "The place is dead, looks like."

"Maybe they ran out of oil. Long trip to bring lamp oil all this way."

"And candles. They don't have any candles."

"Nothing up this way but miles of desert," Buttons said. "Could be they ran out of oil."

"You said that already."

"I know, and that's still what I reckon. They ran out of oil and candles, and all the folks are sitting in their homes in the dark, sheltering from the rain."

"Or asleep." Red said.

Lightning scrawled across the sky like the signature

of a demented god, and for a second or two, the barren brush country was starkly illuminated in sizzling light. Thunder bellowed.

"Buttons, you sure we're in the right place?" Red yelled. Rain drummed on the crown of his plug hat and the shoulders of his slicker. "Maybe this isn't Cottondale. Maybe it's some other place."

"Sure, I'm sure," Buttons said. "Abe Patterson's wire said Cottondale is east of El Paso and just south of the Cornudas Mountains. Well, afore this storm started, we seen the mountains, so that there ahead of us must be the town."

Red said. "What the hell kind of town is it?"

"A dark town," Buttons said. "Remember the first time we seen that New Mexican mining burg, what was it called? Ah, yeah, Buffalo Flat. That looked like a dark town until you seen it close. Tents. Nothing but brown tents."

"With people in them, as I recollect." Red said. "Well, drive on in and let's get out of this rain and unhitch the team."

"Yeah, the horses are tuckered," Buttons said. "They've had some hard going, this leg of the trip."

"So am I tuckered. I could sure use some coffee."

Buttons slapped the ribbons, and the six-horse team lurched into motion. Lightning flashed and thunder banged as nature threw a tantrum. As it headed for a town lost in gloom, the Patterson stage was all but invisible behind the steel mesh of the teeming downpour.

Cottondale consisted of a narrow, single street bookended by rows of stores, a hotel, a saloon, and a livery stable. A large church with a tall bell tower dominated the rest. The town was a bleak, run-down, and windswept place. The buildings huddled together like starving vagrants seeking comfort in each other's company. It was dark, dismal, and somber. Silent as a tomb, the only sound the ceaseless rattle of the relentless rain.

Buttons halted the team outside the saloon. A painted sign above the door, much faded, read THE WHEATSHEAF. "We'll try in here."

Red shook his head. "Try in here for what? Buttons, this is a ghost town. It's deader than hell in a preacher's backyard."

"Can't be. Ol' Abe said we have a passenger . . . what the hell's his name again? Oh yeah, Morgan Ford. He's got to be here and a whole passel of other folks."

Thunder rolled across the sky.

When it passed, Red looked around and said, "Then where the hell are all them other folks?"

"Sleeping the sleep of the just, that's where. There's a church in this town, and God-fearing folks go to bed early." He angled a look at Red. "Unlike some I know."

Red reached under his slicker and consulted his watch. "It's only eight o'clock."

"Farmers," Buttons said. "Farmers go to bed early, something to do with all that plowing they do at the tail end of a horse. All right. Let's try the saloon. Day or night, you ever seen an empty saloon? I sure as hell haven't."

The saloon was as empty as last year's bird nest. Cobwebbed and dark, the shadows were as black as spilled ink. The mahogany bar dominated a room with a few tables and chairs scattered around a dance floor. A potbellied stove stood in a corner. Red thumbed a match into flame and held it high. The guttering light revealed pale rectangles on the walls where pictures had once hung, and the mirror behind the bar had been smashed into splinters.

"Ow!" The match had burned down and scorched Red's fingers. Irritated, he repeated, "Like I said . . . we're in a damned ghost town."

Buttons had been exploring around the bar and his voice spoke from the murk. "Three bottles. All of them empty." Lightning flared as Buttons stepped toward Red in the dazzle, and he flickered like a figure in a magic lantern show. "We've been had. This is what they call a wild-goose chase."

"I don't think the Abe Patterson and Son Stage and Express Company is one to play practical jokes," Red said. "Abe never made a joke in his life."

"You're right. Abe wouldn't play a trick on us," Buttons said. "But it seems somebody is, and if I find who done it, I'll plug him for sure."

"Unhitch the team and let the horses shelter overnight in the livery stable. I'll get a fire going in the saloon stove and boil up some coffee."

"Fire will help us dry off. Damn, Red, this was a wasted trip."

Red smiled, "It's on the way back to the Patterson depot in San Angelo. We didn't lose anything by it."

"Except a fare," Buttons said.

"Yeah, except a fare. But I reckon Abe Patterson can afford it."

Buttons closed his slicker up to the neck and stepped toward the door. Red lingered for a few moments and decided that the chairs would burn nicely in the stove. He craved coffee and the cigarettes he could build without the downpour battering paper and tobacco out of his fingers.

Button's voice came from the doorway, sounding hollow in the silent lull between thunderclaps. "Red, you better come see this. And you ain't gonna like it."

Red's boot heels thudded across the timber floor as he walked to the open door. "What do you see? Is it a person?"

"No, it's that," Buttons said, pointing.

A hearse drawn by a black-draped horse stood in the middle of the rain-lashed street. Just visible in the murk behind the large, oval-shaped windows was a coffin, not a plain, hammered pine box, but by all appearances a substantial casket made from some kind of dark wood accented with silver handles and hinges.

"What the hell?" Red said.

"I don't see anybody out there," Buttons said. "Who the hell is in the box?"

"Maybe our passenger."

"Red, don't make jokes," Buttons said. "I'm boogered enough already."

"Let's take a look out there. A hearse doesn't just appear all by itself."

Red Ryan and Buttons Muldoon stepped into the street that was suddenly illuminated by a flash of lightning that glimmered on a tall, cadaverous man who wore a black frock coat and top hat and seemed uncaring of the rain that soaked him. The man's skin was an ashy gray, as though he spent too much time indoors, and he held a hefty Bible with a silver cross on the front cover in his right hand, close to his chest.

"Well, howdy," Buttons said. "Who the hell are you?"

Lightning shimmered, turning the rain into a cascade of steel needles, and thunder boomed before the man spoke. "I am the Reverend Solomon Palmer of this town. You have come for our dear, departed brother Morgan Ford, have you not?"

Rain ran off the brim of Buttons' hat as he shook his head. "Not the dear departed Morgan Ford, mister. The alive and kicking Morgan Ford."

"Alas, Brother Ford passed away two days ago," Palmer said.

"From what?" Buttons stepped back, alarmed. "Nothing catching, I hope."

"From congestion of the heart," Palmer said. "I watched his pale face turn black and then he gave a great sigh and a moment later he hurried off to meet his Creator." The preacher clutched his Bible closer. "He was a fine man, was Brother Ford."

"He was a fare," Buttons said. "And now he isn't. There ain't no profit in dead men for the Abe Patterson and Son Stage and Express Company."

"Ah, but there is," Palmer said. He smiled, revealing teeth that looked like yellowed piano keys. "Come with me . . . Mister . . . ah . . ."

"Muldoon, but you can call me Buttons. And the feller in the plug hat is Red Ryan, my shotgun guard."

"Come with you where?" Red asked. "Me and Mr. Muldoon are not trusting men."

"I will do you no harm," Palmer said. He glanced

up at the black sky where blue lightning blazed. "Only the dead are abroad on a night such as this."

"Cheerful kind of ranny, ain't you?" Buttons said. "I'll have to see to my horses before I go anywhere, and I'll take care of your hearse hoss." He shook his head. "I don't believe I just said that."

"Hearse hoss," Red said. "It's got a ring to it."

"Yes, I'd appreciate it if you'd take care of my mare," Palmer said. "I think you'll find hay in the livery, and perhaps some oats."

"And where will you be?" Buttons said.

"Right here, waiting for you." Palmer looked stark and grim and bloodless as the storm cartwheeled around him, putting Buttons in mind of a corpse recently dug up by a resurrectionist.

The horses were grateful to get out of the storm and gave Buttons and Red no trouble as they were led to stalls and rubbed down with sacking before Buttons forked them hay and gave each a scoop of oats.

Buttons had been silent, deep in thought as he worked with the team, until he said, "Red, what do you make of that reverend feller?"

"He's a strange one."

"You mean three pickles short of a full barrel?"

Red nodded. "Something like that."

"He said that there's profit in the dead man. Did you hear him say that?"

"More or less."

"Do you believe him?"

"Enough to listen to what he has to say."

"Here," Buttons said, turning his head to look behind him. "He ain't a ghost, is he?"

"A what?"

"A ghost, a spook, a revenant . . . whatever the hell you want to call it."

Red smiled. "No, I think he's just a downright peculiar feller. Man must be crazy to live in a ghost town."

Buttons pointed a finger. "See, you said it, Red. You said *ghost*."

"I was speaking about the town, not the preacher. Let's go hear what he has to say."

CHAPTER TWO

The Reverend Solomon Palmer led Red Ryan and Buttons Muldoon to a cabin behind a tumbledown rod and gun store that still bore a weathered sign above its door. The thunderstorm had passed but had left a steady rain in its wake, and when Red and Buttons stepped inside, their slickers streamed water onto the dirt floor.

Palmer lit a smoking oil lamp and a mustard-yellow glow filled the cabin. Red noticed that a well-used Winchester stood in a gun rack and hanging beside it a holstered Colt exhibited even more wear. He decided right there and then that there was more to the Reverend Palmer than met the eye. The man might be a parson now, but that hadn't always been the case . . . unless the firearms belonged to someone else.

A log fire burned in a stone fireplace flanked by two rockers. A small dining table with a pair of wooden chairs completed the furnishings. Above the mantel hung a portrait of a stern-looking man in the uniform of a Confederate brigadier general. The old soldier had bushy gray eyebrows, a beard that spread over his chest, and he bore a passing resemblance to Palmer. The cabin had an adjoining room, but the door was closed. The place smelled of pipe smoke and vaguely of blended bourbon but had no odor of sanctity that Red associated with the quarters of the clergy.

"Help yourself to coffee," Palmer said, nodding to the pot on the fire. "Cups on the shelf." The man removed his top hat, revealing thinning black hair. He set the hat down on the table. "Are you sharp set?"

"We could eat," Buttons said, a man who could always eat.

"Soup in the pot, bowls on the shelf, spoons on the table," Palmer said. "Eat and drink and then we'll talk about Morgan Ford."

The coffee was hot, black, and bitter, but Red found the soup surprisingly good. "Good soup," he said after he'd finished his bowl.

"I spent some time as a trail cook for old Charlie Goodnight," Palmer said. "I learned how to make bacon and beans and beef soup because it was one of Charlie's favorites."

A cook could acquire a Colt and a Winchester, but Red figured he'd never use them the way Palmer's had been used. He still put a question mark against the reverend's name.

Buttons burped more or less politely and then said, "Tell us about the dead man in the box."

"Brother Morgan Ford came to Cottondale ten years ago, hoping to outrun a reputation as a gunman, and in that quest, he succeeded," Palmer said. "He built the saloon, but when the town died, Morgan took sick and died with it. Him and me, we were the only two left. I remained to take care of him in his last weeks, as was my Christian duty."

"How come the town died?" Red said. "Looks like it was a nice enough place with a church an' all."

"At one time it was," Palmer said. "But then the farmers who wanted to grow cotton here discovered that the cost of irrigating the land ate up any profits. One by one, defeated by the desert, they pulled stakes and left until only Morgan and me remained. Three days ago the cancer finally took him and he gasped his last."

"And lost me a fare," Buttons said.

"You still have a fare, Mr. Muldoon," Palmer said. "When Morgan lay dying he told me to contact his only living relative, a niece by the name of Luna Talbot, and ask her if she would bury him. Needless to say, I was surprised that Brother Ford had a niece, but using El Paso as my mailing address, since mail is no longer delivered to Cottondale, I wrote to her and she replied and said yes. She wants his body and will pay to have it sent to her. Apparently, Mrs. Talbot has a successful ranch due south of us on this side of the Rio Bravo. In every way, she seems to be an admirable young lady."

"And you want us to take the body to her? Is that it, preacher?" Buttons said.

"Yes, I do. That is why you're here. I contacted the Abe Patterson company in San Angelo and made all the arrangements."

Buttons shook his head. "Nobody made arrangements with me that involved picking up a dead man. The Abe Patterson and Son Stage and Express

Company doesn't carry corpses, and if it ain't there already, I plan to write that down in the rule book."

"Five hundred dollars, Mr. Muldoon," Palmer said.

"Huh?" Buttons said.

"Five hundred dollars, Mr. Muldoon." A heavy cloudburst rattled on the cabin's tin roof, adding to the reverend's suspenseful pause. "That is the amount of money the grieving Mrs. Luna Talbot is willing to pay for the safe delivery of her loved one."

"I reckon that from here it's around two hundred miles to the ranch you're talking about," Buttons said. "That's a fifty-dollar fare."

"And indeed, you are correct, Mr. Muldoon. The Patterson stage company gets fifty and you keep the rest." The reverend smiled slightly. "Because of the unique nature of the . . . ah . . . delivery, Mrs. Talbot is prepared to be generous."

"Red, what do you reckon?" Buttons said.

Before Red could answer, Palmer said, "I have a sufficient length of good hemp rope to lash the coffin to the top of the stage. We can make it secure so that Brother Morgan can take his final journey in peace."

"Without falling off, you mean?" Red asked.

"Precisely," Palmer said.

Buttons and Red exchanged a glance, and finally Buttons nodded. "Get the rope, Reverend."